THE PACIFIST'S SWORD
M.S. UDDIN

THE PACIFIST'S SWORD

First published in 2018 by M.S. Uddin, United Kingdom.
ISBN 978-1-9164419-0-3

Credits for the Cover Design – Waz Islam
XLVI Press
www.XLVIMediaGroup.com
www.SaifTheWriter.co.uk

Acknowledgements

Yes, I have finally written and published my very own novel. The first of many, if God wills. On that note, let me begin by saying it was with Allah's grace and guidance that I managed this much. I am *very* grateful that I have a functioning body and mind, because many of us—myself included at times—take such a thing for granted. I pray that I continue to receive *His* guidance and blessings.

A special thanks to my family for being patient with me and creating a strong foundation of support, something that is so vital to a writer's journey. To Alamin Farooque and Masum Ahmed, my closest of friends and family, who have supported me on my many ventures and paths, and I hope will continue to do so.

To the people that have worked on this book with me: Stephanie Diaz, who brought my book to life with both realism and creativity; something only a good author and editor could bring about. Thank you for believing in my story. Leesa Wallace, my editor, who has taught me much in such a short time. Thank you for your patience and effort! Madeha Rahman, you were the first person to read the whole book and give me feedback. You probably weren't even expecting to play such an important role but thank you once again!

I was born and raised in East London, thus I'd like to thank the Borough of Newham. I am grateful for everything that has been provided for me and all the lessons learned living in his amazing borough.

My past is one that bleeds into this book, including the amazing times I had growing up in Newham, the time I witnessed the Olympics 2012 and all the commotion and excitement that came with it, the pleasure of living in a diverse and mostly peaceful community, as well the cultural and social issues I've experienced. Many of us grew up surrounded by gang violence, muggings, robbery, knife crime, acid attacks, discrimination and racism. Some of us even suffered from a lack of good housing and education. I'm mentioning all of this here because I'd like to acknowledge that these things should not be an excuse for you to give up, there are tough times and there are

3

tougher times, but we get through it with love, kindness and empathy. Every hurdle is simply that, a hurdle, not a wall.

After months of wondering whether to self-publish or traditionally publish my book, I chose the former, simply because I am an entrepreneur at heart, and I want to show the children of Newham and London—and perhaps one day the world: if the doors are difficult to open, then create your own doors and your own path. You do NOT need the best grades, you do NOT need to be from an elite background or have a LOT of money, and you do not need 100,000 followers to pursue your dreams, especially when it comes to writing. You need to work hard and believe in yourself, carry a productive and kind attitude, and help as many people as you can along the way. This is my recipe. If I am one of the first British-born Bangladeshi novelists from London, and if I—who didn't do great at my English GCSEs—can do this much, with a laptop and an idea, then I know there are thousands of others that can do the same.

On that note, I'd like to thank XLVI Media Group and my team for all the support and work behind the scenes. Without a team of like-minded people, a journey like this would be impossible. I'm glad to be a part of this project, and it feels amazing to bring young creative people together, to support and guide them towards their version of success.

To Charavell, one of the most genuine people I've ever met, thank you for your constant support and energy, your drive for success felt parallel to mine so I guess our success is in alignment (Insha'Allah). Waz Islam, the genius behind the design work of my novel. We all know people judge a book by its cover, but with you around, I didn't worry about that judgement. To my uncle Redwan and his family for being some of the most supportive relatives I have.

I'd like to reserve a special thanks to all the Authortubing community around the world, from those uploading helpful and amazing advice about writing, to those uploading motivational and uplifting videos for the dark days of authors, and those that have used this platform to create bigger things for the community: A special thanks to Vivien Reis, Kaila Walker, Kristen Martin, Bethany Atazadeh and Dahlia Burroughs. A special thanks to Jenna Moreci for her all her amazing work across several platforms online, for her especially entertaining videos and my favourite novel thus far from an Authortuber.

Finally, to my readers, you. For reading this book and taking the leap with Arthur as he takes on the forces of inequality, intolerance and injustice. Let us hope the world you're about to read about remains fiction.

I hope you all continue this journey with me, thank you.

Dedication

In memory of Hafiz Mudoris Ali, Fahmida Zaman, and Uncle Anam Uddin.

Also, in memory of all the victims of the Grenfell Fire, we will never forget...never.

Prologue

Lillian pulled her collar closer to her face to avoid the harsh gusts of wind that battered against her as she hurried through the streets of Whitechapel. Her hair moved as if it had a mind of its own, and she soon gave in to the futility of fighting nature. Tears flew from her face the moment her eyes produced them. She picked up her pace, anxious to get away from the Dark Quarters. Disgust lodged deep and thick in her stomach from what had happened tonight. It was bad enough that she was beaten and bruised by her last visitor, but even worse that she hadn't consented.

The wretched oaf hadn't even paid her. Rent was due soon and she was already short on her weekly earnings. She would have to work extra hard tomorrow. She bit her lower lip hard at the thought of it, puncturing her soft tissue. She wiped a trickle of blood away from her mouth and continued her hurried strut.

She turned onto a narrow brick-laid road. Had she been here before?

A murder of crows swept over her head, accompanying her travel. Perhaps it was a sign to let her know she wasn't alone. She turned down another road. The bitter stirring of the wind had swept along a drizzle.

'Wait…' she began to mutter. 'This isn't the way home.' She cursed her lack of concentration before turning back.

A dark figure stood before her.

A scream almost leapt from her throat. Almost. Perhaps she would have been forgiven for it, too. But there were all sorts of people walking the streets at night; she was one of them. There was no need for a woman to cause a scene, especially this late at night.

'Sorry I didn't see you th—' She stopped. Her gaze fell on the mask he wore – a grinning face with a long curly moustache.

She wanted to step back, wanted to break into a run. Her limbs disobeyed her. Something was wrong.

'Can't move, can you?' The voice was distorted, she couldn't tell if it was a man or woman. The stranger's demeanour stirred with something sinister, yet familiar. Who was it?

The air grew heavy and she could feel her heart beating furiously with the wind. She struggled to move her legs, struggled to speak. Her body ingested a deep wave of terror.

'I wish you just listened to me, Lillian.'

1. The Pacifist

Arthur

The first revolution had ended the monarchy. The second had ended resistance. The third had ended all forms of old-culture in London, from libraries and museums to universities, theatres and religious buildings. Arthur was born after the fourth. He could remember Mr Hudson telling him all sorts of fascinating stories. Stories that were told to Mr Hudson by *his* adopted father. Stories of the Golden Age of Technology, where every man, woman, and child was connected by a powerful god-like force; they called it *The Internet.* That was close to ten years ago, and Mr Hudson had moved on to the Beyond.

Arthur stared, with bated breath, at the dusty brown notebook on his desk. Its leather exterior looked at least two decades old. Fingerprints and crease marks decorated the cover. He must have been at least the fourth or fifth owner of this illegal item. A long list of names was scribbled on the inside of the first page, but only one name mattered to him. His fingertips scrolled through the list of writers and stopped at *Lucy.* His sister's name.

With nervous fingers, he flicked through the pages and found her familiar handwriting. His heart pumped faster, pounding against his chest like clouds teasing for thunder. This was all she had left him after her disappearance. A month he had searched for her, scouring every broken road and hidden alleyway of Whitechapel for signs of his sister. It was only after he had ripped through their apartment for clues that he had come across the most valuable legacy she had left behind: her immortal words, written in a journal shared by many before her.

A turn of the page would fill his mind with her words, a simple flick of his fingers.

He stood up, almost knocking a candle off his desk. He couldn't do it. He couldn't bring himself to read something that would leave his mouth with a sour taste. What was she going to say? A journal entry about why she had left him? Or even worse, a suicide note? There had been too many of those happening all over the slums recently.

Pain gripped the broken shards of his insides; the bitter feeling of emptiness filled the large gaping hole in him. A contradiction of feelings.

He noticed a tiny black creature scuttling across his desk. He quickly scooped the spider in his hands and walked over to the window, carefully letting it scurry across his palm and into the unsettling wind that taunted the streets. He detested the idea of being the reason behind the creature's short life.

He ran a shaky hand through his hair and peered outside his window again, just to make sure he wasn't being watched. The streets of Whitechapel looked nothing out of the ordinary. In fact, there was nothing to see at all. The darkness held strong against the light of the moon; long poles that were once called streetlights stood redundant. The streets were almost empty, as there were very few car-homes in Whitechapel. Most cars had been dismantled, their parts used for other purposes or sold for food.

Arthur watched a man climb inside a small blue Volkswagen, pull the seat back, and fall asleep. His tattered, brown overcoat doubled for a blanket. The car was missing a door, but that didn't matter, as the old man probably had nothing worth stealing.

Turning away from the window, Arthur moved back to the candlelight at his desk. He couldn't bring himself to read his sister's words, not yet, so he decided instead to read someone else's writing. The date was scribed in the top corner: *2074*. Thirty-six years ago.

Dear Readers,

I don't know when you'll read this, but I hope by the time you do, things have gotten better. The White Arrow Party has secured control across London. Their stupid wall has trapped us out for over twenty years now. I can't remember what the inner-city of London really looks like anymore, I've only heard about it from my parents. Skyscrapers once stood towering over us, but when I look around now, the only tall structure is the wall itself. What's going on behind it? God knows.

There's no electricity for anyone in Whitechapel. Things are getting restless here, fighting breaks out almost every day. But that's what happens when you lump together people of all backgrounds and status.

No, maybe I'm wrong. The differences don't matter, not when we're united by poverty. Especially since the last air raid on the Hamlets, as we've been trying to rebuild a town almost from scratch. What a cruel and twisted reality. For God's sake, even Royal London Hospital is shutting down. What will happen to us now? Oh, and don't get caught with this book. You should know it's illegal to write anything in a book. The White Arrow will have your head for it!

- Daniel

No one ever signed with their full names. Arthur reckoned this was because they worried about getting caught. What Daniel said was true; the White Arrow Party—a group of fascists determined to horde all the electricity and power for the "True British"—certainly was one to fear. But what does being *truly* British even mean? Arthur had been raised to be tolerant to all walks of life; Mr Hudson had raised him that way ever since he was a young boy. He was a man that chose to be amongst a group of people known as the Tolerant, although the White Arrow supporters called them the Traitors. His reward was banishment from the city; to live and die with the outcasts in the slums.

He closed the book and squeezed it underneath his mattress.

He reckoned he had a few more weeks to read it before another White Arrow house inspection. He took one last glance around his modest room, from its narrow shape where two pieces of furniture could be stationed to the rough laminated floor—how fortunate he was, many would kill for such luxuries. They couldn't afford two rooms, so Lucy took the bed and Arthur would find comfort on the floor. As Arthur climbed into bed, a tinge of guilt accompanied him.

Tomorrow it was his turn to work the dump shift. Even if there were no laws in Whitechapel anymore, the bedbound old Mayor, Mr Murray, had still kept some order in the small community. Arthur believed in it. He had nothing else to believe in. His sister had been the strong one between them, but in her absence, Arthur only had unanswered questions to accompany him.

He blew out the candle and waited for sleep to haunt him once again.

***

The next morning, Arthur dressed in his usual dirty blue jumpsuit. He walked through Cavell Street, where he lived, and made his way towards the dump site. With all the drainage problems in Whitechapel, people had been forced to resort to more traditional ways of getting rid of their waste.

He passed the familiar, imposing building made of metal and glass that, a century ago, had marked the centre of trade and transport in this part of London. The old Whitechapel station stood desolate and oblivious to most.

After ten minutes of walking, a stale scent filled Arthur's nostrils, making his nose wrinkle. A mountain of green and brown unpleasantness welcomed him as he arrived at the large site at the edge of town. The dawn shift had just ended; uneven holes were dug across the site, waiting to be filled. He approached his work with bravery, and eyes that stung. He wrapped a cloth around his nose and mouth to try to block the smell—even though it was pointless—and picked up an abandoned shovel.

The stench of excretion created an almost unbearable atmosphere. Arthur watched as some townsfolk shovelled for a few minutes before retreating to safety. He tried not to let it deter him; the work had to be done. This was the world they lived in. He just prayed that his eroding boots would last him the day.

'You there,' someone called out—a scrawny fellow with a fisherman's hat on.

'Me?' Arthur pointed at himself.

'Yes, Blondy. Do you see anyone else working so close to the dung? What's your name?' His accent was strong. He must have been from one of those faraway European countries that Mr Hudson had mentioned a few times.

Well, it's not Blondy. 'My name's Arthur.' He knew, with his short, blond hair, he raised a few brows in Whitechapel. Most blond people were living in Inner London, safely behind the walls, in the comfort of their warm homes that were supplied with electricity. They were eating lavish meals regularly, sipping proper British tea, and basking in their ignorant tranquillity—or so he had heard.

'Artar…? Just Artar? That sounds posh, doesn't it?'

'Ar-thur.' He enunciated the syllables in his name. 'Arthur will do just fine. You?' He met the man's eyes, before noticing the man's bandaged arm. He was a cripple. He held his shovel in his good right arm.

Arthur wondered how he was going to work with one arm. But then, if this was his only option for work, what choice did he have? The blessing in disguise was that cleaners were not discriminated against based on how many functional hands they had. It wasn't strange for him to meet new people at work, many people travelled into Whitechapel for work from time-to-time. The man's pale complexion and brown hair—and his distinct accent—definitely showed signs of a former citizen of the fallen EU. Things had changed after Britain had left the European

Union almost a hundred years ago.

'My name's Lukas.' He itched his bandaged arm with his good one, dropping his shovel clumsily in the process. 'Say, how come you're not a Peacekeeper? You look tall and strong enough. Why are you out here cleaning this dung?'

This wasn't the first time Arthur had been asked this. Why wasn't he a Peacekeeper? Why didn't he train himself to wield a sword and fight against those who disturbed the peace?

'Well.' He smiled and spoke in the politest tone he could muster. 'That's my business.'

The truth was he had no interest in ever holding a sword. Harming others was not something he ever wanted to do.

Lukas shrugged and continued his work.

Over the next hour, Arthur kept noticing the cripple talking to himself. Or maybe he was talking to Arthur? He tried not to pay him much attention.

The community here was split into different sectors. There were those who harvested and supplied the food; those who built new homes and focused on sheltering people; and then there were those who cleaned up the environment, making sure that Whitechapel didn't end up like some of the neighbouring areas; full of disease and battling other issues linked to unsanitary conditions.

Other roles existed as well. Special roles like doctors, nurses, and even a Peacekeeper called Gareth. Mr Hudson was the last teacher in Whitechapel, but after his passing, the children all had to be schooled at home.

'Hey, Artor. Did you ever think you'd end up here when you were a child?' Lukas babbled. 'Earth to Artoooor?'

Lukas' voice faded away as memories flooded Arthur's mind.

She was with him only a month ago, learning together, working together, eating together. She wasn't his real sister, but they had both grown up under Mr Hudson's care. Both adopted, both equally loved as children. He had never felt like he didn't have a family—that was important to him, especially when he couldn't remember his real parents. This was the irony of his life: he was gifted with a brilliant memory but couldn't even remember his parents. Not since the episodes started.

Sweat trickled down the side of his face as he lifted his shovel and dumped the contents into a third hole now. The smell made him wince. He tried to breathe in from inside his jumper, but the stench was so strong it seeped through the holes of the fabric. He tried to ignore it. He had been brought up to accept that everyone had a role to play, especially in times like these. Working together for the community gave him a rewarding feeling, even if it meant cleaning up other people's waste.

'Oi, you there!' grunted a short man from across his heap. Arthur didn't notice him at first, but when he did, his eyes immediately flicked to his bulging belly. A grin shone on his stubbly face. 'Since you're almost done with your heap, how about you help me with mine?'

The man had been at work for at least as long as him, yet his share of waste had hardly been touched. Arthur took a closer look at the man. He had seen him a couple of times at the local tavern; his long pointy nose was something he wouldn't forget, since it reminded him of Inner London's Big Ben. The man stared back at him, waiting for his response.

'Sure.' Arthur finished his last few scoops before turning to the man's heap.

He sneered. 'Well then, I'll leave you to it.' He threw his shovel to the side and immediately turned around to leave.

'W-wait! You want me to do your work for you? Where are *you* going?'

'I've got things to do. You seem to enjoy this anyway.' He didn't look back at Arthur, but continued walking.

'Everyone's got to play their part. How else are we ever going to make this work?' Arthur pleaded.

The man waved back at him, already quite a distance away. 'Make what work? The world is broken. Happy shovelling!' he shouted back, before bursting into a fit of husky laughter.

Arthur tried to not let it get to him. He tried, but his hands gripped the shovel so tight he could almost feel the wooden splinters pierce his skin.

'Where the hell did you go, Lucy?' Arthur said out loud, almost shouting.

The skinny figure of Lukas poked his head around his heap, unaware of what had happened. 'Hey, Artor. I told you my name is Lukas, not Lucy.'

'I wasn't talkin—you know what, never mind.' Arthur slammed his shovel into a new pile of dung and continued to toil away. 'And my name is *Arthur*!'

Was the world really broken beyond repair? Was this when his life would start to tumble downhill? Lucy would have told him off for sulking. She would have scolded him for being so disheartened. Of course there was hope. Of course his life was going to get better.

If change does not come, then you create change. That's what she would have said.

Arthur swung his shovel a little too fast and lost his balance. Hope, that was all he needed. Hope. His legs wobbled, and the force of the shovel pulled him down, face first into the repugnant heap he had only just begun to shovel.

Hope.

2. The Assassin

Tina

The sound of dripping water echoed from a broken pipe somewhere along the bare corridors of the old school building. Tina didn't bother trying to find the source of the noise. The echoing soothed her; reminding her of a familiar feeling of abandonment. The white light of the moon cast a dreary shine on the hallways. A month had passed since she moved to Whitechapel. She had purposely chosen an empty building, away from the town centre. Away from people.

There were plenty of desks, broken computer screens, and pieces of paper littered across the room. It looked ancient, like it had been abandoned decades ago. There was even a docking station for the old virtual reality devices that children had used many years ago. She had found a clean supply of water from one of the still functioning sinks in the boys' toilets and deemed it to be a good place to settle. After all, clean water from a tap was rare in these parts.

Sometimes she wished she was back in New India, back at her own school. Surrounded by people who knew her. But she quickly pushed that thought out of her head. She had chosen this, and she wouldn't go back on her decision now. Besides, things were peaceful here.

Sometimes she would hear children gathering together outside, talking about how the eerie sounds and movements coming from the building meant it was haunted. Tina did her best to fulfil their fears. Sometimes she would stand in the right position by the window and let the moonlight turn her small frame into a large shadow of a woman. Her daggers would dance; the white light devouring their imaginations. It worked every time.

Ever since the Battle of the Bridge four years ago, she had decided to leave her past behind, but the escape was a façade as her memories would resurface and eat at her. Even when she fought them off through meditation, her mind would conjure a darker battle within. Sometimes she wondered if it was worth living at all. Wouldn't all the pain simmer to nothingness if she just let her life end? But Larsson wouldn't let her do it. It would kill him if she did.

Tonight, she crawled into her makeshift bed and pulled her blanket over her head. It was cold. She would need to find a lighter or a matchstick tomorrow—candles, that's what she needed. It was all she needed.

For someone that had mastered the art of assassination by sixteen, the one thing she hadn't come to grips with was sleep. To sleep after living in the shadows; after spilling blood; after being torn by the temptations of vengeance, was an absolute luxury. It happened every night. Nightmare after nightmare, she couldn't escape. It was always the same vivid images: the fire–that godforsaken fire–the smoke, the burning of her home. The Soulhaven; a pub that she grew up in. Her father and brother waking up to the sound of an explosion, and her father's face as he watched a second explosion take her brother's life. His last words before he flung her fourteen-year-old body out of the window to save her from the fire. Then there was that woman, the woman who had lurked in the shadows, the one who had caused all of this.

A knocking, always a knocking. Knock. Knock. The sound before the fire. The purple stained lips of that woman again? Knock. Knock. Knox.

Weariness wrapped around her body like a cloak, her eyelids closed like the Great Gates of London, and it began again.

People, hundreds of people. All equipped with swords, lances, bows, spears–so many devices to kill. All ready to take the life of the people standing opposite them. She was one of them; she was ready. Her daggers—No, they weren't there. Instead, she was holding—an arm! It was fresh; blood squirted out of the severed limb. Dark red filled her blurred vision. She screamed. But the scream found its way into someone else's shrill laughter. A thud, knock. Knock. Knox.

There she was, Knox, the lady of the shadows. But her face never came into view. What did she look like? What grotesque form of a face did she have that would do justice to her evil laughter? Tina felt her eyes burn as she glanced down at the familiar body held in Knox's grip. Who was it? The laughter continued, increasing in volume as the seconds passed. The tempo changed. The pitch changed. Cackling, hysteria.

Let it stop. Please let it stop.

But it didn't. They say nightmares last for a few minutes but Tina felt the full force of the time that her body took to recuperate. It was as if she were trapped in a hole that sucked at her soul until her memories and imaginations were bled dry. The so-called minutes turned into torturous hours.

The shrill sound of laughter eventually drifted into reality and Tina opened her eyes. A bead of sweat travelled down the side of her face—no, it was a tear. The laughter wasn't laughter, but the sound of a malfunctioning school bell. The sunlight pierced segments of the room from behind the cardboard that hugged the windows. She reached to her left with as much energy as she could muster, and threw her dagger at the square box on the wall. Death introduced itself to the school bell, and silence blossomed.

She found herself darting to the boys' toilets and throwing water over her face. The wet face of a teenage girl reaching adulthood stared back at her from a mirror. Her black hair curtained across her forehead and fell right above her eyes. The length of her hair trailed behind her head to her shoulders. Dark circles around her penetrating eyes contrasted with her now-pale skin. Would Lars scold her for not taking care of herself properly?

A minute passed before she realised she was still staring at her reflection; within a year, her petite and slim body had managed to add a few inches to her height. She would be nineteen in a few days, yet she could still get away with impersonating a child. A blessing in disguise at times. Behind the allure of a young women, she had more experience in the art of combat than most people triple her age. She was, after all, a graduate of the New India Martial Arts School.

Tina headed back to her classroom and moved the brown boards by the window. Sunlight flooded the lonely room, accompanied by a soft warmth. It was time to work.

She had scouted most parts of Whitechapel by now, but there were still a couple blocks she needed to survey before she could conclude her knowledge of the town's geography. She always found it reassuring when she knew every road, building, alleyway, gap, crack, and shadow of the infrastructure in the town she decided to settle in. Every escape route.

Today she would map out the eastern roads of Whitechapel. She wrapped herself in a cloak and found her way to the roof of the building. This was her entry and exit point—she never used a door. Why would she? It wasn't the way of an assassin. She leapt off the roof and began her descent to a nearby ledge. Every step was light, every turn was swift, every movement was measured with an elegance of speed that made her look like a bird soaring across the rooftops, or so Lars had once said to her.

3. Whitechapel

Arthur

Arthur was around nine years old when he first discovered his ability to recall memories in precise detail. Lucy had misplaced her silver necklace somewhere in her room but couldn't figure out where it had gone. She had treasured it greatly, as it was one of the only things left to her by her mother. Arthur had been able to vividly retrace both his and Lucy's steps and found that she had simply left it resting on top of a dusty unused shelf. A special piece of jewellery like that could have been sold for a good fee in the market.

Last year he'd stolen a glance at one of her journals. She'd snapped it shut when she realised he was looking and gave him a lecture about privacy. It was a telling off he would never forget, but he also never forgot every word etched into the deteriorating page. They had instantly filled his belly with curiosity—words like democracy, hypocrisy, anarchy. Words he had never heard before.

The early morning sunlight illuminated the corners of his room. As he sat by his desk, reading through the journal, he pictured every word, sentence, and paragraph on the pages he read. Reading wasn't something he enjoyed doing, but he wasn't just reading anymore. He was experiencing the thoughts and journeys of every writer in the journal.

After the Cultural Revolution many years ago, when the burning of books had taken place, journals like this started to be written. They were kept hidden and never spoken about in public, but always passed along from one daring individual to another.

Every time there was news of the next White Arrow raid on

an area, the journals would be secretly ushered to another place. Thus, the White Arrow would never be able to find it, and consequently, the book never stayed with one owner for longer than a few weeks.

Arthur flicked through the pages, adventuring the days of hundreds of people. He had handled many journals over the years, but this one was special. It was close to midnight now and the temperature had dropped. His fingers hovered over the candle, grasping the warmth that escaped by the second. He opened the journal with his cold hand and turned to the page he had last read.

Dear WhoeverTheHellFindsThis,

My name's Willy. This is the first time I've written anything down, so I'm not expecting this to be perfect. But I do think what I'm about to write is important. Well, it's important to me. I hope you find it easy to read. But anyway, look, today was the 44th annual Anti-Muslim day.

Arthur flicked his eyes over to the corner of the page to check the date: 2076

Today I saw something horrible. I mean, I've seen plenty of horrible things in my life but this was just the worst of the worst. I hope you never have to see anything like this or...worse. So, I'm sitting at home, minding my own business, then BAM. I hear a window smash in the house next door. Now, I know I'm living risky when I'm living next-door to Muslims. But man, I did not see this coming.

I look out the window and see a bunch of masked men walking into Mr Ali's house, and they didn't look like Peacekeepers. In fact, I wouldn't be surprised if under the masks they were townsfolk from Whitechapel. Anyway, they walk in, and I hear shouting. Mr Ali telling someone to run away. 'RUN, GET OUT QUICKLY. THEY'RE COMING,' he shouts. Anyway,

*I'm brickin' it here, thinking this is some White Arrow raid, so...
I do what I do best. I barricade the door and mind my own
business. I mean my dad told me about what they did to Muslims
in China! Nobody did anything to help them there, right?*

*Call me a coward if you want, but if you had been there,
would you have done anything different? What help could I have
given Ali?*

*Alright, fine, so I feel terrible. I guess that's why I'm writing
this down. The next day, I left my house and took a quick glance.
The door was broken down, and there didn't seem to be any
sounds coming from inside. Of course I didn't go inside. Maybe
they got away.*

*Heck, aren't all Muslims gathering in North London
anyway? The scramble for areas has been going on for ages.*

*Anyway, I guess if there is any God out there, I'll probably
get punished for not loving my neighbour? Or perhaps God has
bigger fish to fry. He's got the whole world to fix, and it's
slipping out of his hands right now. But that's none of my
business. If you're reading this and making your puny
judgments, then let me ask you this—would you have done
anything different? Knowing that your life, your family's life,
and your future was at stake?*

Arthur slammed the book shut and cursed. He would have
done something different, of course he would have. When the
world was so hell-bent on dividing humans, why should anyone
sit and accept it? Reading journal entries like this really did irk
him.

Sometimes he wished he didn't remember things so well.
But understanding the past helped him deal with the frustrations
of the present; it gave him a reason to want to change things.

Change. A word that people took too lightly. Everyone
wanted it, but no one was willing to do anything to make it
happen.

***

After breakfast, Arthur began his rubbish collecting duties. He walked from home to home, car-home to car-home, collecting all the rubbish that was left out from the night before, and throwing it all into his cart, which he would cycle to the rubbish dump. When he returned to the dump site after his second round of collections, he noticed Lukas shovelling away at his produce. The large heap of waste was being shovelled at an agonisingly slow pace. He waved at him with his one good hand; his shovel fell to the floor as he did so.

'Mornin' Arthur! Looks like you were beaten to it today,' he called out.

'Beaten? I'm the only collector on duty today,' Arthur replied, sounding nonchalant. He had learned not to listen to everything that came out of Lukas' mouth, as yesterday the man had spoken endlessly about crows. The reason the Internet had been destroyed was because of crows, apparently.

'Are you sure, Arthur?' He pointed towards a heap of rubbish Arthur hadn't spotted earlier. Again, Lukas' shovel dropped to the floor. Arthur picked it up for him before turning back to the rubbish and frowning. This was strange. He was sure he was the only collector on the rota.

'Doesn't matter. The more the merrier, right?' Lukas beamed stupidly.

Morning turned to afternoon and Arthur returned to the dump after his final round of collections. In the distance, he could see a panicked looking Lukas calling for him.

This time Lukas' voice struck Arthur's attention. His voice was trembling. 'Arthur, I don't know how…I was just shovelling and then I found…'

Arthur almost slipped as he climbed past the brown and black garbage bags. When he finally reached Lukas, he wished he hadn't. There, hidden beneath the decaying heap, was a body. Lifeless. The pale skin looked rough in the gleam of the light. The mere sight of its lifelessness made Arthur's stomach churn.

He and Lukas quickly freed the body from the clutches of

decaying waste and pulled it into the sunlight. Again, Arthur wished he hadn't. The women's face was unrecognisable, sliced and chopped in all different directions, as if a butcher had attempted to be an artist and failed on an unpalatable level. The blood was drying, and her clothes were torn. From the colour of her skin, it looked as if the woman had been dead for days. Arthur really hated his knack for details right now. He couldn't stare at what was left of her face any longer, but his eyes trailed down to a patch of blood near her legs. And of course, he wished he hadn't looked there. In fact, he wished—for the first time in his life—he had just stayed in bed today and abandoned his duties.

The women's genital parts were horribly mutilated.

Arthur turned around and added to the foul stench with last night's dinner.

He slowly wiped his mouth. He couldn't look at the body any longer, but he didn't need to.

'Who the hell did you see doing rounds before me?' he demanded.

'I-I didn't see their face, I only saw them leaving, but they had a hood on and I-I—' Lukas was clearly in shock. His shovel dropped again. This time neither of them made an effort to pick it up.

***

Some stories lied. But Arthur believed there was always an element of truth behind them. He had read hundreds of journal entries over the last few years but there were some special stories written. Stories the writer had warned every reader not to ever forget, like the stories of the great World Wars, world-changing assassinations, and holy wars and purges. Stories of bravery and slavery, of corruption and colonialism. Stories lost into the future as history never fell into conversation anymore. It was too risky.

There was only one story which drew to his mind now. A

story that made him shiver with fright, lock his windows and doors, and pray to a God he didn't believe in when he was only thirteen years old. The story of Jack the Ripper, the infamous murderer from over two hundred years ago. A man who brutally murdered the women of Whitechapel.

He could picture it as clear as day, as if the victim were laying on the table in front of him right now; her green dress dirtied with blood and rubble. Her face askew, flesh hanging waywardly defiling the natural state of human creation. The body—Arthur shook his head. Surely this was all the work of his imagination? He had tried to convince himself for hours, but what he had seen was an exact replica of the murders described in that story. He needed to warn people.

The Wayward Tavern was bustling with unusual commotion. The shouts and jeers of drunken men filled the bleak atmosphere. Arthur retold the story of finding the bloodied corpse around a hundred times to the townsfolk that gave him a chance to tell it. He answered question after question from all the locals.

Shock and concern were one of the numerous reactions that soon turned to relief and humour. Greg, a careful-eyed bald man with a heavy cockney accent, listened eagerly, before bawling with laughter.

'Well a' least it was a worthless woman,' he grunted, before entertaining himself with another gulp of beer.

'Yeah mate, I heard it was one of them women from the brothel. I wonder if she got paid before she go' killed,' Stu interjected, his eyebrows raised as if he were truly concerned.

Arthur gritted his teeth. Surely there was a man in Whitechapel who wouldn't react like this?

'What's all the commotion here?' Gareth had walked in and joined them by the bar. 'I'll have the usual.' He winked at Mary-Anne, the barmaid. She got to work while masking a blush.

Gareth had a way of enticing people. His presence brought the crowd to a quiet murmur.

'So, does anyone want to tell me what's going on? I've been

hearing all sorts of talk on the way here.'

'Young Arthur 'ere,' Greg pointed a dirty finger at Arthur, 'found a body.'

Gareth raised his eyebrow at Arthur. 'The body at the dump?

'It's not just a body!' Arthur sounded exasperated.

He breathed in, before recounting the story another tedious time for Gareth. Every time he repeated his account he had to revisit the memory of this morning. Images of the woman's mangled body filled his mind with immense detail: the remnants of life, the colour of murder, the design of the killer... 'You see, I've been told all of this before, a long time ago! It's definitely the work of this Jack the Ripper!'

'Jack the Ripper? Never heard of him.' Gareth looked at Arthur the way an adult would look at a child trying to explain the boogieman under the bed. 'Are you sure you're not letting your imagination run a little wild?'

'No, I've never seen anything like this before. The person was murdered in the exact way they described the infamous Jack the Ripper's killings.' Arthur stood his ground against such a tall and fierce-looking man. As he stood so close to Gareth, he noticed just how broad his shoulders and chest were. He was probably well into his thirties, a decade older than Arthur was. Strength was a necessity for Peacekeepers, and Gareth fit the bill.

'And I'm assuming you see more dead bodies than a Peacekeeper?' Gareth's patronising tone rung clear in the air.

The tavern fell silent.

'N-no, that's not what I'm saying, bu—'

'I've heard enough, kid. There was a murder, I'll try to catch the killer. It's nothing new. That's all there is to it. Let's not spread any nasty rumours and create any panic.'

The townsfolk all nodded and murmured. His words sounded mature and correct. But it frustrated Arthur. What did he mean by *try* to catch the killer? He knew his words would be lost with them today and it was pointless to continue arguing.

Instead, he finished his drink and left the men to their own chatter. As he left the tavern, he caught the eye of Mary-Anne. Her concerned face was quickly masked with a—

'Thank you for coming, have a nice day.' And a brisk smile.

The sun had reached its highest point, shining a blindingly bright light down on Arthur. The irony; such a bright light during a dark time. Why didn't people care about this woman? About this murder? About Jack? Did they have any idea what they were up against if they were dealing with a modern-day Jack the Ripper?

Greg and Stu thought so lowly of women, it disgusted him. But he knew it wasn't just these men. Most people in Whitechapel thought like them. *Fools*. A woman dying wouldn't mean much to the people here.

Even the women themselves devalued their own gender. They didn't believe they were equal to men simply because they believed they couldn't do what the men could. Men were *supposed* to train to fight and protect them; women were *supposed* to do their duty by looking after their families. It was that simple to them. Lost were the days of equality Arthur had read about.

It was beyond frustrating.

He approached a crossroad and walked down Fairclough Street on his right. He passed by Mrs Gower's clothes shop, where the kind-hearted woman spent most of her time knitting and weaving new clothes. Beside her shop was the popular pizza shop. There was nothing like a good old stone-baked pizza. In an hour's time, there would be a long line of people queuing up. Farther along the road was the Dark Quarters and the brothels that Stu had mentioned earlier.

Just then, in the reflection of the glass of the building, Arthur noticed the movement of a dark figure behind him, somewhere on the rooftops. He turned around.

Nothing.

He squinted, in vain. Surely he had just seen a child running across the rooftop? He picked up his pace and kept looking towards the roofs, but the sunlight interrupted his vision. He gazed away. There! In the reflection of another window, he saw a dark-hooded, short figure. He turned, and just like that, they were gone.

Was he seriously imagining things now? He searched into his memory and recalled the two glimpses he had just seen. He wasn't wrong. There had definitely been someone there, running across the roofs.

The Ripper?

4. I Can See You

Tina

The sun stole away from the reaches of clouds and begun its descending fury on the roofs of Whitechapel. Tina found her usual position—the shadows—behind a chimney on the brick-top roof of a bakery. The smell of fresh produce filled her lungs and made her inner childish urges itch and her stomach growl with frustration. Her mind, however, was occupied by another thought: she had been seen by someone. A man with blond hair. From where he had stood, he had looked a slim yet slightly bulky figure of at least six feet. It wasn't strange that a person would notice someone running on the roof, but she wasn't an ordinary person. She had been shadow-stepping across the roofs, and she was *good* at shadow-stepping. So why did he look up twice? He shouldn't have been able to notice her this much. The look on his face had been a mixture of fright and determination. Something told her this wouldn't be the last time she saw him.

She walked to the edge of the roof and gazed down at the bustling street. A long queue had formed outside the pizza shop. Men, carrying heavy loads in their cart, walked by the bakery. Children on their bicycles raced past. Women with babies in prams waltzed along the pavement, avoiding the carts. Tina stretched out her hands and shaped the biggest figure she could, trying to attract their line of sight. One of the men looked up and seemed to glance at her. He squinted, almost like he was trying to focus on her, but couldn't. After a few seconds, his head dropped, and he continued his chores as if he hadn't seen anything.

Her eyebrows knitted together. How had the blond man seen her?

The rhythmic moving from the bakery below was slowly overwhelmed by another sound. Another rhythm. It came from the building a few houses down. It sounded muffled at first, but Tina's sharp hearing allowed her to hear more.

Someone was playing an instrument, a piano? All music was outlawed in Whitechapel, just as it was across many areas allied with the White Arrow. Ever since the third cultural revolution years ago, public gatherings, books, music, art, everything that expressed a person's feelings had been banned. Failing to follow this rule could lead to arrest or worse.

How interesting, she thought.

She crept across to the building and rested alongside the chimney, listening to the sounds getting clearer. It was a women's voice, and she was singing.

> *You can hold the knife but,*
> *You cannot tempt me.*
> *I can see things that*
> *Nobody else sees.*
> *You can cuff my wrists and,*
> *Hold me to reason.*
> *You cannot tempt me,*
> *To tell me what my worth is.*

Her voice sounded young and beautiful. Her words were well thought out, and dangerous. She sat there listening, verse after verse, as minutes turned to hours. But the music continued.

> *If you gave me a pen,*
> *I would write you a poem,*
> *Sing you a chord,*
> *And fight with your demons.*

> *If you gave me a knife,*
> *I might carve out my soul.*

Pray for your cause,
And tell you my woes.

Tina fought the urge to peer through the window and steal a closer look at this wondrous vocalist. Instead, she took out a large sheet of paper that was folded in her bag, and a pencil. She surveyed the roofs and the streets below and began to map out her findings.

Eventually, her growling stomach interrupted her, so she found her way down to the shops and picked up some food. She had brought enough money with her from New India to buy what she needed to live off—not that it mattered. Nobody ever noticed her walking in or out of shops. She could have stolen the food, as most people with her abilities might have done, but of course, somebody back in New India would scold her if they found out. Most definitely Master John. So she always left some money by the counter. Her small, quiet and unnoticeable presence allowed her to slip in and out of a shop without any attention.

So just *who* was that blond guy who had noticed her? The thought kept nagging at her like an irritating itch.

The sun had begun to set, and with it, the shadows formed armies. She hopped across the roofs and found her way back to the large square rooftop of the school. Before she entered, her ears picked up an abrupt and sharp sound. It came from one of the blocks she had just passed. In all her years of combat and training, Tina knew exactly what it was, but she denied it for a second.

A bloodcurdling scream, then choking, like someone was gagging for air. Then silence.

I'm here to live in peace and quiet, she told herself. Getting involved in other people's business was not on her agenda. But she knew, if Lars ever found out she had ignored something like this, he would roast her. Figuratively, of course. *Goddamn it.*

Someone was about to get killed, and as much as she wanted to just ignore it, she couldn't. She grinded her teeth. Then—in half-a-blink—she dropped her bag on the roof and turned towards the sound of the struggle.

How troublesome.

She arrived at an alleyway, a light-forsaken gap sandwiched between two tall buildings. A hooded figure was bent down, their hands moving in an erratic fashion, a knife in their hand, covered in dark red. The smell of decaying food, fresh meat, and blood filled the air. She crept closer and saw a body on the ground by the cloaked figure. A woman's body cut up and mutilated.

A deep burning fury leapt through Tina's body. Her fingers wrapped around the hilts of her daggers in an instant, a well-practiced and natural reaction. She flung one towards the disgusting figure a few metres from her. They avoided it, jumping to the side and crashing into the trashcans. Tina's breath caught in her throat.

Something was wrong. The figure in front of her had just shadow-stepped, albeit a weak and clumsy step. Just who was this person? They were wearing a mask; a curly black moustache painted on a white frowning face. Was there another assassin in Whitechapel? No, it couldn't be—their form lacked practice and experience. They must have moved out of pure instinct.

'Whew, that was close. If I hadn't felt your murderous intent, I probably wouldn't have even noticed you were there.' They spoke through a voice distorter; it must have been attached to the mask. Tina couldn't tell who she was up against, whether they were old or young, someone she knew or didn't know. 'So, what is a young lady like yourself doing here? I've never seen *you* before.'

Tina stayed silent. Her eyes rested on the lifeless corpse of the woman between them, before looking back at the mask. She heard movement behind her and turned to see the same blond-haired man she had seen earlier. He stood at the entrance of the alleyway.

'Who's there?' he called out.

He clearly hadn't seen anything yet; he must have just heard the crashing of the trashcans. But what was he doing in these parts anyway?

Tina turned back to find the masked person had disappeared into the darkness. *Damn.* Just when they were right in front of her. She needed to leave the scene as quietly as possible.

She began to walk away, blending into the shado—

'Don't move. I can see you.' It was the man behind her.

The same thought resurfaced. Just how was he able to see her when nobody else noticed her?

She faced him, swallowing hard. Was she nervous? Why would she be? He was unarmed. It couldn't be possible—it had to be some sort of a fluke. She could simply walk past him unnoticed. She picked up her dagger and took one last glance at the mutilated woman behind her, before silently walking out of the alleyway. She took two quick shadow-steps towards the man, sidestepping him.

He didn't notice. She was too quick.

But then his head turned and faced hers directly as she attempted to pass him. His eyes bore into hers. He fully acknowledged her presence. His eyes were like Larsson's; burning with the fury of a star and yet as composed as a cloudless night. They intrigued her.

But she couldn't have him running back and telling people about her existence. How troublesome.

5. Pizza

Arthur

His heart pounded against his chest, screaming the word *danger* at his ignorant mind. But his legs had a mind of their own and chose to freeze to the concrete. This little girl was dangerous. His mind frantically sought out rationale. He could just about make out an outline of a body in the dark, farther ahead. His eyes cast down at the girl's daggers. They weren't bloodied. He focused on her body, in a way that made him a little embarrassed, but he knew the moment he looked away she would slip out of his vision.

'Tell me who you are and what you saw.' Her hazel eyes and her pale face contrasted with the rest of her all-black attire.

'What are you, a Peacekeeper?' she fired back. Her voice didn't match her youthful looks. She spoke every word as if it were a command.

'No, my name is Arthur. I'm…' Well, what was he going to say? *I'm looking into a recent murder that was committed in the exact same way that Jack the Ripper used to kill his victims in the 1800s? Oh, and I think you might be Jack, but I'm not sure.*

'Listen, there isn't much time, it's almost dark. Go and report this, then come find me by the school up ahead. Come alone and don't tell anyone,' she commanded. 'And no, I did not commit this murder.'

Goosebumps ran up Arthur's arms as she spoke. She was so calm, as if she was used to seeing such horrors. She didn't commit *this* murder, she said, but which murders had she committed then? Arthur was not filled with assurance but nodded at her anyway. He wouldn't dare attempt to bring her in by himself.

Before he left, however, he walked over to the slain woman and engraved her into his memories. Her corpse hugged the dirty floor, her fingers curled at the touch of dirt as if she were clutching onto the very last earth moments before her life was ripped away. Signs of purple bruising ran across her sleeveless arms, her neck and torso were stained with dark-red.

He noticed the little girl gazing at him, her eyes searching, and her brow arched as if she were curious at the sight before her. Ever since he had discovered the first body, he couldn't wrestle with his mind to delete the woman from his memory. As much as it brought him great disdain, he knew these vivid images could come in handy afterwards, at the very least he could now compare the two victims.

He turned around and found himself alone in the alley, the girl had vanished into the night. Without another moment's delay, he sped through the streets.

After a few minutes, he found what he was looking for. Attached to a nearby pole was a brown pedestrian box. He flung it open and pulled out a whistle. It was small, but it would produce a very high-pitched sound, enough to alert other whistle-blowers.

An hour passed as he gave Gareth a statement. The Peacekeeper directed the clean-up crew—which consisted of Stu, Greg and Eve—to the scene of the crime before addressing Arthur.

'Two bodies of women were found with identical injuries and causes of death. Surely you believe me now?' asked Arthur.

'I don't want to hear any more of your Jack the Rapper theories, so keep quiet about this,' Gareth warned him. 'And as you're the first one on the scene… don't leave town.'

Gareth didn't wait around to entertain Arthur's claims. He wanted to convince Gareth, refute and rebuttal his denials, tell him he was a fool for not believing him. But the thought of meeting this mysterious girl pushed his frustrations aside.

He left the scene of the crime and made towards the school.

Was he going insane? He was blindly trusting a potential killer with his life. The thought of the little girl being a threat to him was something that would have made for a round of laughter in the Wayward Tavern, but they hadn't seen her. They hadn't experienced her cold demeanour, her nimble and sharp movements, her lustful daggers. The one thought that kept festering inside him was that it could have been Lucy dead in a rotten alleyway. Next time it could be.

He was already halfway towards his destination when another thought crossed his mind. Maybe he should tell someone where he was going? He wiped a bead of sweat from his face. Who would he tell anyway? Gareth wouldn't care much. Also, he wouldn't want to draw him out only to find out he'd wasted his time. Maybe the girl wasn't going to be there? If anything, perhaps he would've told Eve, his neighbour and friend. She had moved into Mr Hudson's building several years ago. Although, back then she wasn't a mortician, but a nurse studying under Dr Dovedi. They were the only people who were permitted to read books, but only for the sake of learning for their profession.

His belly rumbled. He couldn't tell if it was out of fear or hunger at this point.

Shops were now closing for the day. He noticed a pizza shop in the near-distance and sighed. If things took a turn for the worst, perhaps the ripper would allow him to have one last meal.

***

The landscape of Whitechapel had altered and grown a little since the bombings in 2052. It had taken a good part of half a century to build a new town out of the rubble. He followed the path that now twisted and inclined towards higher ground. He was approaching the road that led to the school that was supposed to have been abandoned for several years. He couldn't remember ever needing to come to this part of Whitechapel. At least twenty minutes passed before finally, in the distance, he could make out the grim-looking building. Vines ran down the side and the windows were boarded up. The road was full of dirt and deteriorating litter. He made a mental note to clear this up on another day, if he lived that long. It would take him another fifteen minutes to walk to the ominous building.

He needed to focus. He was about to walk towards his potential death. *Stop being so pessimistic*, he kept telling himself. Perhaps the little girl was that at heart, just a little girl. His stomach growled. *Not now.*

The moon had replaced the sun as the solemn object in the sky. Arthur had never wanted to visit this school before. He had, after all, heard many ghastly rumours about it being haunted. Children all over Whitechapel would talk about eerie noises and ghoulish screams coming from inside. He never believed them, but it certainly didn't entice him enough to take a stroll through these neighbourhoods. He passed by several deteriorating and uninhabitable buildings leading up to the school. A gust of wind brought forth the smell of damp, and the unkempt grass had morphed into large bushes capable of playing an innocent game of hide and seek, or a murderous game of—

A screeching sound made him spin around frantically. The black school gates opened, on their own. If this girl really was the murderer, perhaps he was the worst victim of all. The fool who was walking right into her trap. The *only* thought that kept him from running away was the idea that Jack didn't kill men. But would that spare him? After all, perhaps she wasn't Jack the Ripper, but an ordinary killer who didn't discriminate against genders. The irony was simply unnerving.

He stepped through the gates. The doors lay hanging by a single hinge. A loud groaning sound induced shivers into Arthur's body. The hairs on the back of his neck stood tall, ready to jump out of his skin. What was that sound?

He clenched his fists. Why was he being so stupid? He was here for a reason. Justice needed to be dealt for the women who had been brutally killed. But more importantly, he wanted to get to the end of these attacks before it got out of hand, just as it had done two hundred or so years ago.

If this girl really was the murderer, then he would confront her, somehow. If she wasn't the murderer—which he hoped she wasn't—then perhaps she could be the very help he wasn't receiving from the rest of the town. After all, *she* was the one who'd asked him to come here. Was it simply the wrong time and wrong place for her in the alleyway? Or did she arrive there on purpose? What were her intentions?

The moonlight illuminated only the bare hallways; the rest of his sight was filled with darkness. From the shadows, by the bottom of the stairs that probably led to a labyrinth of corridors, he saw the girl appear. She wasn't holding her daggers, which brought him some relief. A small smile was drawn on her face.

'Oh, chill your boots, I usually make that screeching sound to scare away children.' Her eyes fell to his hands. 'Wait! Did you bring me food?' She licked her lips. She sounded so casual, like they hadn't just crossed paths at a murder scene only a few hours ago.

He nodded. 'I thought you might have gotten hungry.' His own stomach growled at him.

He would definitely write about this. He was meeting a potential killer, at an abandoned school, at midnight, with a margherita pizza. He decided to summon some bravery and walk towards her, but she was gone. *Where did she go?* Questions raced into his head. He looked down and gasped. She was standing right next to him now. Her hand was out, beckoning for the box of pizza. He leapt back in surprise. How in God's name did she get there? He could have sworn he was just staring at her by the stairs.

A hazy memory passed over him. He could remember seeing her now. She had simply walked over to him. Why hadn't he noticed her? Was he simply not paying attention? What was up with this girl? His brow creased in confusion.

'I find it strange too,' she replied as she opened the box and ripped a slice of pizza. 'I find it strange that you can even notice me so much.' She beckoned him to follow.

Arthur didn't understand what she was talking about, but he

decided to silently follow her. Even in the dark, he could make out her small figure. Her black hair fell to her shoulders and the way she walked was unlike anyone he knew. Her steps were infrequent, both small and large, while her pace was both quick and slow, almost undecided. He struggled to keep up with her. After a minute of walking up dirty staircases and down corridors filled with cobwebs, they arrived at a classroom. He surely would've got lost if he'd come by himself, and how he would leave this place was beyond him.

VR12, the sign on the door read. A virtual reality room, the most redundant classroom today. Arthur wondered what virtual reality was even like. The girl set the pizza on a desk. Why was she even here?

'Umm...' he began.

The girl walked over to the window and placed a wooden board across it. Had she seen him coming from there? The moonlight struggled to penetrate the boards hugging the windows, bringing the room to an almost complete darkness save the candlelight emanating from each corner of the room. 'Yes?' She looked his way.

'Why do you stay here? I'm sure the townsfolk could have accommodated you with a room in town.'

She looked at him like he was missing the obvious. 'Yes, that's why I'm staying here. Away from the town, and away from people. But let me save us some time. Sit,' she commanded him as if she were years older than him.

She pointed to a small chair that some poor child would have sat on years ago. Its plastic red frame looked ready to snap with any weight. Arthur's lips pressed together. How was a little girl like her telling him what to do? But he followed her finger and carefully found a safe position to rest his weight.

'My name is Tina. I came from New India, a couple of areas east of here.'

Arthur knew exactly where New India was. It was the area that was famous for its predominantly Indian population; it was the second or third largest slum area, made up of the old eastern towns; starting from the borders of the Deep Slums and stretching north-east, all the way across Kingsland to the corners of the Shamal. This was just one example of how London had divided itself after the revolutions.

But Tina didn't look Indian at all. If anything, her olive-skinned complexion, combined with her dark hair, made her look a mix between an Arab and a European. Many people of different backgrounds used to come to Whitechapel during the rebuilding of the town.

She continued, 'I didn't, and haven't committed any unlawful or unjust murders, or any murders in Whitechapel for that matter.' Arthur shifted in his seat. She hadn't admitted to never murdering anyone ever, just not in Whitechapel. 'I don't know who has been killing these women, but you should definitely keep looking into it. I may be an assassin but I'm not the same killer.'

The last words took a few seconds to sink into his over-spilling bathtub of consumption. The chair snapped, and he clattered to the floor.

'Wh-what? An assassin?'

''Yeah … but I'm a good assassin.' She replied like it was a perfectly understandable statement.

'A *good* assassin? Does that even exist?' He picked himself up and found another chair.

'What are you, fourteen? Of course good assassins exist,' she snapped as if she couldn't believe what she was hearing.

'I'm twenty-one actually, and aren't you a little too young to be… an assassin?'

She looked him up and down, before looking away. 'I'm turning nineteen next week.'

Arthur's eyes widened. The girl's petite frame made her look younger than she actually was. More courage filled his insides. The logic made him feel silly. So, she was an eighteen-year-old assassin from New India, the area famous for its culture and education.

'Am I right in assuming that you're from the New India

Martial Arts School?' Her eyes lit up as Arthur asked.

'Oh, you know about NIMAS? Yeah, I graduated from there a year ago.' She sounded excited, like a child hearing praise.

Graduating from NIMAS certainly *was* praiseworthy. It was known as one of the toughest schools of the new age, with the best masters teaching a variety of ways of fighting. In a world where conflict was common, learning at NIMAS was a privilege beyond measure for some.

Another thought dawned upon him. 'How come you're telling me all this? If you say you're here to keep yourself to yourself, why invite me here? Why tell me anything?' He tried to choose his words as carefully as he could.

Her eyes pierced into his.

'I know I can trust you. You live alone, in a small apartment on Cavell Street. You clean streets and sort garbage during the day, and you have a good sense of morality from what I've picked up. Plus, you trusted me enough to even come here without telling anyone. Wait, you didn't tell anyone, did you?' She shot a fleeting glance towards her daggers, which were resting by the whiteboard, where the teachers used to put their whiteboard markers.

Arthur raised his palms and immediately assured her he hadn't. 'So, you've stalked me,' he said.

She rolled her eyes. 'Did you not hear?' She looked at him as if she was trying to decipher if he was genuinely forgetful.

'No, I get it, you're an assassin. Reconnaissance is part of your role.' He paused. He had never met an assassin before, though he had read that they were people of darkness and blood. But perhaps not everything he read was true. 'You *can* trust me. If you don't want anyone to know about you, then that's fine by me. As long as you're not killing anyone here or committing any other devious actions.'

'Well, you're the only devious one here, visiting an innocent eighteen-year-old girl at midnight.' Arthur shot her a blank look. She laughed. 'Anyway, there's your answers. Now I've got a question for you.'

Arthur nodded slowly.

'How is it you could notice me earlier?'

Arthur frowned. 'Are you supposed to be invisible or something?'

She shook her head. 'I've learned to hide my presence, and my aura, to such a level that most people don't seem to even pay attention to me. It makes being an assassin a lot easier. But you've been able to notice me all day.'

He recalled back to during the day. Things were starting to make sense now.

'That's not entirely correct, I only started to notice you through the reflections of the window. I wouldn't think to look for someone on the roof.' His lips pressed to the side as he began to think. 'It may have something to do with the fact that I can remember everything I see?'

'Hmm…' Tina reached for another slice of pizza. 'I still don't get it. What's that got to do with your ability to see something your mind shouldn't be able to register?'

The question stirred in the silence, as Arthur tried to piece together an explanation.

A candle wavered in ignorance and the shadows around the room danced with it. Arthur finally understood. He leapt up and walked over to the Whiteboard, using his sleeves to wipe away the dust.

'Lemme try to explain.' He grabbed a black marker and prayed it worked. It did. He drew a circle. 'This is me.' Then he drew another circle farther away. 'This is yo—'

'Why am I a circle?'

'Fine, what do you want to be? A triangle?' She had sparks of immaturity about her. It calmed him, reassured him.

'Whatever, carry on.' She rolled her eyes.

He did his best to explain it, drawing arrows and dotted lines. 'Like you said, you've trained yourself to not be noticed as much, and in addition, you're small.' That earned a glare from her. 'You're able to hide your presence well, and at times, fall out of a person's focus. Your presence—or whatever you want to call it—is suppressed so that their brain simply doesn't register you being there.' He drew an arrow to represent movement. 'Well, not until you move, which is when their eyes pick up movement, as they should. But it's probably because of your small frame and genuine speed that you're able to move almost as if you're invisible for a second.' He put his hands to his stubbly face and tried to rephrase. 'You simply look like you phase in and out of their line of sight.'

'Okay *sir*,' she said mockingly. 'I think I *know* about my own abilities. What I do is called shadow-stepping, to seemingly phase in and out of someone's line of sight, but why is it *YOU* can see me?' He could see her fidgeting with her fingers, growing impatient.

'Well, if you let me finish, my memory records everything my eyes see. My brain is registering your movements and I'm seeing it as a memory. You're slipping out of my attention temporarily, but you're not really escaping what my eyes are seeing and what my memory is recording. In other words, I can see you move.' He tried his best to make sense of it all. Even someone like him, who had always been quick to analyse and understand things, found this unique concept a mind-bender.

Tina didn't show any signs of confusion nor complete understanding. Instead, she stood up and pushed a table aside to create some space. She bent her knees and took a step back. She looked as if she was about to dash towards him. Her lips curled as if she was trying to comprehend his explanation. She readied herself. Arthur complied; he focused on her stance, her body, her eyes. He would try to see her move, to see her Shadow-Step, as she called it.

She dashed to his left, disappearing into the very darkness of the—no she wasn't gone, it was almost as if he was watching her after-image. She was unbelievably nimble and light on her feet. She had swerved past chairs, moving at breath-taking speed. Before he knew it, her face was an inch away from his, her eyes shone with a beautiful shade. Her daggers were suddenly in her hands and poked at his ribs. A satisfied smile was drawn on her lips. She had even picked up her daggers in that movement?

'No.' Her warm breath bounced off his skin, as she leaned in and whispered. 'It's not that you can see me move at all. You can remember my movements, only after I've moved. At best, you can use your memory to predict where I'm going, and at worst, you're seeing me too late.' She leaped back and grabbed another slice of pizza.

He gulped. A bead of sweat slid down Arthur's face, and his rapid heartbeat started to slow. This girl was crazy. It made him wonder, just what kind of monstrous people graduated from NIMAS?

She looked at him and seemed to register his fear. 'Don't worry, Arthur. I would never hurt you. Your eyes are too similar to Larsson's.'

'Larsson?' But she ignored him.

'You better head home. It's already late.'

He nodded.

But he wasn't finished yet. He needed her help. He needed to get to the bottom of whatever was going on in Whitechapel. They quietly walked back through the maze of corridors and out of the school. Although the meeting was odd and frightening, he felt like he had made a friend of her. He hoped.

She thanked him for the food and led him out of the school. Before he reached the gate, he turned around and met her gaze.

'I need your help. I need to stop these murders from happening. My sister has been missing for over a month and I'm worried that I'll find her body next.' He found himself struggling for saliva as his throat turned to a desert. 'You're an assassin. Together, we can save these women's lives and put this Jack the Ripper copycat away.'

'Who's Jack the Ripper?' But she didn't wait for an answer. 'Look, I'm sorry about your sister and for the record, the person I met today in the alley is definitely one of the townsfolk. I could tell as much from the way they spoke.'

Arthur nodded quietly. She would make such an asset in his

search for this killer.

'And anyway,' she continued, 'what are you going to do once you catch him? Hand him over to the White Arrow?'

Arthur couldn't think of a response. If he caught the killer, Gareth would most definitely hand them over to the White Arrow. The same government that had caused this mess in the first place.

'The answer is no," she said. "I want no involvement in any of this. I just want a quiet and peaceful time here in Whitechapel. Let the Peacekeeper deal with this killer. Go back to cleaning the streets.' And with that, she closed the gate and slipped out of sight before Arthur could respond.

He couldn't believe she had refused him. Wasn't she a graduate of NIMAS? Leave this to a Peacekeeper? He gritted his teeth.

Why was it that the people with the power to do something were the ones who always acted the most selfishly?

6. **Lucy** Hudson

Arthur

The next day felt as ordinary as it could have been. The townsfolk didn't speak about the murders from the previous nights; they simply carried on with their lives. Even though two women had been murdered in cold blood. Surely there should have been some level of tension, if not hysteria?

He was working the lower streets today, picking up litter—cans, bottles, cardboard boxes, and other mundane materials. Lukas had cycled the cart full of bins and was waiting for the waste to be deposited in them. The man with one working hand had resumed his composed, and frankly weird, state. Speaking about crows, bees, wolves and today, it was vampires. Arthur had once read a journal entry about these mythical characters. Bloodsuckers. Lukas reckoned the murderer was one of them, who preyed on young women's blood. Arthur, who had been in a sullen mood since last night, found this lifted his spirits a bit. Although he knew there were no such things as vampires, or creatures that hide in the shadows and feast on the blood of humans, at least someone other than him was thinking about it. Even if vampires were the wrong way to think about it.

After all, he had read enough to know what kind of vile creature had caused these deaths. To not only slash the throat of these women, but then to also mutilate their bodies…there was only one type of killer that could perform such a heinous act, and it was no vampire. He couldn't imagine the horror of finding Lucy covered in blood—

He shook his head.

Whether Tina helped him or not, and whether the townsfolk believed him or not, he had a moral obligation to help people.

He didn't need Lucy to tell him this anymore. He needed to work smarter.

After returning from work, he brainstormed all his ideas before deciding how he would go about his search. Arthur thought about listing all the people he knew who thought of women as inferior to men, but that would've included at least three-quarters of the townsfolk. Longer than the amount of space on his page. He didn't want to waste paper unnecessarily; it had cost him a half-pound for a sheet, which was almost a day's wage. Not to mention, as a street cleaner, he wasn't licensed to scribe.

He needed to be more specific. He started to list those who worked with knives or other sharp objects—like the barbers and butchers—and those who had any past grievances with women. Which, from his memory, were a couple men; including Gareth and his cronies.

The journals about Jack the Ripper were very inconsistent with details. They described the horrors of the killings, the ritualistic symbolism and methodical tact of the action, but they never really confirmed who the killer was in the end. It was always left a mystery. But not on Arthur's watch—Whitechapel would get its justice this time.

He drew out a long list of thirty-six names. He made sure to put any personal bias to the side, and to write every name that fit the criteria. Including Tina.

He wasn't angry at her. Well, he wasn't anymore. If anything, *he* was the one being selfish. To ask a young girl, who wanted to live in peace, to get involved with something that she shouldn't need to, was a selfish thought.

He sat for a moment and analysed the list of names. Did this make him some sort of detective? Mr Hudson had told him a story once, about a famous detective living in the heart of London.

What was his name again?

Arthur wished at times that his memory extended to remembering everything he heard, but unfortunately, his gift was limited only to sight.

After a few minutes, he'd drawn up a rota. Working around his duties he would need to visit these people, one by one. He would ask them questions and hopefully gather clues, or better yet, see if he could trick their tongue for information that could incriminate them, or someone, or just point him in the right direction.

This is what detectives do, right?

The image of the woman by the dumpsite flashed through his mind: her limp corpse splattered in red, her neck bulging with torn flesh. He squeezed his eyes shut to try to block the image out, but then something made him stop. Instead, he tried to recapture it once more. Something looked odd. Her neck—there was something odd about the flesh—the cut. What was it? A sickening feeling tore through his guts the longer he pictured her. He needed to think of something else before he puked in his own room.

The ultimate question was: who would go this far to kill someone? The people of Whitechapel were generally peaceful folk, but that didn't mean they were an innocent bunch. Starting with Gareth, the Peacekeeper, there were many in Whitechapel who simply wanted to exploit their positions for their own gain. Lucy had warned him of this. He just needed to know which one of these men would go so far as to kill another human being in such a grotesque manner.

Several minutes passed in contemplation. Dark clouds clustered together, and the sound of rain teased his windows. Arthur decided he would start his investigation tomorrow. He really was sounding like a detective now.

Sherlock Holmes. That was the name.

A distant drumming sound filled the room as the rain began to build momentum. His eyes fell to his desk-drawer; he pulled it open and retrieved Lucy's journal. His hands ran across the creases of the brown leather book. Some of the pages had writings that were dated back over fifty years, and some were recent. *2107.*

Dear Reader,

A new wave of resistance has begun across the slums. Well, I say resistance, but it's more like a method to keep the peace. Strong groups of warriors have banded together and begun to control areas across the slums; a new power structure. Most of them with good intentions; protecting the people and the environment, as well as upholding some level of justice. Can you imagine? A superstar line-up of Peacekeepers.

I think it's brilliant, after so many years of anarchy, even if it comes from only the strongest people. It isn't a democracy, but it surely is better than being under the control of the White Arrow. They call these groups "Guilds". I hope that most of them keep their good intentions and don't abuse it. A friend of mine spoke about a new one that was formed in New India. They sound amazing. They are a group of young graduates from NIMAS. I think they called themselves "The Ruh." But what a talented bunch they are: The colossus figure Toby Welder, the master marksman Kisuke Neel, the dangerously skilled swordsman Larsson Dennith, and the genius from the rebel family, the leader of the Ruh, Sebastian Armstrong. I'm sure there are more members of this guild, but heck, people like this surely are a breath of fresh air in these dark slums. A fearless generation of people.

-Syria

Arthur stopped reading, frowning at the page as something caught his attention. He had heard one of these names before. He scanned them again until he found it. Larsson. He had heard that name from Tina. Was she acquainted with him? She was from NIMAS too. He decided he would ask her about this later. She said she wouldn't help him, but that didn't mean he couldn't visit her again.

He leaned back and rested his head against his timbre chair. Whitechapel didn't have a guild, but if it did, surely these kinds of murders wouldn't happen. Perhaps if there were a group of strong Peacekeepers patrolling the area? Gareth and his men weren't enough. Although he did control the area, there were still plenty of devious characters causing trouble from time-to-time. His main priority was always to keep the community from panicking by hushing up any troublesome events. But in times like this, when the community needed to be aware and protected? Simply keeping these murders quiet wasn't the right thing to do, was it? Arthur was no Peacekeeper or warrior, but his moral compass certainly pointed him in a different direction than Gareth's.

His fingers rustled past a page that had a corner marked, Lucy's entry. She had written in it months ago, before her untimely disappearance. He could remember her sitting on the bed, watching him, making sure he wasn't peeking.

He wondered if she had decided to travel to another area, but that was a rare thing to do. Her stuff was still here, and surely she would have taken her belongings with her, even if she wanted to leave in secret. Next week would mark the second month of her disappearance. A deep rotten feeling grew in his gut once again, and he squeezed the journal with his fingertips. Would it do any good to hold on to the hope that she was still alive?

She is *alive*, he told himself, firmly. *She'll come back, one day.* But with all these women being attacked and left for dead, it was growing harder and harder for him to believe.

He couldn't shake the thought that the next body he found could very well be hers. He didn't want to think about that, didn't want to imagine it…but it was true. Was he giving up on Lucy or was this the real reason why he felt so strongly towards catching this killer? This copycat. This evil, wretched, fiend.

His fingers snapped open the page his sister had written in. If he was going to feel this terrible tonight, then he would let these feelings swarm him altogether. If Lucy was really dead, then he would have to be brave enough to face her in his own way.

His heart was thudding against his ribcage as he stared down at the page. There was no date.

Dear Arthur.

Did I shock you? Of course I'm addressing you. There's no point addressing anyone else, and knowing you, you're nosy enough to read my writing one day. If you're reading this and I'm not around, then take heed little brother, and pay attention to what I have to say. I'm about to tell you a story, a story of how the world came to be. Call it the new Genesis, but I've spent an ample number of hours studying the writing of others, reading hundreds of illegal books, all to understand the history that was lost.

You are the perfect person to write for. Why? Because you're able to remember and you're emotional, so I know you'll do something about it! I'm about to tell you why the White Arrow started their cultural revolutions, their purges, their deletion of written words. Why nations turned against each other and how the Great Cyber Age came to an end.

Arthur felt a wave of emotions crash through his psyche. His insides burned like the core of a flame, tightening in his chest; his head ached with anxiety. He read her words carefully. Every time he blinked, his vision became obscured from the streams of tears that poured uncontrollably down his cheeks. He just wanted to be in her arms right now, he just wanted to hear her speak. He wanted her to tell him the story, not for him to read it.

I'll start with this, however, before I begin my story. The darkest days of humanity are the days when art lies forsaken, languages are lost in translation, culture is buried and burned, and history is forgotten, unwritten. I leave you a task—to save this city, this country, and this world.

You might be thinking you're unworthy of such a burden, but that's not true. Even if we're not related by blood, you are a special person. Trust me, I've studied your bloodline. You are my hope. So here it is.

He shivered as he read the last line of the page. His arms were decorated with goosebumps. He was about to read, possibly, his sister's last words. *A story of how the world came to be? And what does she mean, she studied my bloodline?*

Holding his breath, he turned the page.

Arthur had always been a person who was extremely strong, mentally. He never let things like pride stifle him, he didn't care for his reputation, nor was he worried about what the townsfolk said about him. He didn't care that he couldn't wield a sword properly, and he never avoided backbreaking hard labour if it meant he was doing his part for the community. He was the man who never let anything break him mentally. The rain cascaded against his window, almost to mirror the storm that he was fighting inside him.

His sister's pages of writing had been ripped from the book, leaving behind only a ragged edge of the margin. They were all missing, like her. To say he felt broken wouldn't be correct.

His pristine, robust, glass of mental strength was simply shattered.

7. Chin Up

Arthur

'Chin up, Arthur,' Bart whispered, peering over Arthur, snapping him out of his melancholic daydream.

A bottomless and heavy dark hole eroded away at his stomach, twisting and churning with every question and lingering thought he had about those missing pages. Someone had ripped them out of the journal, but why? He squinted hard, as if to squeeze out every bitter feeling coursing through his mind.

'No, no, chin up.' Bart motioned with his own chin before bringing his cut-throat blade close to Arthur's skin.

Bart the barber was the first person Arthur had decided to pay a visit to. His small shop sat on the long road of shops, in between the Wayward Inn and the local grocer. He had known Bart since he was twelve-years-old, when Mr Hudson had adopted him. Signs of weariness and age had grown on Bart's face and hands. He was probably well into his fifties. His greying brows hovered over Arthur with a frown.

He could not imagine Bart to be involved in any way, not at his age and not with his kind and quiet personality. His eyes shone with concentration behind his steel-framed spectacles.

'Bart. Have you heard of the recent deaths in Whitechapel?'

'The poor women found in godforsaken places? Yeah.' Bart pulled the cut-throat away to wipe it against a towel. 'It's a sad, sad time for this town.'

'Do you think it could have been done by anyone here?' Arthur asked, remembering what Tina had told him.

'You mean by one of the townsfolk?' He straightened up and wiped the blade on a cloth before continuing. 'I'm not too sure. I couldn't imagine anyone from here doing such a thing.' He paused to give Arthur a longing look. 'Are you looking into it?'

Arthur would've nodded had his neck not been at the mercy of the old barber's blade. The irony of the situation didn't sit well for him deep down. What if Bart was the Jack the Ripper copycat? Was it wise to ask him questions whilst being held at knife-point? The thought teased him. He answered the question with a smile.

'I just think someone should take an interest in the fleeting lives of our people. The women here are already shunned. It's almost as if our world has gone back to the dark ages.' Arthur stopped himself before he flew into a lecture that would definitely sound patronising to this man who was more than double his age. 'Have you ever heard of Jack the Ripper?'

Bart finished the shave and stowed his tools away. 'Will that be all today?' he asked politely.

Arthur nodded, wondering if he had said something that offended him. He paid the man with a small silver coin. Something that looked like the old twenty pence coin he had seen once in a journal.

'It's a dark road you're attempting to walk down, Arthur.' Bart eyed him with a stern frown that reminded him of Mr Hudson. 'I've seen you grow into a fine man. Mr Hudson would be proud of the work you're already doing in Whitechapel. Keeping the streets clean is as respectable as keeping the streets safe in my opinion.' With that, he turned away to clear up the blond straddles of hair that dirtied his floor.

**

'Did you know...' Lukas began, in his strong European accent. Today he was talking about crows again, the black-feathered ominous flying creatures.

They were collecting bottles on Fairclough Street, scouring the cobblestone road for their day's worth of wages.

'And they always hop. If you ever see a crow with both legs of the same length, then this would be a freak of nature. Crows hop because one leg is longer than the other.'

Arthur felt the light breeze caress his neck; it cut through his smooth and stubble-free skin with a light touch. He stopped walking. Again, the image of the dumpsite woman's corpse filled his mind. The neck. There was something about the way it was cut.

Lukas' voice snapped him back to reality.

'Isn't it ironic? A flock of crows is called a murder, and you've seen murders take place in Whitechapel.' The man with one arm in a sling beamed at him disturbingly.

Sometimes what Lukas said felt insensitive and alarming, but the feeble-looking cripple looked as innocent as a child learning to walk the streets of Whitechapel for the first time.

'This way, Lukas.' Arthur pointed down Christian Street.

Several days had passed since the first body was discovered, and Lukas had stuck with him for every shift they shared. They were *buddies* according to him, though the only thing that constituted this was the fact they had discovered the body together. The conversations they shared were often pointless and random, but Arthur felt comfortable talking to him. He put up with his wacky theories and in returned, Lukas listened to what Arthur would say. In a strange way, he appreciated Lukas' company. After all, nobody else cared to listen to him. He had told him about Jack the Ripper and all the gruesome things he had learned of the vile killer of the 19th century.

'So the killer would have to be someone with knowledge of the human body. Maybe it's that pretty nurse lady?'

'Eve?' Arthur hadn't got around to speaking to Eve yet. He had last seen her cleaning up the second corpse in the alley. 'I've known Eve for so long. I don't think she would be involved with this.'

'Still, Arthur, you're a smart young man, you can't rule anyone out.' He beamed stupidly again.

Arthur rolled his eyes. 'Yes of course, Lukas, I'll even keep you in mind too with your one good hand and brilliantly devious mind.'

'Aww, thanks buddy. But wait, what are you keeping me in mind for again?'

Just then, Arthur noticed the familiar figure of Tina racing across the rooftops. He drew his eyes to the brown tiles of the buildings that hadn't been worked on for decades.

'Is that a crow hopping across buildings? Didn't I say crows did that? Nasty rats they are, distrustful creatures.' Lukas squinted his eyes to try to get a better look.

Arthur didn't bother telling him who it was. The assassin wanted privacy, and he would give her that. Instead, he tore his gaze towards a poster that was stuck on a glass window in front of him. He had not seen it here before.

CIRCUS COMING TO TOWN, it read. The circus came to town every year, and Arthur attended it religiously. The poster was hand-drawn with an expert eye. Three clowns were standing in front of a large candy cane coloured tent. Curiosity and the thirst to be caught off guard with mind-boggling performances always drew him. But he would prefer to not go alone again.

He cast a quick glance at Lukas, who was now in a deep conversation with his reflection in the glass.

Arthur sighed.

8. The Melancholic Melody

Tina

Tina embarked on her morning routine. She left the school to survey the area, working from west to east, just as she was taught. She had almost finished sketching out the layout of the buildings, with every road and alleyway, every business and building of function. What surprised her about the large landscape of the area—which bordered between the Stepney Marshes and Aldgate—was the number of buildings that were left desolate and empty. Broken dust-decorated windows and boarded-up doors flagged these buildings to her attention. She made a note of them before leaping to another rooftop.

There were very few trees that flourished in this town; a tall oak stood at the heart of the town as a lonely figure of nature. Besides the scattered remnants of patches of green, Whitechapel's murky industrial town stood in stark contrast to New India.

Reconnaissance was the only task Sebastian had given her when she had departed from the Ruh, her guild, almost over a year ago. To travel to different areas and understand the layout and populace of each. He hadn't told her why he needed this information, but the leader of the Ruh was always up to something.

The air rustled her hair with every leap. She took no more than three steps on each rooftop before climbing to another. Her knees bent with every landing, and her hands swayed by her side to weigh her flight. She carefully applied everything she'd learned from the New India Martial Arts School. Within half an hour, she had swept across the town with a keen eye, noting the deteriorating and broken structures.

She had heard from Master John that there was a Mayor, a man with delightful humour. But she hadn't seen him anywhere in all her time here. Whitechapel was typical in its struggle to maintain social order. The only form of leadership she could observe was the local Peacekeeper and his group of men. She had watched them a few days ago, when a man called Gareth barked orders to his crew. His tall stature and broad shoulders cemented his role as the alpha of Whitechapel. She couldn't observe his strength as there weren't any obvious signs of trouble. A good sign. It was strange, however, that there weren't more official Peacekeepers here. A town without a Peacekeeper's guild was unusual.

Supplies from behind the White Arrow walls would arrive fortnightly. She would see people queueing up for food that would last them for a few weeks, material that would be used to make new clothes, and other supplies that looked as if they would be used for medicinal purposes.

One of the most sought-after supplies were batteries. People relied on them as their only source of energy, but just like in New India, they were expensive and only the wealthy could afford them. The rest of the townsfolk had to get them through illegitimate means. Batteries could power many redundant pieces of age-old technologies, including some heaters to use during colder seasons or clocks to help keep order.

Nothing out of the ordinary here; the White Arrow delivered to most law-abiding areas in similar fashion.

The outer ring of Whitechapel was decorated with patches of land used for agriculture and the rare cattle breeding. Vegetables grew in neat rows, a *very* good sign considering the surrounding towns were suffering from poor harvests.

During the night, she would see groups of people come into Whitechapel and head to the Dark Quarters. A few roads that were lined with brothels and other businesses that made her insides squirm. A few days ago, she had spotted Arthur there, walking into one of these buildings for a few minutes with his brown satchel weighing him down, only to leave a few minutes later looking pleased with himself. She hadn't expected him to be a customer of the Dark Quarters. She'd followed him back to his home. She needed to know more about him. She'd watched him through his window as he sifted through his satchel and pulled out a big stack of books. Illegal journals.

After turning him down, she had made it a task to see how Arthur reacted. He took to his daytime duties of cleaning the streets religiously. He never missed a shift, and she never once saw him complain where others did. There was something about him that made her feel at ease, whether it was the gentle and faint pulsing aura that emanated from him or the determined look he had behind his eyes. The one thing that she had acknowledged after meeting him in person was his honest and naive intentions. She knew he meant well.

Tina turned her attention to the burly Asian man who had drawn his cart to Pinchin Street. She was sure she had seen him once before, perhaps during the winter in New India. She would need to find a way to report back to the Ruh, and she felt the wood merchant would make for the perfect messenger. But she would have to observe his routine and character at least once more before she was sure.

She decided to spend the next few hours on the roof of the singer. She had grown fond of the talent and always felt comfortable there, listening to the melancholic and soothing voice of the woman, whom she still hadn't seen. But Tina didn't care; she just craved for more of the rhythmic sounds that emitted from the building. She leaned against the chimney and listened carefully. Every key that was struck danced in the air and mesmerised her senses, floating a warmth into the cloudy sky.

The one thing she relished in her stay away from New India was the brief escape she had from her duty as an assassin. But no one was watching her now.

Tina closed her eyes and absorbed the variation of pitches in the women's voice. Her head rocked slowly to the rhythm of the piano as it moved from a low pitch to high. She could see her brother's face, sitting in Lars' pub, *The Soulhaven*. She remembered sipping the hot chocolate her father made her. They were watching the snow fall from the windows in the dimly-lit corner.

A group of men sat in discussion, the heroes, The King's Arm they called them. Lennart, Khalid, Astal, and Master John. Their warm presence illuminated the dark setting of the pub. The music picked up pace, creating an intense feeling inside her. The piano chords were played with such precision and speed, and were perfectly matched by the woman's voice.

The heavens opened up, releasing a soft downpour of rain, but Tina didn't move. She sat rooted to the roof, listening to the most beautiful piece of music she had ever heard. The rain coursed through her hair. What was this song called?

Curling up into a ball, she leaned her head back against the chimney bricks. Tears began to stream down her cheeks without her permission, and a wave of memories flushed through her like a dam broken, bringing the wrath of uncontrollable water, twisting and turning in her mind. The memories changed as the music changed its intensity.

She saw flashes of fire—heard her father's voice—an explosion. The windows were thrust open, bringing a glimmer of hope as the wind and rain invaded their rooms, but it only made the fire worse. She could hardly breathe with all the smoke. She heard her brother's last gasp as a second explosion took him. Her father wailed as he held Reza in his arms. Her brother's eyes were open and white. Her father placed him on the floor before turning to her, lifting her into the air and throwing her out of the window, into the inky darkness of the night. What did he say to her before he did so? Everyone from the outside was shouting at him to jump out. She remembered her body falling, landing safely. Then she looked back up at the window, waiting. Not understanding why he wasn't coming.

'It's your turn now, Papa, jump,' Tina whispered to herself. 'Just jump. Don't leave me.'

Her heart ached, and her lips trembled as the cold rain

balanced the fire in her mind. She couldn't tell the difference between raindrops and tears at this moment. The singing reached its highest and most melancholic note, then came to an end. Everything always came to an end.

The rain stopped falling on her, yet she could still hear it. She flinched, almost gasping aloud. Lost in her reminiscence, she hadn't noticed someone standing right next to her. She quickly wiped her eyes with her sleeve.

Arthur held an umbrella in his hand, covering them both. A sombre and silent look crossed his face. How did he manage to get up here? More importantly, had he seen her cry? Her eyes tried to find meaning in his, but her mind came to rest when she saw the dark circles around his eyes. Had he been crying too?

He sat down gingerly, making sure he had enough grip to not slip off the roof. He leaned back against the chimney with her.

'Are you here to ask me to help you again?' she muttered, avoiding his eye contact. She felt bad for turning him down earlier, but she wanted to test his resolve.

'No, that's my burden to deal with. It seems you have your own.' The words rolled off his tongue as if he had already come to terms with her rejection.

The next song began. They sat in silence, listening to the masterpiece being played below. The minutes felt like hours. She didn't feel troubled by his presence, nor did she feel she needed to leave. They were both soaked now, but Tina didn't mind, and Arthur didn't seem to either. But why did he look so upset? She didn't think her rejection would make him like this. Something else must have happened. She was sure of it.

'Mary-Anne's voice is beautiful, isn't it?' He broke the silence with a voice that reflected his soft nature.

'The barmaid from the Wayward Tavern?' She recalled from her earlier surveillance.

He nodded. 'And the daughter of the Mayor too.'

So this was Mr Murray's house.

She looked up at Arthur. His blond hair and white face

glowed in the sunset, a different type of glow to her half-Iranian and half-Italian complexion. His aura felt calm and yet so unlike any she had ever felt before. It was something peaceful.

Mary-Anne began to hum below them.

Tina remembered the time she was first introduced to the idea by Master John. Aura: the innate power that every human being could harness with the right mental and physical training. Students spent countless years trying to perfect it. Those who successfully mastered it were able to push their bodies to the limit and achieve great things. With aura, Kisuke never missed an arrow, even with his eyes closed. Toby could lift unbelievably heavy things, and Lars could sense the presence of others without seeing them. It wasn't magic, just a way to heighten your senses. But Arthur was different; he radiated with an aura that felt innocent and pure, like it wasn't meant for fighting.

'Umm, earth to Tina, you've been staring at me for a minute now…' His grey eyes shined back at her.

'I…sorry, I never noticed the colour of your eyes,' she muttered, before changing the subject. 'Why did you come here?'

He looked across the roof and waited a moment before answering. 'I've seen you sitting on this roof before. I guess I'm noticing you more than usual, maybe because I'm always looking at the roofs now. You know, just in case I spot other young assassins roaming the roofs of Whitechapel.' He turned and faced her. 'You're part of the Ruh, right?'

This caught her attention. Had he learned this from the journals he read? She nodded. 'If you want to speak about this, let's go somewhere else.'

***

By the time they arrived at Arthur's house the sun had set, encompassing Whitechapel in the familiar eerie darkness, only accompanied by the faint moonlight hidden behind the clouds. It took Tina longer than usual, as she had to walk the streets with Arthur, after he had assured her that he would fall to his death if he tried to free-run across the roofs like her. They climbed a second flight of stairs, passing many doors along the way. Each one had a nameplate stuck on them. Arthur's room had the name "Lucy."

'It's my sister's name. She's…gone now,' he explained. Was this the reason behind his sullen appearance earlier?

The room was simple and small. A bed lay behind the door, a desk stood by the window, and a bookshelf was filled with various items. Everything besides books. There was also no wardrobe.

'A bookshelf without books,' she muttered, as she took a seat on his bed.

'Just in case I get an inspection. In this era, books are not meant for bookshelves. But—' he lifted up a floorboard by his bedside and pointed at a box that lay in a hole, '—for hidden places like this.' He pulled the box out and lifted the lid. Inside was a stack of journals. 'This was my sister's.'

Did she die? Tina wanted to ask but didn't know if the topic was too sensitive. She decided to leave that for another time. 'So, what did you want to ask?'

'I read some entries about New India, and a group of Peacekeepers called the Ruh. They mention Sebastian, Larsson, and others, but they never mention you. What exactly is the Ruh?' His words were coordinated well, except he kept pronouncing the name wrong.

He handed her a glass of fresh orange juice and some pastries he had fished for in a cupboard.

She gulped the juice down, thinking about just how much she should tell him. 'It's pronounced *Rooohh*, with a heavy H sound.'

'Oh, it's Arabic.'

She nodded. 'Ruh means Soul in Arabic. It's a guild made up of seven people, formed by Sebastian Armstrong. Most of us were a new generation of students all graduating from NIMAS at the same time. A lot of people don't know the Ruh has an assassin. Besides, I'm the youngest of them and graduated after most of them.' She pulled her cloak aside to reveal her daggers. 'Each one of us specialises in different skills. We decided to form a guild to help protect people and to eventually change the slums.'

'Change the slums? What do you mean? The slums are huge in London, how can one group hope to change everything outside the White Arrow wall?' His brows knitted together, seemingly in deep thought.

She shrugged. 'You'll have to ask Lars if you ever get to meet him. But he wanted to change the slums and help the people.'

'My sister…wanted me to do that too.' Silence fell with the sullen tone in Arthur's voice. He turned to her. 'So, that means you're a Peacekeeper too?'

Tina knew where he was going with this. She nodded. Being a Peacekeeper meant that she had a duty to ensure peace and stop any forms of violence or harmful actions.

'Seems like you've already got a Peacekeeper in Whitechapel,' she said nonchalantly.

'Don't start. Gareth does everything to keep things quiet rather than confront the problem at hand. He just likes to feed off the title, I doubt he really knows what it is to be a Peacekeeper.' Arthur sat down, and his hands made a fist that rested on the desk.

'And you do?'

'What?'

'You know what it means to be a Peacekeeper?' Tina shot back.

He shook his head. 'I just know that I want peace and equality. I don't want Whitechapel, and London in general, to be full of anarchy and violence.' He was very non-confrontational. Tina wondered what would happen if she kept provoking him.

'Peace? Isn't that what the White Arrow wants too? Why don't you join them then?'

He looked at her as if she had cracked a poor joke, then burst into laughter.

'My entire life I've been reading about this White Arrow organisation. I've seen the way they conduct business here from time to time. They believe Britain is for the pure-blooded and Aryan. There is nothing in my spectrum of morality that fits into the ideals of the White Arrow. I don't wish to divide people, segregate them, or have any fascist views.'

Tina liked the sound of him. As nimble as he looked, he had guts. After all, he'd just committed verbal treason. 'So, why don't you tell me how far you've got with this Jack the Ripper case?'

His eyes widened. 'Wait, what? Are you kidding?' He scrambled for his notes and lists.

This man had the moral fibre of Larsson and some of the intellect of Sebastian. He was like a hybrid version of them. 'I have a feeling that you're someone worth working with,' said Tina with a shrug. 'So, count me in. This will be a long night.'

'I wanted to ask you…' Arthur began to speak. By now, Tina had registered how his face looked when he was thinking. 'Did you notice anything weird about the victim's neck?'

Tina frowned. 'I didn't get a clear look in the alley. What are you thinking?'

He shook his head. 'It's probably nothing.'

She raised a brow. 'So are we officially calling this killer Jack the Ripper now?'

9. The Nurse

Arthur

The next morning, Arthur woke up to an embarrassed Tina. She profusely apologised for falling asleep on his bed, and he assured her it was not a problem. He didn't blame her, it must have been rough sleeping in a school all the time. He couldn't usher a young girl out in the dark, assassin or not. It reminded him of when Lucy was here. His back, however, ached from sleeping on the floor.

A knock on the door made them both jump.

'It's me, Eve,' came the familiar voice of his neighbour.

Tina shot him a look and mouthed something like: *Who is that?*

He gave her a calm glance back and whispered, 'Don't worry, she's a friend of mine.'

Arthur unlocked the door. Her appearance, as usual, made his eyes flicker and his stomach turn. Her dark-brown wavy hair rested on one side of her head, leaving a side of her neck bare and beautiful. He pushed these thoughts out of his head and welcomed her in. She was carrying a bag.

'I thought I heard another voice last night. Here, I've brought you breakfast.' She smiled and passed Arthur the bag of buttered bagels.

'Wow, thank you, that was really thoughtful.' And then he remembered—Tina didn't want to be seen or known in Whitechapel. He passed her a quick glance, but she was already staring out the window, hiding her face. Eve looked from her to him.

'Well then, Arthur! I've got work to do for Gareth. Killer on the loose and all. Have fun!' She winked at him before leaving.

Arthur sank into his bed. *How awkward*, he thought.

'She's the town's nurse and mortician. A really smart person, really helpful too.'

Tina raised a brow.

Arthur pressed his fingers against his eyes and massaged the ridge of his nose. 'Anyway…shall we get to work?'

***

Over the next few days, the mysterious assassin from New India became not so mysterious, as he learned a great deal about Tina. They tracked the people on their list, watching them, interviewing them, checking their alibis. Arthur did this while trying not to be too pushy. After all, he didn't want to attract any unwanted attention from Gareth for meddling in Peacekeeper business.

While Arthur worked on the streets of Whitechapel, Tina stalked each person and noted their day-to-day activities. She called it *observing* instead of stalking. Her previous surveillance of the area also became an asset to their search; they were able to figure out a lot of the townsfolk's routine, and where they would usually be. Although this didn't lead to a clear alibi for many of them, it gave Arthur an idea of the general movement of the townsfolk. It also told him a lot about what Tina had been doing in her spare time.

In the evenings they would often climb up to the roof and listen to Mary-Anne's singing whilst indulging in freshly baked cheese and tomato pizza. Arthur would ask Tina to tell him stories of New India and life outside of Whitechapel. He had never been outside of Whitechapel, not that he could remember anyway.

He was fascinated by what she spoke of—stories of swordsmen who could hypnotise you and control you. Stories of the Shamal, a town full of Muslims in the north, and a great warrior called Khalid. Stories of the red-haired hero Lennart Chance, the most dangerous man in all the slums north of the river, the man who was at the centre of the rebellion against the White Arrow.

Having read so many journals, his mind would often take him on journeys outside of Whitechapel. Allowing him to see, feel and hear through some of the more detailed and well-written entries. But the need to fulfil his duty to the community always brought him crashing back to reality. However, things were different now, his sister was missing now. One day perhaps—

'A RAID! A RAID! THE WHITE KNIGHTS ARE COMING!' Someone shouted from across the road.

***

It all happened within a few minutes. A White Arrow unit arrived in town on functioning Tesla vehicles. Functioning was a crucial detail, as Arthur had never witnessed electric powered cars driven by anyone else other than the White Arrow. The electric powered beast was like a mechanical assassin, fast and silent. No one had heard their arrival from the edge of town. Arthur could make out four figures dressed in white cloaks protruding from each of the three silver Teslas. It was still such a bizarre sight; to see a functioning vehicle run on electricity in the slums. But he had no time to waste now, within a few minutes they would be moving from home-to-home, exposing, arresting and punishing those with illegal goods.

Arthur found himself moving like a gust of wind down the narrow brick roads, fear fuelling his run and paranoia giving him an extra push. The thought of his journals being confiscated or worse, burned, made him remember all the things that Lucy mentioned in her entry.

The darkest days of humanity are the days when art lies forsaken, languages are lost in translation, culture is buried and burned, and history is forgotten, unwritten.

He gasped for air as he skidded 'round a corner. Tina had

bolted for the school the moment the raid was announced. It was more than likely that she wouldn't be seen until they had left, as finding a member of the Ruh in these parts would be like hitting the jackpot for the White Knights.

Raids weren't uncommon, but every time they occurred it always had Arthur on edge. His own crime of hoarding books would have easily won him an audience in one of the infamous detention centres, followed by a few years of labour by the walls. But it was the sight of White Knights that frightened him the most; they were warriors from the city that had been trained to deal with any signs of rebellion. They were strong and ruthless, they were the enforcers of every cultural revolution and purge. Many stories floated the slums, the most popular of which was the Battle of the Bridge; the famous showdown between the White Knights and Lennart Chance four years ago.

He turned into Cavell Street and walked up to his door. His fingers fumbled at the lock, sweaty palms made the simple task of opening a door difficult. In the corner of his vision, he could see four white cloaks, turning onto the road. His door clicked open, and in a quick movement he rushed inside and bolted up to his room. He felt as if he were moving at three times his usual speed, as was his heart. He found himself briskly scooping up all the journals that lay about his desk, as well as all parchments and pens, and depositing them in a box that lay beside his bed. He dropped to his knees, pulled a floorboard out from under his bed and pushed the box into a small hole—just about big enough for the box—before placing the wooden floorboard back.

He should have passed these journals on ages ago, it was safer that way. But he didn't want to just yet; he could potentially lose even more valuable information if he did. The thought of his sister's lost pages still haunted him, itching at his very soul.

A loud crash sounded from downstairs, someone shouted, and the sound of boots stomping drew closer. Arthur opened his door and almost jumped as he found himself staring into the mask of a White Knight. Black and red lines defined the facial features. It was the eyes that caught his attention. The sharp rectangular slits of the mask glowed, it was unlike any light he had ever seen before, as it was neither the light from a flame nor the light from the sun. Was this a form of city-technology? The White Knight's broad figure was wrapped in a white trench coat that trailed to the knees, a badge with the party crest was stuck on his chest. A circular logo with an arrow piercing through it. Under it was the slogan: *Making Britain Great Again.* As if Britain could only be great with one race acting more superior than another.

A sword hugged his waist. No doubt every White Knight would be skilled swordsmen that could rival most slum warriors, rival even Sebastian and Lars.

***

He had never been this close to a member of the raid-force before. His heart thrashed against his chest and his mind fought the numbness that coursed through his fingers. It was like standing in front of a sinister being that had crept out of a nightmare, ready to punish, to terrorise, to kill.

'Step aside.' The man or woman's voice was distorted behind the mask.

Arthur didn't need to be told twice, not that they would repeat themselves anyway. After a few minutes of rummaging through his room, flinging clothes and other items around, the White Knight stood beside his bed, the eyes of the mask glowing once more.

From the other rooms, Arthur could hear the shuffling of feet and the sound of items being thrown around, furniture being moved and muffled voices.

The White Knight pointed at his desk.

'What purpose does this have?'

'It's a desk...' The words rolled off his tongue, and regret tumbled after it.

'I know what it is. I'm asking you what purpose a desk has

for you.'

Arthur blinked. What could he possibly say to him? That he used it to write? To study? To read? Every answer would lead him straight to a detention centre.

'I…' Tears started to form at the corner of his eyes. 'I…I used to sleep on it, before my sister went missing,' he lied.

'You used to *sleep* on this?' Even behind the distorted voice, Arthur could hear the bewilderment in their voice.

He nodded, wiping the traces of false tears with his sleeve. Anything to avoid conflict.

'And I take it this bookshelf is used for something other than books?'

'Yes clearly,' Arthur said, pointing to a stack of clothes and other materials he had hurriedly thrown on the shelves.

'Your name?'

'Arthur Hudson.' Arthur watched as the eyes of the mask lit up once more.

'Your name and address have been noted on our system.'

Just then, a loud voice boomed from Eve's room. 'BOOKS FOUND.'

The White Knight hurried out of his room, Arthur followed him.

'What the heck is going on here?' Eve's voice rang out from downstairs. She must have just entered.

'They're inspecting our rooms.' Arthur whispered to her as she reached the top of the stairs.

Another White Knight approached them.

'Do you live here?'

'Yes,' Eve replied flatly.

'Are these books yours?'

'Yes. I have permission to read these books, look.' She rummaged through her bag for her credentials before passing over the sheet of paper. 'You see? I'm a nurse. I'm allowed access to these books.'

The eyes of the mask flashed and Arthur peered closely at it. He had read about some of the technology of the previous era and wondered if these masks took pictures like the old camera. If it did, that would mean that they had taken a picture of his face and his room, as well as Eve's face and her credentials. Arthur shook his head, maybe he was getting too ahead of himself.

'Your credentials have been verified. We have chosen to pardon you this time.'

A smile crept onto Eve's face.

'However, we will be confiscating these books. You will no longer be permitted to read any book that isn't produced by the Party.'

Eve's face grew pale. 'Wait…what?'

The White Knights moved in quick fashion, stowing all her books into a bag before pushing past them.

Arthur stood motionless. Did they understand what they were doing?

'But you *can't* take my books! There isn't a doctor here in Whitechapel anymore! I'm studying to become one!'

Arthur gritted his teeth. 'People will suffer if no one knows how to heal people!'

Their voices fell on deaf ears, or perhaps the helmets blocked them from listening to sane people.

'As of today, no one in the Hamlets will be allowed *any* books unless they are produced by the White Arrow. Whether it is for medical necessities or not. Furthermore, due to the number of violations noted across Whitechapel, we have concluded that within a fortnight, the White Arrow Party will discontinue its gracious services towards this town.'

Arthur hurried after them as they left the building.

'Wait, what does that mean?' he asked.

But the White Knights ignored him.

'It means there won't be any more supplies coming from the city. The town is sure to suffer now,' Eve spat, eyeing the White Knights with a fury that Arthur had never seen from her before.

In the distance, he could see Eve's books being piled up in the middle of the road. Eve had returned to her room, probably not wanting to see what happened next. One of the White

Knights stood by the books, his hand outstretched. He was holding some sort of cylindrical object. Arthur squinted for a better look but quickly took a step back.

A loud gushing sound was followed by a long stream of red that engulfed the books. Fire. Arthur's jaw clamped shut and his legs wouldn't move. His eyes remained focused on the scene before him. He could see the withering pages turning to ash, the leather spines and covers of the books melting to the floor. This was how the past hundred years had been deleted, how power was stripped from the people and freedom along with it.

Shouting from across the street could be heard above the roar of flames. Two people were locked in an argument.

'That's our food. We need that to survive,' shouted one of the townsmen as he followed a White Knight out of his house.

'The White Arrow supplied you with enough fruits, vegetables and grains, growing your own is against the law.' The white cloaked enforcer dropped a basket of food on the floor and began the incineration.

He felt powerless watching, yet the only power he *did* have was the ability to remember this sight, to remember the way the fire devoured humanity. He wanted more, he wanted the power to put an end to this.

***

A few days had passed since the raid. News of the White Arrow's announcement to stop supplying Whitechapel had spread across the town, eventually being calmed down by Gareth. He assured the town that he would make a deal with another town to ensure the basic provisions would be supplied. How Gareth was going to do that was beyond Arthur.

To make matters worse, another body was discovered. This time on the borders, by the deserted buildings that bridged the gap between Stepney Marshes and Whitechapel. Before Arthur and Tina could arrive at the scene, the body had already been taken by Gareth, and as usual, he ensured panic didn't spread by assuring everyone it was an accident that had occurred in a neighbouring town and that it had nothing to do with Whitechapel. It felt like Gareth was sweeping everything under the carpet to avoid hysteria. To let the townsfolk feel oblivious to any danger. But Arthur knew better.

Eve had conducted the post-mortem, so he decided to check in on her that evening. It was time she knew about this Ripper too.

When she ushered him in after a few taps on the door, Arthur saw no signs of being flustered or frustrated by the raids earlier in the week. She still had enough knowledge to do her role as a nurse and mortician.

'Sylvia Rendall, a young woman who lived in the Marshes but worked the Dark Quarters,' Eve told him. 'Seems like she was wandering the streets at night, looking for extra commission.' She hesitated. 'There was something a little odd about her death though. I found it quite…strange.' Her eyes gleamed with an interest that perhaps only those who understood the world of science would share.

'What do you mean?' Arthur asked.

'The body was missing an organ, a heart to be specific.'

'That is strange…' Arthur stroked his chin in deep thought.

'Indeed… I mean, why take a heart, right?'

'No, it's not that… Jack the Ripper *did* take an organ from one of his victims, but it was half a kidney. Well, this was from the stories I've rea—I mean heard about.' Arthur winced as he bit his tongue in frustration. He'd almost let slip about his illegal activities.

Eve shot him a peculiar look.
God, she looks beautiful.

'It's okay, Arthur. I know you read journals.' She let out a hearty laugh. 'I think you're quite a brave young man.'

Arthur's eyes widened in shock. How did she know? He felt a little embarrassed.

Eve reached for his hands, encompassing them in hers. Arthur felt his heartbeat rise and his face warm. He hoped he wasn't turning beet red.

'You can come to me whenever you need me, Arthur, just like the other time. With your sister gone, we need to stick together, right?'

Please don't call me your brother, please don't call me your brother.

'You're like a br—'

Arthur jerked his hands away. 'Sorry Eve, I've just remembered I've got to go somewhere! We'll speak later, okay?'

He bolted from her room and ran outside. God, what was he even thinking? She was easily several years older than him anyway. Arthur had never really understood or experienced the feeling of love. Mr Hudson's wife had passed long before Arthur was adopted by him. He hadn't really seen a true form of love. His experience was never a first or second-hand account, but a third-hand account, from love letters and written confessions in journals.

He pushed Eve out of his mind, forcing his thoughts back to more important issues. Damn, he had completely forgotten to ask her about the victim's neck. It was the same kind of murder, and another mutilated body, but this time, the body had been opened up. This time, there was an organ missing.

10. Satisfy the Soul

Arthur

After another day of working through their list, crossing out more unhelpful names and potential suspects that had led them nowhere, Arthur and Tina decided to retreat to Mary-Anne's roof. It was her day off from the tavern, and as usual, she was playing a beautiful piece. The bright chords were played with a wistful allure, working in a delightful symphony with the singing of birds that only the pair of them could truly appreciate from the roof.

HICK. Arthur grumbled. He had been dealing with the constant annoyance from his body all day. HICK. He held his breath. HICK. Took a swig out of a bottle of water. HICK. Held his breath and put his head in between his legs. He must have looked terribly silly in front of Tina. HICK.

She watched him with a frown.

'If you really want your hiccups to stop, try this.' She turned and faced him. He never could figure out how she kept such a well-maintained balance on a slanted roof. 'Look at me,' she commanded.

He did so, staring right into her sunlit golden-brown eyes. What was he looking for exactly?

'Concentrate on your breathing, breathe deeper, and will for your hiccups to stop. Feel the energy flow from your body to your head, and then back to your stomach.' She looked deadly serious.

HICK. He followed her instructions, focusing his—HICK—energy as she said. HICK.

A few seconds passed, and his chest didn't feel like it was

going to implode.

'It's gone?' He couldn't control the astonishment in his voice.

'Well, of course it's gone. You don't need any silly gimmicks to get rid of your hiccups. You need to use just a fraction of your aura.'

Arthur shifted on the tiles. 'I… I didn't know I had any aura.'

Her eyes narrowed. 'Don't be silly—everyone has an aura. It's just most people aren't trained to use it, but it still exists within them.'

Arthur wasn't sure if he fully believed that. He knew aura was a feature that was growing more and more common in people, but it was still a new science to humankind. A result of exposure to radiation, they said.

'You *do* know what aura, is right?' She passed him a fleeting look. 'I imagine an educated person like you would.'

'I've read about it, I know it's a new scientific and psychological discovery. They say they discovered it in humans around forty years ago? Caused by all the E-Smog, Wi-Fi, and other forms of small-level radiation that humans were exposed to for decades.'

Tina nodded slowly. Her eyes searched him as if she was trying to keep up with his explanation.

'Right…okay, I don't know the history about it but it's simply a part of everyone. It's like a form of energy that we can harness inside us. I'm probably not going to explain it that well, but it can help us do certain things better, amazing things—but it's not magic.'

'Yeah, I get it, so it's not superpowers. Just a way for people to enhance some of their own qualities?'

'Yeah, I guess… What an individual may take a whole lifetime of concentrated training to master can be achieved in a few years.'

'You must have gone through a lot to get it to this level.' He imagined she had gone through a painstaking amount of training in New India.

'I'm not that great at using aura. But yeah, NIMAS was tough.' She paused. 'I've got some really important memories there.'

He nodded. 'Memories are important.' The thought of his sister flooded his mind.

Tina looked at him as if she could see the worry consuming Arthur's mind.

'Tell me about your sister.'

The wind swept over the roof, and Tina clasped her hair to stop it from flying around. It had grown to find a way further down her shoulders now.

'Her name was Lucy. We weren't related by blood, but we grew up together. She was the one that showed me the journals in the first place. You would have liked her, she was always learning about people from all over London. Telling me about all the awful things the White Arrow Party did, all the purges and raids. She told me about the Battle of the Bridge. You were there, right?'

She nodded. 'Four years feels like a long time ago.' Her lips twitched as if she wanted to say something. 'Is she—'

'Dead? I don't know.' His eyes were glazing over. 'One night she just…didn't come home.'

'You shouldn't give up. If you keep looking, there's always a chance you'll find her,' Tina said.

Arthur forced a smile. The assassin was certainly warming up to him.

He knew he shouldn't think of Lucy as gone. But with all the recent deaths, Arthur didn't know what to think. 'What were you doing before you went to NIMAS?'

'We used to live in the Greenlands. Me, my brother Reza, and my father.' She fidgeted with her fingers. He could tell there was a great amount of weight in her words, especially when she mentioned her father. 'We lived with other families in a pub, the Soulhaven it was called. It was owned by Larsson's family— well, we call him Lars as he hates being called Larsson.' Arthur gave her a sheepish smile before turning away.

'He's like a brother to me.' She spoke fast. 'He's always looked out for me, and I've put him through hell at times. But…' Her voice broke off.

'You don't need to talk about it if you don't want to,' Arthur said.

She shook her head. 'Let's just say…Knox happened.'

There was movement below. Arthur shifted. He wondered how long the music had stopped playing for. The front door swung open and Mary-Anne strode outside, her crimson-brown hair neatly tied in a bun. She walked to the middle of the road and turned around to face them. A curious smile painted her face.

'Well, I thought I heard someone talking from the roof. What on earth are you doing up there?'

'We…we were just…' He felt himself turn red.

'If you wanted to listen to my music, you should have just asked.' Mary-Anne sighed before squinting. 'Oh, you have a friend with you too. Please, come inside. Father could use some new company.' She motioned towards the front door.

Why hadn't Tina hidden herself? Arthur passed her a quick look, but she simply shrugged.

'Let's go meet the Murrays.'

They found their way to the ground and followed Mary-Anne. From the outside, her home looked larger than most, but Arthur still couldn't help but gawk as he entered. Large was an understatement. A massive chandelier hung from the ceiling as they entered. Candles illuminated the large wooden staircase that spiralled before them. The solid-wood flooring blended well with the cream-coloured walls. It put the floorboards of his own room to shame. His mouth dropped as she led them passed a large dining area that could have fed a dozen people and then into a room at the back.

The warm ambience ushered them in as if they were returning home. A large piano was posted by the window and in the corner of the room was a bed. Mr Murray lay there. He was well into his seventies the last time Arthur had seen him. The old Mayor of Whitechapel was a man Arthur had great respect for, a very docile voice of reason. His greying hairs were combed behind his ears and his face had wrinkles that looked like tributaries of the old River Thames. Running Whitechapel in his old age had taken a toll on his health a few years ago, and he had left it in the hands of Dr Dovedi—that was until the doctor died.

They took their seats on the couch by the bed. 'Mr Murray, it's me, Arthur,' he said to a frail-looking figure who eyed them as they walked in.

'Arthur? I don't know any Arthur. Which Arthur?' He babbled incoherently for a second. 'Oh yes! Young Arthur. How are you? How is your sister? Lucy hasn't visited me in a while.' It seemed like he was suffering from some level of dementia.

Mary-Anne and Arthur exchanged nervous looks.

'Father, are you hungry?' She made towards the kitchen.

'What? Hungry? No—yes, actually I am. And bring some tea for our guests too. We haven't had many guests since…what year is this?' His eyes searched like a little boy parted from his mother in a market, before finding calmness in familiarity once again. 'And who is this young lady?' He diverted his gaze to Tina. He held out a wrinkled hand.

Tina took it, wrapping her fingers around his palm. 'My name is Tina, sir. I'm from the New India Martial Arts School, I've heard a great deal about you from my friends.' Arthur couldn't help being startled by her introduction. Tina trusted him with her identity? He was sure he had never spoken about Mr Murray to Tina.

'Your friends?' Mr Murray looked at her as if he was trying to remember if they had crossed paths before.

'You knew a man by the name of Lennart Chance? He used to travel with Master John.'

This was news to Arthur.

'Ah yes, young Lennart. God, I must have last seen him over a decade ago. And how is John? He always amused me with his satirical banter.'

'…They're great.' Something about Tina's delayed response made Arthur question the truth behind it.

'Ah, I remember it like it was yesterday. They really helped me deal with some trouble in Whitechapel. Say, do you guys have the time to listen to an old man's story?'

They smiled and nodded.

'Good, good.' Mr Murray turned to Arthur, his brows shaped with confusion and his eyes weary. 'And who are you?'

'Arthur, sir. Arthur Hudson, son of Bartholomew Hudson.' Arthur wondered if Mr Murray would ever recover from this. He wished he would. The man had so much life in him still.

Mary-Anne walked in with a tray of food. She set four cups on a mahogany desk that was probably worth more than everything Arthur owned.

The rest of the afternoon was filled with Mr Murray's stories. Being around them made Arthur feel warm, like he belonged to a family again. Mary-Anne played the piano and sung her soulful music to them. After every song they applauded her, as she, in his eyes, was proof. Proof that no matter how dark a place could be, no matter how broken a person might be, there was always a way to lift the blanket of darkness and satisfy the soul.

11. Don't Get Close

Arthur

Only two days after their evening with the Murrays, Arthur began to hear rumours circulating the town. People who frequented the brothel were gossiping about some townsfolk having gone missing. This kind of news didn't strike everyone as important or shocking. Times were tough in Whitechapel, and not everybody could earn their keep in conventional ways. Some women would prowl the night looking for customers; sometimes they turned up the next day, sometimes the day after.

'Arthur!' Bart called his name from across the road. He dropped his bag of rubbish and walked over to him.

'Is everything okay?' asked Arthur.

Bart's eyes were dark and wrinkled, as if he hadn't been sleeping well. He drew closer to Arthur and whispered, 'I don't suppose you've seen Mrs Gower? Her shop has been closed for a few days now and it doesn't look like she packed up and left anywhere.'

Arthur gaped. The reality struck Arthur hard. People had started to go missing. But there were no signs of killing? No bodies being discovered?

Lucy.

He shook his head and promised to help look for Mrs Gower after his shift. As he was finished moving the rubbish another thought struck him. Where was Lukas? He hadn't seen him on duty for a couple days now, strangely enough. He hoped he was all right. Jack the Ripper only went after women, right? But there weren't any missing people in the old stories… Was this really the work of Jack the Ripper? Or were there two psychopaths on the loose?

He needed to find Tina and work through their list, faster.

***

Arthur ran his index finger down the list of potential suspects, crossing out the ones they had visited today. He and Tina were sitting on the roof of the pizza shop, hiding behind the shade of a large chimney that exploded with the warm aroma of cheese.

'Who's next?' Tina asked. She blew on her colourful pizza and watched steam fly into the sky, before devouring the slice.

'Mmm, someone close to home,' he mumbled.

'Oh.' She raised her eyebrow. 'Your hot neighbour-girlfriend-mortician-nurse-friend.'

'No, just my neighbour-mortician-nu—'

'Yes, yes I get it. So where is she now? It's almost 6:00 pm.'

Arthur scanned the roofs, looking for the cluster of buildings where the old hospital used to be.

'Eve will be leaving her lab soon. Let's see if we can catch her on the way out. Though I don't know what we'll find with her, besides her reports on the victims.'

Tina frowned. 'Because she's your friend?'

'Not just that, I've known her for years.' He looked away from Tina. 'When I returned home after finding the first body I was in such a state, she comforted me and helped me through the shock.'

'I'm sure she did,' Tina said wryly.

Arthur ignored her. Instead, he stood up and started to make his way towards the rooftop door.

'You know, there's easier ways to get down from here,' Tina said, pointing to a ledge farther down from her view.

'There are also better ways for me to break my legs,' he replied with a laugh, before shutting the door behind him, as he climbed down the stairs and into the side alley.

After ten minutes of striding across the light-seeping streets, they arrived at Eve's lab. It was a building situated in the broken and abandoned infrastructure that was once called the Royal London Hospital. The towering presence of the building did very little to ignite any feeling of hope that would be expected of a hospital. The doors were chained shut and a padlock hung on the chains.

'Looks like we came a bit too late. Maybe she just left?' Arthur asked.

'Does she need to padlock her door?' Tina frowned. 'Even her bedroom door isn't secured like this.'

'This place is always locked like this. It used to be Dr Dovedi's clinic.'

'Who's Dr Dovedi?'

At that moment, a sharp scream breached the air, causing a flock of nearby crows to caw back. Arthur swivelled on the spot, trying to discern the direction of the scream.

'Something's happening. Let's get moving,' Tina whispered, before launching herself down the road. Arthur followed.

If it was a Ripper attack, then it definitely wouldn't be in the middle of the road. They quickly scanned each alleyway they passed. Though with the sunlight quickly diminishing, it became difficult for Arthur to see anything clearly. Tina, on the other hand, didn't slow down. She moved with confidence, as if her eyes were trained for the dark.

She came to an abrupt halt, almost knocking into him. A finger pressed against her lip, she signalled to an empty alley on their left. Abandoned buildings bordered the neglected and empty street they were on now. Another area at the outskirts of the town.

Arthur carefully turned the corner, then broke into a burst of movement. His heart leapt to his throat as he saw Eve slumped against a wall. A bulky cloaked figure stood pressed against her, holding a knife to her throat.

'WHAT ARE YOU DOING? GET AWAY FROM HER!' he roared. He knew no matter how much sound he made, there was no one besides him and Tina around. No one else to help them.

The cloaked figure began to laugh a deep, hoarse laugh. The mask over the brute's face obscured everything but his barely visible eyes.

'Get… off… me,' Eve barely managed to squeak.

Arthur didn't know if he should move towards them or not. The knife now touched Eve's skin; a small cut was beginning to form. He needed to think of something, quick. A thought crossed his mind. What he needed to do was divert Jack's attention. He would have to trust Tina to understand what he was doing and act quickly.

Arthur raised his arms wide and high, showing the masked killer that he didn't have any weapons. He slowly edged forward, blocking more of the Ripper's vision. 'Hey, wait…wait! Look, I can give you money. Here, how much do you want? I'm sure I definitely have a really old gold pound somewhere.'

Those eyes behind the mask seemed somewhat familiar, like he had definitely looked into them before. Arthur continued to wave his arm, trying his best to misdirect him. It was working; Jack relaxed his grip on Eve slightly. His eyes focused on Arthur's broad stance and moving hands so much, that he hadn't noticed Tina slip by both of them.

She stood behind him now, a dagger in one hand. She swung at the arm that was gripping Eve, causing the masked figure to flail backwards. Curses flew into the air as blood began to drip from his arm. Arthur used this opportunity to grab Eve and dash back out onto the street. Jack didn't wait a second longer. He pulled open a door that neither Tina nor Arthur had noticed and flung himself into the building, bolting the door behind him.

'I'm going to follow him. Meet me back at mine later!' Tina shouted at Arthur.

Arthur carried Eve to a nearby bench and gently rested her on it.

'Are you okay? Are you hurt?'

She shook her head, but she was shaking. 'Just a bit of a

shock, and a small scratch.' Her eyes glazed with tears. 'Thank you, Arthur. If you hadn't found me I don't know what would have happened. With all these horrible murders happening, I…'A tear escaped her eye. 'I thought for a second that I'd be the one ending up on a mortician's table this time.' She sobbed into his arms.

'Don't worry, you're safe now. I'll find him, I promise.'

***

At quarter past eight, in the refuge of the night, Arthur met Tina at the school. His memory was finally successful in navigating him through the corridors to her classroom.

'Any luck?' he asked as he stepped into a dimly lit classroom.

She shook her head. 'I don't understand. When I looked inside, there was no one there. I thought he was hiding at first. So I watched every exit. I watched mice run out of the building, but not him. The building was empty.' She sounded genuinely disappointed.

Arthur sighed. 'What struck me as weird was that I never fancied a Jack the Ripper copycat to be hungry for money. From what I read, his killings were more ritualistic and motivated by his gory passions, not for copper.'

Tina bit her lip. 'I never did ask but, who was the real Jack the Ripper in the 1800s?'

'That's the strange thing, we still don't know to this day. There were several accusations thrown around and many suspects who would have perfectly fit the character of Jack. But no one was ever pegged with the crimes.'

Arthur took a seat at the desk and noticed a strange drawing on the whiteboard. A large square was drawn neatly on the board. Inside the square were rows and columns of circles.

'Is this how you pass the time?' he asked.

Tina walked over to the board, stopping a few metres before it. 'Nice flailing fish movement today.' Her lips hooked into a small smile.

'Well, I did what needed to be done,' he replied gingerly.

'No Arthur, you did what would've worked well with *my* movements.'

Arthur knitted his brows. 'Was that the wrong thing to do?'

She shook her head. 'It was perfect for *then*. But what would you have done if you were by yourself?'

Arthur leaned back in his seat. If he had been by himself, he would probably have forced himself to jump at the killer. But he knew if he said that out loud he would be scolded for the thought. He probably would've had no chance of survival, let alone saving anyone else.

'See?' Tina had looked at him now like she genuinely was a teacher in the room. She pointed at the whiteboard. 'Do you really want to catch this killer? Do you really want me to help you?'

She knew the answer and probably wasn't even looking for a response, but Arthur made it a point to declare it out loud. 'Yes of course I do, people are dying!'

'Then I'm going to have to teach you a few things to at least keep you alive. You have no problem with that, right?'

He shook his head but stopped midway. 'I don't want to learn how to wield a sword, or any weapon for that matter.'

Tina rolled her eyes. 'For God's sake, Arthur, this is a pretty dark world we're living in. How do you expect to survive without—'

'I expect to survive without killing anyone.' He could feel himself heating up, and his voice was rising. 'I've read enough and felt enough to know that I don't want to inflict death on another person. I can see how it affects people—I can see it in your eyes, Tina. You have the eyes of a killer, and as much I love looking at your eyes, I don't want them.'

Silent sparks flew between them as they were locked in a battle of glares. Arthur could almost feel the burning radiation of willpower between them. Here he was, staring down an assassin, convincing her of his pacifism. He didn't mean to offend her in any way, but he wasn't willing to lose himself. If there was one thing he wanted to remember Lucy by, it was her resistance to violence. His own mind had been nurtured this way, an unusual way in a world full of conflict.

Tina broke the silence. 'Fine, I'll continue helping you, and I won't teach you the ways to kill. I'll teach you a few things to help you stay alive, but you'll be learning under my conditions.' She paused to mutter, 'And stop looking at my eyes.'

She beckoned him to stand next to her and face the board.

He nodded and did so. 'So, what is this?'

'That's what I want you to tell me. What exactly do you see?' She was looking at him now, watching him scan the board.

'Well, I don't really get if this is a trick question or not but I guess it's quite simple. I can see a large square. Inside, there are sixteen rows and columns of small circles.' As soon as he finished his analysis he felt a searing pain graze the side of his head. His body rung like the bell of Whitechapel's church. He staggered backwards before catching himself on a nearby table.

Tina had leapt up and punched him.

'What…what was that for?' He rubbed the side of his face.

'You answered wrong. Don't complain about pain now. You might not want to train yourself to inflict pain on others, but you surely won't get away from feeling pain yourself. I'm going to enjoy being around a…'

'A pacifist.'

'A pa-ci-fist like you.'

He glowered at her amusement. But what did she mean, he got the answer wrong?

'Take a look.' She nodded at the board. 'You missed the triangle.'

'What triangle? There isn't any—'

'Look and stop talking nonsense.' She made to swing a kick for Arthur's stomach, but this time he predicted her movement, and smothered the impact from her foot in his hands.

He scanned the board again and noticed the small triangle on the bottom right of the square. 'Oh… I see it now.' He paused for a moment. 'I understand; my mind assumed they were all circles for efficiency right? It filled in the blanks even though my eyes were seeing something else. It's like a magician's trick. They misdirect people by making their minds assume things rather than actually understanding everything in their view.' He looked back at Tina and noticed her face tinged with a slight red. Was she blushing or annoyed at him again? 'What?' he asked sheepishly, before noticing what he was doing.

She gritted her teeth. 'You're *still* holding my foot.' She swung her other foot, which connected with his chest, forcing him to recoil to the floor. Her body flipped in the air and began to fall gracefully. She used her hands to catch her descent and push herself up before she reached the floor. With elite athleticism, she swung her body back to a standing position again. Arthur couldn't help his eyes widening in amazement.

'You're a pretty surprising person, Arthur.' Her frown made him wonder if they had both witnessed the same thing.

'What do you mean? You're the one who just did some fancy acrobatic flip.' His eyes creased with confusion.

'You caught onto my movements and stopped yourself from getting kicked in the guts.' A smirk graced her face as she looked away.

Arthur sighed before glancing around the broken classroom. 'Now I wish classes were like the old ages; less painful.'

A sudden thought crossed his mind. Was he becoming a punching bag for an assassin?

***

Tina

When Arthur had left, close to midnight, Tina was faced with the familiar dark feeling of loneliness. She offered to walk him home. After all, it was late and there was a killer or two roaming the streets. His refusal made her even more annoyed at his lack of combat ability. He really was a dunce at fighting. How could any child grow up in a world like this without knowing how to fight? It made no sense.

As annoying as he was, she enjoyed his company. It made sense for her to work with him; he was loyal and fierce for a nimble-looking person. He could barely throw a punch, but his ability to read a situation was exceptional. Perhaps one day she would introduce him to Sebastian, as he spoke like him, after all. All full of complex explanations and annoyingly weird words. But whenever he lost his composure he reminded her of Lars, full of stubbornness, spirit, and stupidity, a different type of strength. Her own body would get into better shape if she had a sparring partner—if this could even be called sparring. Why was she thinking of Arthur so much anyway?

You have the eyes of a killer, and as much I love looking at your eyes, I don't want them.

If anyone else had said this to her she might have taken offence. But he loved looking at her eyes? Tina found her way to the bathroom, and slapped water onto her face like she was trying to slap the thought of him from her mind.

She savoured a quick and much-needed shower. A smile crept onto her face as she appreciated the clean flowing water, albeit only functioning in the boy's bathroom. A few minutes later she had changed into a simple t-shirt and shorts and slipped into her makeshift bed, which was a small mattress covered in cloth from the now-missing Mrs Gower's shop. Her thoughts tangled into a labyrinth of memories and ideas, eventually succumbing to the anarchy of her mind.

For too long she had not slept well, haunted by memories of the past that shifted into horrible nightmares. For too long she had stalked the idea of vengeance against the Shadows of London. The villainous group of professional killers. But tonight, she didn't feel so alone, as ironic as it sounded. She had made friends here in Whitechapel, even though she wanted to seclude herself.

Perhaps sometimes change couldn't be controlled. She would have to treat the blessings like her ordeals; she'd simply live with them and accept them. As she began to drift off to sleep, another thought infiltrated her mind.

Don't get too close to him.

12. Magic

Tina

The next morning, Tina found Arthur collecting bottles by the narrow pavements of Fairclough Street. The cobblestone flooring mixed with broken tarmac made for an unusual setting, and an awkward footing at times. A blanket of stratus clouds hugged the sky selfishly, weakening the glow of the sun.

After listening to him talk, she had come to understand the economics of his role in town better. Every bottle he collected could be sold for five pence each; for every street he swept, he would receive two pounds. On a good day, he could earn himself just over eight pounds.

Arthur caught her movement and beckoned her over. He was getting better at recognising her presence.

'Morning, sleep well?'

She looked away and felt herself tinge a slight red. She'd slept unusually well. 'Mmm.'

He peered at her, oblivious to the dangerous thoughts surfacing in her mind.

'What are you lost in thought for?' He didn't wait for a response. Instead, a sheepish grin broadened his face. 'Anyway, when we first met, you said you were turning nineteen soon. When is that?'

The question threw her off completely and brought her crashing back to reality. Her brows furrowed at the thought. She was nineteen today. She had completely forgotten, lost in all the commotion over the last few days. 'Today is the 18th of October, right?'

Arthur nodded, placing a box of bottles on the pavement. His slightly tall frame made her seem like a young teenager standing next to him.

'Well, then my birthday is today.'

He beamed at her. 'Excellent, Happy Birthday! I've got a surprise for you.' He picked up his box of bottles and began to lift it onto his cart.

'Wait, no, don't do anything.' What could he be planning? A flurry of thoughts made her heart race. 'I don't like surprises,' she added.

'There's clearly plenty of things I do that you don't like. This will have to be another one of them,' he replied without looking at her. 'Anyway, meet me here in an hour.' He left before she could respond.

***

Arthur

It was approaching 2:00 pm by the time Arthur had successfully dragged the reluctant spectre of the assassin to the small park between Fairclough Street and Ponler Street. His satchel clung to his side, weighing him down with the numerous journals he had brought with him.

The park that would have been otherwise green and dull was instead full of spirit and noise today. The circus was always an eventful occurrence and it visited Whitechapel at least once a year. Despite the vibrant entertainment and the colourful allure of the abstract acts that were performed, Arthur always made sure to visit for another reason. Hidden behind the facade of loud music and the crowds of people that travelled from neighbouring areas, there was an undeniable amount of socially unacceptable things that occurred during the spectacular hustle and bustle of the event. It was a hot spot for trading illegal goods.

Tina followed closely behind him as he led her through the bustling crowd and the lines of stalls. People of all colour and language buzzed in excited chatter, while the merchants were calling for every bystander to taste their colourful delicacies. The smell of freshly baked cakes and biscuits elevated their noses and filled their lungs. Rare savoury treats were openly left on display, tempting the attention of pigeons and, of course, Lukas' favourite ominous flying creatures, crows. A colourful spectrum of drinks glistened in the light, ranging from freshly brewed beers to exotic-smelling teas.

'This reminds me of New India,' Tina mumbled behind him.

He pointed to a small tent, which had a sign that read: *Silk Road*. Arthur ducked behind the drape that served as a door and entered a dimly lit space.

Immediately, a scrawny little man with a thick white beard, dressed in a brown cloak rushed over to them. Juvayni.

'Salaam! Can I interest you in a newly made pajama? And I do insist you tr—' He stopped himself the moment he had recognised Arthur. 'Oh Arthur! I take it you're here for the usual?

Arthur smiled and nodded.

Juvayni scurried behind a screen, leaving him alone with Tina for a few minutes.

He returned with a small bag. 'I'm afraid I haven't got too many today. It seems like the Party has confiscated quite a lot this year. Oh, this one is special though!' He handed Arthur a red leather-bound book, before whispering, 'This one has entries from the Emir in the Shamal. Khalid Ibn Umar, the great swordsman himself.'

Arthur noticed the glint in the man's eyes. He quickly searched the bag and began to fish through the journals, giving them a quick flick through to make sure the pages weren't blank. He replaced the new ones with the ones in his satchel, before placing a gold coin in the vendor's open palm.

'Oh, and here's your usual batch of paper,' Juvayni said, passing over several sheets of white paper.

Arthur placed them all neatly in his satchel. He hoped he had brought enough money with him.

'How's business been, Juvay?' Arthur asked him.

This was the third time he had met the Muslim man. Juvayni was the name of a famous scribe around a thousand years ago, a scribe who attained great power and tried his best to save as much of the literature and written knowledge from the destruction of that time. It was a fitting name for someone who smuggled books of knowledge from place-to-place today. He wondered if it was his actual name.

'It's been pretty slow this year. We've travelled from the Great West, through the Churchlands, Kingsland, the Shamal, and most of the Hamlets. It's been mostly peaceful though.'

'He's a smuggler?' Tina's whisper cut across the tent. She had been floating around, studying the delicate fabrics that were laid out on a small table. 'Do you have any...' She paused and walked over to him, as if she was trying to figure out if she could trust the man. 'Any weapons?'

Juvayni's eyebrows rose, but he nodded. He turned from Tina to Arthur. 'My, Arthur, did you go and get yourself married whilst in the space of a year?' He patted Arthur's back.

Arthur's cheeks flushed. 'No, no, nothing like that. This is a friend of mine.' He turned his back towards Tina to spare himself from the deadly glare that felt as menacing as her daggers.

Juvayni indulged in a full-bellied laugh and continued to pat him before delving once more behind the screen that shut his activities out from prying eyes. He returned with a couple of knives and a bow, handing them nervously to Tina.

He leaned towards Arthur and whispered, 'Will she be okay with that, Arthur?'

'Oh yes. More than most actually,' he replied with confidence. 'Any good shows this year?'

'Oh yes! There's a new act. They call themselves "Breaking the Fourth Wall."' A grin painted his face. 'They're so clever and funny. Not everyone can understand what they say but they have me in tears.'

'I'll take this.' Tina held the bow. She was about to fish for some money before Arthur stopped her.

'It's your birthday today, so you don't get to pay for anything.' Tina looked more annoyed than happy, but Arthur didn't care. He took the bow and carefully stowed it in his satchel, stretching the leather slightly.

After bidding farewell to Juvayni, Arthur led Tina towards the large candy-coloured striped tent in the centre of the park. The clouds had begun to gather just as the people had, in large numbers, darkening the sky from the afternoon glow.

'Yo Arthur!' a voice called.

He turned to see the figure of Percy approaching.

'Who's that?' Tina asked hesitantly. Arthur could tell she was doing a full analysis on him. From his tall and skinny teenage demeanour to the grey hoodie and black snapback he wore.

'A friend of mine, one of the local kids.' He engaged Percy in their usual handshake, which consisted of a firm grip and a slight shoulder barge.

'Whaaz good G? I haven't seen you in time. Where you been?' His deep voice hinted at his late stage of puberty. His choice of words always made Arthur feel like he came from a different age, or even a different world altogether.

'Ah, you know me, Percy. Busy keeping the streets clean. How's the rest of the boys?'

'I hear that. Nah, they're all good. When are you gonna hear us perform? We've been grinding, you know? Hey listen, I saw you on your ones here and I thought we could both go check out the new act they got lined up.'

Arthur shifted slightly, wondering if Tina would be okay with that. 'Actually Percy, I'm not here by myself you see...' He pointed to Tina, who was standing right next to him. As usual, her aura and sense of presence showed little signs of her existence, just the way she liked it. Arthur smiled at Percy apologetically.

'Holy sh—' He slapped both his cheeks simultaneously. 'I didn't even see you there! Oh my god girl, are you a magician or something? Ouch.' He started to rub his face as he realised he had slapped himself too hard.

Tina snorted. A slow smile crept onto her face, like she was amused. 'My name is Christie. Nice to meet you. I'm a friend of Arthur's and I heard there was a circus in town, so I decided to come to Whitechapel and check it out.' She stretched out a hand. She sounded so genuine that it made Arthur question whether she had even told *him* her true identity. She shrugged when she caught his surprised look.

'My name's Percy.' He shook her hand. 'I'm the lead rapper of my group. Some people call me the local troublemaker, others call me the Badman of Whitechapel.' He beamed with pride.

'Oh my Go—Percy, that's not how to introduce yourself.' Arthur turned to Tina. 'Percy here is a smart lad, one of the finest youngsters around. He's extremely gifted with music, too.'

'Yeah yeah, anyway, I didn't know you were on a date… so… I guess I'll leave you to it.' Percy looked hesitantly between the pair of them.

'Oh no, we're not dating!' Arthur blurted out, too quickly. He noticed Tina's eyes narrow.

'Oh… in that case, would you mind me tagging along? I promise I won't cause no trouble.'

Before Arthur could respond Tina had already stepped forward. 'That's perfectly fine with me. Shall we?' She raised her arm to allow Percy to loop his own by her side. She had said it with such quick venom, as if her words were meant to sting.

Arthur found himself speechless. He shook his head, before following behind them.

***

Arthur watched as people from all over flooded into the main event. The large tent surprisingly held the massive groups of people that funnelled their way inside. They had fortunately managed to find themselves seats at the front by the wooden circular stage at the centre. Loud cheers erupted from the crowd as each act introduced itself. Arthur had seen many of them in previous years, but it was always fascinating to watch the faces of the audience. The people *oooh'd* and *ahhh'd* as each act took to the stage. Perhaps shows like this were fascinating for those who could not hold the memory of the previous year's entertainments. But for Arthur, who could recall every act with precise detail, it became a repetitive spectacle. A spectacle though, nonetheless.

Tina sat in between Percy and him. They watched the welcoming act and each act thereon with great energy and romance. Dazzling as each show was, Arthur could not help feeling slightly bored. If the assassin enjoyed the show, her excitement was certainly not displayed publicly.

A loud voice boomed above the crowd. Arthur didn't understand how they were able to project their voice that loud, but assumed they must be using batteries.

'AND FOR OUR NEXT ACT, OUR NEWEST ACT… LADIES AND GENTLEMEN, PLEASE RISE AND GIVE A FANTASTIC WELCOME TO…' A drum roll sounded from all around them as the audience rose to their feet and started to murmur with excitement. '…BREAKING THE FOURTH WALL.'

A piano started to play fast as three clowns waddled onto the stage. Each was dressed as a typical clown should be, with a red wig that looked as if it belonged to somebody's great-aunt, a large red nose that stole the attention away from their eyes, and colourful, baggy attire. One was considerably taller than the others, walking on stilts. He surprised the closest of the audience to him—who gasped—as he began to swing his body left then right like a pendulum.

'My name is Raita. Nice to meet you.' He tipped his imaginary hat towards the crowd, who waved back at him.

A clown with a wooden puppet in his hand made his way towards the other side of the stage, stealing the attention of the children by making the inanimate body of a doll speak and dance. A ventriloquist. 'My name is O'Reilly!' The puppet spoke in an Irish accent. 'I'm just a character in this clown's novel.'

'Oh really?' The children tried to mimic his accent.

The clown closest to them began to mime. His white latex gloves took hold of the air as if there was a rope that Arthur couldn't see. He tugged on it, then mimed his struggle to pull an invisible something from an unknown somewhere. Arthur had never seen this act before. His body slid toward the edge of his seat; his mind yearned for new substance. A chalkboard on wheels floated onto the stage from behind the curtains and wheeled its way towards the centre, yet nothing was attached to it. Besides the imaginary and invisible rope that only the clown could see and feel. It came to a halt by the clown's large red boots. He took a step back and raised his hand. A piece of chalk rose and began to move. The crowd erupted into a deep *ooooooh*. He pointed at the board and the chalk began to write, free from the grip of the clown but not his control.

My name is Mind. I'm glad you are all literate enough to read this.

The three clowns began their acts one by one, leaving each side of the audience in tears of laughter. The sound of thunder reverberated around the walls with the end of every act and the birth of every applause. Arthur soon grew familiar with each clown's way of communicating. Raita would shout downward as if he were speaking to the very ants living in the cracks of the earth's crust. O'Reilly, the puppet, would rock its head and contract its wooden jaw to crack rude jokes. And Mind would write his replies magically on the board, whilst engaging in activities in the art of miming.

'What's on your mind, Mind?' O'Reilly cackled.

One day I was walking down the streets of Kingsland. I tried to be a good person. Bear in mind, entrepreneurs like myself have a mind to helping people. But every time I try to, they always say.

'MIND YOUR OWN BUSINESS?' bellowed Raita from behind him.

The jokes were not all funny, but it was the facial reactions, the delivery, and the timing that kept the crowd amused.

For our next act, we're going to do some MIND-READING.

The fancy white handwriting curled at the end of every last letter for added effect. From what Arthur could make of the handwriting, it didn't suit the clown at all. Arthur had seen handwriting like that many times from all his reading. He could recount every person who wrote in that style, and they were always women.

I'm going to look at people in the crowd and guess a name of someone important to them. Ready?

The clown scanned the crowd, his emerald eyes swinging from left to right. The piano played in a satirical fashion, raising the tension. He began to write once more, his fingers danced in the air, the chalk scribed.

Bethany. Charles. Hussain. Cindy. Jermaine. Fabian.

A burst of commotion followed as the names were written clearly for everyone to see. Arthur could hear chatter from all around him.

'That's my wife's name, Cindy.' The man behind Arthur stood up.

'That's my son, Fabian,' a woman squealed.

Several others laid their claim. Arthur was in a state of confusion; his mind raced for rationality. They must have been planted in the crowd, probably paid for the sake of entertaining the audience. Mind kept turning to glance at Arthur. He shuddered as he began to notice the pattern of looks between the clowns.

'FOR THOSE WHO BELIEVE THIS TO BE A TRICK. DEAR BROTHERS AND SISTERS AND INANIMATE SILLY OBJECTS—'

'OI,' squeaked O'Reilly.

'I TELL YOU, THIS IS NO TRICK. WE HAVE SPECIAL POWERS, YOU SEE.' He paused for dramatic effect. 'THE POWER TO ENTERTAIN.'

More names started to appear on the board. But one name was repeated three times. A name that caused the very warm waters of Arthur's sanity to freeze over, and his mouth to gape as if he had seen three ghosts on the stage instead of clowns.

LUCY, LUCY, LUCY.

Another applause followed. This time, neither Arthur nor Tina joined in. All three clowns jerked their heads abruptly and looked towards them. Their eyes wide and bulging, their smiles turned to a frightful grimace. Was no one else seeing this?

Immediately the room dimmed, as if a sudden gust of wind had crept in and stolen the light from the candles. A shadow blanketed over the stage and the piano slowed. The three clowns were almost lost in the shadow.

'What's going on?' Arthur whispered to Tina.

The room was so dark now that it was hard for the audience to even see each other. Arthur nudged Tina but missed. He turned and reached out. But his fingers only grasped the air.

She was gone.

His heart raced. The piano continued to play. No one in the audience stirred, as if the music was keeping them in a deep trance-like state.

'Percy,' Arthur hissed.

But he got no response. He got up and moved closer to him. Percy was still sitting in his seat, but he was looking straight at the stage. A white grin was barely visible on his face. Arthur turned to see the rest of the crowd. He reeled back in shock. They were barely visible, but he could make out the uniformed stare. They were all grinning into the blackness that had swarmed them. His heart drummed against his chest. Something was definitely wrong. Percy was still breathing, but his eyes were fixed on one point, and his lips in one contraction.

Arthur jumped over the barriers that separated the audience from the performances. He needed to find Tina—he needed to know what was going on.

He leapt onto the stage and walked towards the darkness.

13. Mind Your Mouth

'What's going on here?' Arthur called out.

The clowns weren't on the stage anymore. Was Lucy a name used by coincidence or did they actually know something Arthur didn't?

Arthur called out again.

'Hush,' hissed Raita from behind the curtains. 'It seems our hypnosis didn't affect you. So, come sit down and listen to the grown-ups talk.'

Hypnosis? He remembered Tina telling him about people who were able to hypnotise others, making them motionless or even worse, making them do things without meaning to. All with their own forms of aura. It was an outlawed practice.

For a moment, Arthur hesitated, wondering if he was under any threat. Surely clowns weren't dangerous? Either way, he needed to find Tina. Arthur pushed past the heavy drapes.

A small dark corridor led him to a wooden room—perhaps a large storage room. At the centre of the room was a round table, and the three clowns sat across it on one side. Tina sat on the other. Candles at each corner of the room created a mild glow.

'Tina, what's going on?' Arthur couldn't keep his voice from shaking.

How the essence of a clown could change entirely, just by simply changing the shape of their bright red lips. Raita was now the same height as ordinary human beings. The ventriloquist who spoke for O'Reilly had deposited the doll to the side as he sat across from Tina, his arms folded. Mind was leaning back in his chair, his eyes darting from Arthur to Tina, then back to Arthur.

'Take a seat, Arthur,' Tina said, motioning to a vacant seat beside her.

A part of Arthur just wanted to run back to the town centre and alert Gareth. There was something very wrong about everything here. An eerie silence pierced the stale air. He could imagine this to be a nightmare that would wake people during the night. He hesitated, but chose to stick with Tina instead, taking his seat next to her.

'They're not just clowns.' Tina broke the silence. 'They're assassins.'

'Just like you, little Tina of the Ruh.' Raita sneered. 'If it weren't for you not applauding us earlier, we probably wouldn't have noticed you hiding away in the crowd.'

'Assassins?' Arthur turned to face them. 'What are you doing here in Wh—'

'SHUT UP.' Tina jerked, startling him. '*YOU* can't ask them anything. Keep quiet and watch.'

Confusion and frustration filled his mind. What did she mean? And why was she acting like this?

'She's right, you know.' A woman's voice startled him further. 'We, the Assassins of the West, have rules that you must follow. As a courtesy to the Ruh, and for our own entertainment, we will answer only three questions.' The voice was coming out of Mind's lips.

You're a woman? Arthur was about to blurt out but quickly stopped himself as he felt Tina's nails dig into his forearm.

'Well of course I'm a woman.' Mind spoke as if she truly had read his mind. Had she? Was this even possible?

Arthur's brows rose. Tina must have recognised them too. It irked him to see her like this. She was quiet, and Arthur couldn't begin to unearth what was streaming through her mind. From what he could decipher from the tension in the air and her own posture, she feared the three clowns—or assassins—who sat across from them, but that was all he was certain of. His mind attempted to unravel the situation. An itch to ask questions infuriated him. He wanted to ask them about Lucy.

'So, you've got our attention. Just be aware that it is only because of a favour we owe to Sebastian of the Ruh that we are even conducting this meeting. Our mindless crowd beckons, speak fast,' Raita said. More questions filled Arthur's mind. *How annoying.* How were these clowns connected to the Ruh?

Tina nodded at him.

'I acknowledge your return of favour for a member of the Ruh.' She spoke with a mature and elevated tone. It was hard to imagine she was younger than Arthur at this moment. 'Whitechapel is currently being threatened by an unknown force. Women are being killed and it is not by the work of any assassin. What can you tell me about this?'

The three clowns exchanged eye contact before replying simultaneously.

'The Shadows are returning. History is repeating once more, but it is more than one history.' Their simultaneous response added to the already eerie effect that lingered in the room.

Who are the Shadows? Arthur made a mental note to ask Tina this after. But once again, as if Mind had read his mind, she began to answer his question.

'The Shadows of London are a dark guild consisting of five members. They are all strong warriors born from the darkness of the slums themselves. Wherever they go, the body count rises. They have a never-ending thirst for knowledge, for they believe knowledge to be the key to power.' She leaned closer to Arthur. Her white and red eerie face created a shadow across his. 'They will do anything. *Anything.* To get what they want.'

'You're in a very talkative mood, Mind.' A deep and dark voice erupted from the clown beside her. The ventriloquist.

'And you're not, Riley. As usual,' she snapped back at him.

'My second question,' Tina began. 'Where is Knox?'

The clowns looked at each other once more before replying. 'She is here, in Whitechapel.'

Arthur watched as a bead formed around Tina's brows. She must have been racking her brain for the right questions to ask, questions that wouldn't bare wasteful answers, questions that would provide her with clarity and understanding. The answer must have satisfied her, as a small smile crossed her lips.

She broke her gaze away from the clowns and quickly looked at him.

'My third question. Where is Lucy?'

Arthur's heart leapt, suddenly not knowing whether he really wanted to know the answer, but of course he did. A terrifying tension swept through him, his eyes flickered to the three clowns.

Once again, the clowns repeated their simultaneous movements before replying, 'She is close to the King.'

The King? What did that mean? There was no King anymore. Confusion turned to anger. What a pathetic answer. His mind raced furiously. The clown had easily picked up the frustration in his eyes.

'Calm yourself. Isn't it worth anything to know that she still lives?' Mind asked.

That much was true, and Arthur had to accept that.

'But why can't you answer the question better than that?' he persisted.

Instantly, the clowns leapt to their feet. Tina pushed Arthur back, knocking him onto the hard surface. Her fingers passed over her daggers, but instead came to halt at her side. She entered a deep bow.

'I apologise for the fourth question. Please forgive my friend, he knows not the way of the assassins.'

'He should know better. Don't treat him with ignorance, Tina of the Ruh,' Raita rasped. 'Or perhaps even *you* don't know who he really is? The man from *that* bloodline.'

What did he mean by that? Lucy had written something about his bloodline too. What did his bloodline have to do with anything?

'I think it is time you take your leave, young assassin,' Mind jeered. 'Oh, and Arthur. Do keep me in mind, won't you?'

14. The Memory Bank

Tina

The crowd erupted into a standing ovation as Tina took to her seat as if nothing had happened and no time had passed. The mass of children who had travelled with their parents from surrounding areas screamed with praise for the three clowns that bowed to the audience.

'What an amazing show!' Percy's hands slapped together rhythmically.

Tina ignored him, still lost in her head. She had only heard about the Assassins of the Great West from Sebastian but had never met them in person till now. It was only deep into their performance that she'd noticed their aura starting to hypnotise the crowd. People who had never experienced aura would have been under their control almost instantly. She had stirred some of Arthur's when he'd had hiccups. Perhaps the experience had helped him to repel the low-level hypnotism? Or maybe she truly didn't know enough about him? What did Raita mean by his bloodline? Whom did he descend from exactly?

They left the circus. Percy thanked them profusely for letting him tag along, which Arthur played down. As they stopped to get some food, Arthur remained oddly quiet. Perhaps he was still trying to figure out what the assassins had said about Lucy.

Tina waited for the warm meals to be prepared whilst Arthur dashed to another shop nearby. Her mind was consumed with the information about Knox. Her father and brother's killer was in the same town as her and possibly walking on the same street as her. Was she being watched? Did Knox even know that she was here?

But the thought of Knox swept from her mind with Arthur's return. He clearly hadn't let the new information weigh on his mind for too long, as he held a simple sponge cake with a lit candle in front of her. Tina knew there was something special about the young man before her.

'Happy Birthday!' he beamed.

She found herself lost for words. Why was he doing so much for her? She was a nobody to him. She stared blankly at him, wondering whether she should thank him or—

'Stop thinking and make a wish. You know you can ask for anything. Heck, if any of this ever works—but hey, you only turn nineteen once.' Arthur shoved the cake into her hands.

She could ask for anything? What did she want? It didn't take her long to decide on something.

She blew, letting her wish transform from a small ember to a wisp of smoke, before disappearing into nothingness.

***

By the time they got back to the school, the sun was already setting. The clouds began to camouflage into the sky and a cool air descended on Whitechapel. They placed the food on the desk and began to eat, finishing with the cake.

'So…who were they?' Arthur asked at last. He sipped juice from a straw, making an annoying gurgling sound as the orange substance came to an end. Tina frowned.

'They're members of another guild from the Great West. A powerful guild. I've only heard a little about them from Sebastian, but during his days of travelling with his family, he came across them. He told me they conducted themselves in a different way to others and you had to earn their respect. I'm not exactly sure what he did to earn it.'

'But how do they know so much? Are they psychics?' His brows rose with intense curiosity.

She shrugged. 'I don't know much about it. But they're known for their wit and knowledge. Sometimes the things they know are helpful and sometimes they're not. But they are wise and experien—'

'And strong?'

Tina didn't need Mind's skills to know what Arthur was thinking. She rolled her eyes.

'Yes. If a fight broke out, I'd barely be able to take on one of them at a time. And no, they won't help us. They're very neutral as assassins. They uphold the laws of the land and choose to never get involved unless it suits them. They would never help us, so don't expect them to.'

Arthur sighed. 'I guess not every assassin is like you.'

'I don't think you understand assassins at all.' She paused and wondered whether it was worth explaining it to him, but his eager eyes searched for knowledge. 'Not all assassins are Peacekeepers. Some are strict to their own codes; others veer off onto darker paths. Generally, they aren't hired killers. Most of them aren't swayed by money, but by loyalty and favours. Remember that, Arthur. Favours and debts are worth more than any coin in this world.'

He nodded, before standing up to retrieve a journal from his satchel. 'Thank you,' he said as he resumed his seat by the desk. 'For asking about Lucy.'

Tina shook her head. 'It's fine, I'd got the answers I needed for myself already.'

In fact, she had received more than what she'd expected. A deep and dark feeling inside her stirred as she thought about Knox.

'Knox?' Arthur's face contorted as if he was recalling the eventful meeting.

She nodded. 'The women who killed my family. She's one of the Shadows of London, and she's here in Whitechapel.'

I can finally avenge my family. She didn't want to say what she was really thinking out loud, fearing Arthur's pacifistic reaction.

But he didn't stir. Instead, he opened the journal and began to sift through the pages.

'Thank *you*, Arthur.' She could feel herself going red as she turned and faced the window to avoid his eyes. 'For everything you've done today. I didn't expect this when I came to Whitechapel.'

'What did you expect?' His voice was soft, and she dared not turn to face him now.

I expected to be alone.

She gave him a simple shrug.

'Why don't you read to me?' she asked. 'Tell me a story, teach me something new on my birthday.'

She could hear him flicking through pages. God only knew how fast he read and how much his eyes could remember.

'Haven't you ever read one of these journals yourself?'

She shook her head. She had read some books in NIMAS but that was because she *had* to read them to pass her exams there. She had never really taken an interest in reading anything otherwise, it was such an outdated and extinct notion.

'You've never wondered about the history of this land? Where our ancestors came from? Who was here before that? How the Internet was created? How nuke-warfare ended?' Arthur spoke fast, as if he was reading from his memories.

'Well… not really.' Tina's tone suddenly took a sharp twist. 'I've been fairly busy trying to survive in this current world, so I'm sorry I didn't have the time and patience to read about the past. None of that will make a difference today anyway.'

Arthur shook his head. 'History has been removed to make everyone forget how great we once were, how peaceful society could be and how every race and religion could live in harmony.' His voice drew Tina's attention, his passion resonated both a deep fury and a determined patience, like he believed in every word that he said, and would stand by his morals. In another society, he may have even passed as a nobleman. 'Anyway, I've just finished this one.' He put the journal down and closed his eyes.

She bolted upright. 'Wait, what do you mean you've finished it? You've only just held it in your hands for a few minutes.'

He pointed to his temple, his eyes remaining closed. Of course, he could remember everything he saw, but just how much could his memory take? How did this work exactly?

'All I need to do is understand it now. Give me a minute.'

'You must really love that skill of yours.'

His eyes twitched behind his eyelids. His hands drummed rhythmically on the wooden desk and he sat with one leg raised above his knee. If this school had been functioning, perhaps she could have mistaken him for an actual teacher. A young one.

'My memory isn't always a gift, Tina.' His brows furrowed. 'Sometimes... I have episodes.'

'What do you mean?' Tina found herself drawing closer to the desk. She couldn't take her eyes off him. She wanted to understand him, everything about him.

Assassins are not meant to feel. We are not meant to.

Her years of training had thoroughly cemented this into her. But she felt as if the cement had started to form cracks.

'Sometimes my mind breaks down. I-I'm not able to move or talk or do...anything.' Arthur spoke as if he were embarrassed by this. 'It's only happened to me a few times, but...I end up losing a chunk of my memory each time it does.'

Tina didn't know what to say to him. This was the point where she should comfort her friend, wasn't it? But she was preoccupied with working out what he was trying to say. *Say something.*

'I imagine it must be a strain on your mind. To be able to recall so much information. Surely it's a natural thing for your brain to delete some memory to keep your sanity intact?' This was the best form of reassurance she could give him. If indeed, he was asking for reassurance.

Silence crept into the dimly lit classroom. Arthur still had his eyes closed, as if he were multitasking in his mind. Could his gift not really be a gift? In her eyes, he was already an extraordinary person. His humble and thoughtful characteristics, as well as his inner moral workings, made him a fascinating person. But on top of that, to be able to recall things that he saw with detail made him someone even the White Arrow would be interested in. The thought terrified her. She wouldn't allow it.

'But...' He broke the silence, relieving Tina of doing so. 'What if the next time it happens I forget things that are important to me? Like important information that I've read? Or my sister? Or you?' His eyes snapped open, piercing her hazel with grey.

Why did he have to say that? She picked up the journal on the desk and brought it down on his head with a thud.

'I wouldn't let you forget me.'

He smiled, taking the journal into his palms. His fingers grazed hers as he did so.

Too close, Tina. But her heart shut the thought out with a drumming that felt like music being played out of her chest.

'For the record, I've written journals to myself to help me trigger my memory. I'll write a new one when I get home. In case I *do* have one of these episodes, just find those journals in my room and get me to read it...' His eyes searched deep into hers. Time slowed, or maybe her mind blanked for longer than she would have liked. He wasn't simply asking her to make him read something he wrote; he was asking her to save him if the time ever arose. To save him in a way that was unheard of to an assassin—to make him read.

Tina nodded slowly. She moved towards each window to board it up with cardboard, her usual ritual for the night. Another thought passed through her mind, something that made more sense now.

'Is this why you haven't spoken about your parents? Your... real parents?' The thought of his bloodline crossed her mind again.

He nodded. 'I wish I'd been at an age to write about my parents before they were wiped from my memory. Maybe one day I'll remember something about them. But as it stands, I don't know what the clowns know about me. Maybe...' He was slowly walking over to her. 'You could let *me* do the questioning next time?' He smiled and tapped his journal lightly on her head. 'I've actually got an interesting journal entry that I read a couple of years back. Want to hear it?'

She nodded, thinking back to her wish. If she had been given the chance she would have liked to have made two wishes, as selfish as it sounded. Perhaps she should have wished for more than just vengeance.

***

Arthur

Arthur leaned against the cushioned chair by the desk, sifted through his memories, and began to recite the journal entry that left him with the most questions. The journal entry that had taken both his and Lucy's curiosity to a higher level. One that both frightened him and enveloped him in courage. He cleared his throat and attempted to speak as the brave soul that had written this entry in the first place.

'Dear Reader,

I'm not sure when you'll read this, or where. But this world is not what you imagined. If you opened this book to read a story about a world full of magic, of mythical creatures, gods, demons and valiant knights in shining armour, then I'm sorry to disappoint. But the world is far from such a fantasy. It's the year 2045. People call it the year that everything changed, but it's more like the year that everything ended.

The First Cyber War took its toll on many nations; France, Russia, China, Iran, Japan, USA and even Britain suffered. It was the first war that the world had ever seen fought without soldiers, a war fought virtually. They said the Second World War was a horrific event, but that doesn't even come close. At least in the old wars, the enemies would have to cross borders. The cost of weaponry had become impractical, leading to the end of mass-weaponry being produced by every country. Even nuclear warheads were made useless by hacker groups like the

Anonymous.

When it came to Cyber Wars, hackers would attack a country's security, economy, and resources, deleting and corrupting everything they could until the people starved, and civil war broke out. Cyber Wars ate a country from the inside out.

As powerful as the Internet was, it was the most vulnerable source of power. Nobody could be trusted. Gone were the days where you knew who the enemy was. Paranoia swept through cities as governments cracked down on anyone with access to the Internet. After all, anyone could be a hacker. Whether you were a sixteen-year-old orphan or a sixty-year-old homeless beggar with a mobile phone, anyone with access to the Internet was deemed a threat to the security of the country. Conflict broke out between those who wanted to keep the peace by destroying every form of technology that posed a threat, and those who wanted to hold on to the tools that mankind had created to express their freedom of speech.

The progress that earth had made over the past thirty years was wiped out in three. So much happened in those three years, too much for me to write about. The anarchy ended on the 11th of November–yesterday. I say it ended, but I'm not sure if it ended everywhere. No one knows what's happening in other countries anymore. Communication has been lost even between cities and areas, let alone countries. The extent of the damage was too much.

People didn't just lose their homes, their wealth, and their families. Even before all of that, many lost their sanity. They simply couldn't comprehend living without technology, living without the Internet. The world grew too complacent and too comfortable. Now, well, it's like we're living in the 20th century again.

The monarchy has fallen, and the young King has even gone into hiding, leaving the country without a just leader. Not that the King was ever a leader, but when democracy crumbled, people turned towards the one person they had been praising as a figurehead for decades. Where were the people supposed to look towards next? A God?

A new party has been formed to try to maintain the peace. The White Arrow, they call themselves. Living in London, they're the only group with enough organisation and money to stand on solid ground. But I'm not too sure about them. Rumours have already started to fly around, talking about purges in the north. Refugees, migrants, religious believers, people of different colours and creed are being persecuted, I hear. It scares a black man like myself. God—I hear some people have started worshipping Wi-Fi!

Some crazy rumours even say that the White Arrow has been burning down libraries and museums. I didn't understand why they would do that at first. But, Reader, think carefully. A few years ago, a person would only search for information on the Internet, and if by some unfortunate reason they couldn't do that, they could find information in places like libraries. What if they were all removed from society? What if the only source of information came from the White Arrow themselves? What if society forgot some of the most important things that made humanity strong and wise?

A child may be born in a few years not knowing of the evil that my black ancestors had lived and died through. They will not know of the sacrifice of the Indians or the bravery of the suffragettes when racial and sexual inequality would once again bare its fangs. It hurts me to write this but maybe one day it will become illegal for people to even read? Knowledge is power, after all.

Understand that power can only be received by others if you allow for it. Whether it is a dictator who commits atrocities or whether you are being bullied by someone, they become powerful when you allow them to. The moment you step back, the moment you look away and try to ignore your problems. That isn't pacifism, it's cowardice. Be brave.

This world of mine is one that I, and the people of this age, must take responsibility for. You, the reader of whenever and wherever, have the responsibility of your era. If you choose to do nothing, then you must take the blame for the lack of change, and if you choose to do better than us, then perhaps you'll never fear for your life in the way we do today.

The world is not what you imagined. It used to be better.

-Kingslee

Kingslee's words were ever so powerful and from the very first moment Arthur had read them, he had thirsted for more. A minute passed in silence. Neither wanted to break it nor knew the best way to do so.

'Well, that was… epic,' Tina muttered at last. 'I think… you should read to me more often. Even if you were reading from your memories. I enjoyed it.'

Arthur stole a glance at her. She had been sitting quietly for close to half an hour, watching him and listening intently. She fidgeted with her hair, letting her fingers comb through it before she neatly organised it into a bun. Her hair had grown considerably since he first met her, but then again, so had his.

'If you ever get to meet him, I think Sebastian will really take a liking to you.' She stood up and peeked through the gaps in the boards by the window. 'It's getting late…do you want me to walk you home?'

Arthur shook his head. 'I'll be fine.'

'Good. Meet me in the hall downstairs tomorrow evening. We're going to start your training.'

15. The Warrior

Tina

The wind coursed through her hair, caressing it as Tina jumped from roof to roof. A smile lit her face as she landed with a subtle bend of her knees. The time—or the lack of it—between each jump, created a warm feeling in Tina's stomach. She reached for a higher ledge, gripping it with her fingertips; the cold hard surface welcomed her with each leap. Her light weight and athleticism made her somewhat ideal for parkour. She brushed off the dust from her hands before attempting the next building. Within a few minutes, she had reached Cable Street. She had memorised the layout of the town now. Imprinted in her subconscious were all the important buildings in Whitechapel, as well as all the less than popular routes around town.

She jumped off the old lady's clothing shop and landed on the pizza shop. Tina continued her sprint until she reached a road that led to the rest of the western parts of the greater area of Hamlets. She waited, crouching out of sight.

A few minutes passed before she heard the sound of hooves. The distant echo of a cart bustled into her view; the two-wheeled wooden vehicle squeaked along the road as it was pulled by two dark-brown horses. It was strange to see horses in a town like Whitechapel, they were more common in the Greenlands. The merchant came into full view, he was probably in his mid-forties. He wore a turban that rested just up to his eyebrows and had a beard that had begun to whiten. Tina had observed his routine for over a month now and had figured out his pattern of commerce. He would come to Whitechapel every Monday to trade. She retrieved a parcel from her pouch and held it in her hand, before approaching him in the middle of the road.

He gasped and brought his horse to a stop. 'Woah there. I didn't see you there, young lady!' His Indian accent was as strong and clear as the sun above them.

'Young sir,' she began, as a courtesy, or was it simply flattery? 'Are you by any chance heading towards New India?' She already knew he was.

'Yes, I am. Can I interest you in anything?' He pointed back at his cart full of timber.

She shook her head. 'I've got an important parcel that needs to be delivered to my comrades in the New India Martial Arts School.'

He paused and studied her, before his eyes widened. 'Tina of the Ruh? Is it really you?'

She brought a finger to her lips, silencing him. 'I can't talk out here in the open.'

The man smiled and nodded, accepting the letter from her. 'Consider it done. Straight to Sebastian?'

She nodded. 'Thank you. Here, take this as payment.' She reached into her bag for some coins but was immediately stopped.

'I feel privileged to have even been given this task by a member of the Ruh. I wouldn't ask for money from you. You can call me Magnah the Merchant. Remember me, I'm sure we'll meet again soon.' He gave her a wave, before urging his horses forward, pulling the cart down the dirt road until he became a speck in the distance.

She let out a sigh of relief before making her way back to a nearby roof. At least that was one task out of the way; she had finished her surveying of Whitechapel for Sebastian and had also filled him in on the situation here. It would probably take a week before she would hear back from him. She hadn't heard from him in months, not since living in Kingsland, the place she lived before moving to Whitechapel.

Eventually, she would have to leave Whitechapel too.

***

118

Tina led Arthur through the dirty hallways, across a patch of unruly yellowing grass, and into the school gym. She had tried to rid the place of dust, cobwebs and other signs of negligence a few weeks ago, but it became too time-consuming to maintain the cleanliness. Arthur trailed behind her, gawking at almost everything he saw as if he had never seen a gym before.

The gym was a great space for her to practice her skills and stay in shape. Being an assassin, she was taught that it was her duty to maintain her physique and endurance. A good assassin needs a body that can move like the wind. It can be calm when you want to blend in unnoticed, and razor sharp when you need to kill.

'I don't think even the townsfolk know about the facilities here,' he said.

Arthur passed by one of the heavier weights that she had been using a few days ago, lifting it up and placing it back on a rack with relative ease. 'Maybe one day this place could train a new batch of Peacekeepers.' His eyes glanced from the heavy set of weights to the lifting machines across the room. Except for a couple of machines, nothing was powered by electricity; it was good old-fashioned training.

Tina walked past the row of machines, picking up a pair of blue cushioned pads along the way. She pushed open another door that led to the basketball courts. Arthur *oooh'd* as he entered. The dying sunlight pierced through the high windows on either side, permitting some light into the otherwise dark court. The laminated wooden flooring was lined with white and blue, indicating the rectangular court that children had played basketball on many years ago. A basketball hoop towered down from each end of the court, covered in a browning colour of mixed dust and cobwebs.

Tina moved to the centre of the court where all the light congregated. She turned and passed Arthur an observatory look, analysing the pacifist. A simple black t-shirt stuck to his body, shaping his lean and tall torso. Even beneath his clothes, she could make out the results of all the hard labour he performed. For someone who had no interest in fighting, his body was reasonably well-built.

'What are you staring at?' Arthur asked.

Tina scowled. 'Nothing. Are you ready?'

He nodded slowly. 'What are we doing today?'

'Since you're not learning to fight, I need you to be able to defend yourself.' She threw the pads at him. 'I'm going to attack you. I need you to use them to block me as much as possible.'

She watched as Arthur fumbled with the pads. 'No… you're meant to wear them the other way round.' Tina shook her head. *This is going to be a tiresome evening.*

Arthur held the pads up, steadying himself by planting his foot firmly on the wooden flooring. He nodded.

Tina raised her clenched fist, preparing for non-dagger combat. She took another glance at his posture. He bent his knee and readied himself as she had seen him do once before in the classroom. He looked uneasy, his eyes not finding something to focus on.

'Arthur. This is serious, you know. People are dying in your town.'

'I know,' he snapped. 'I'm ready, come.'

In a quick motion, Tina shifted her body to the left and brought her right fist crashing into Arthur's jaw. A loud snap echoed in the hall. Arthur staggered backwards, his eyes misting over with tears that he vehemently blinked away. He hadn't even moved his pads to block her.

This is going to be a painful *and tiresome evening.*

By the time Tina had finished with Arthur, he was lying on his back with his arms outstretched. Sweat engulfed him as if he had a fever and his breathing was ragged. His body was already decorated in dark blue and purple bruises.

She wanted to treat his training with respect, giving him her full effort and attention. But as time passed, with Arthur consistently receiving the full brunt of every attack, Tina decided to ease up, pulling her punches to not give him any further facial souvenirs.

She couldn't help but frown at his meagre fighting abilities. Was there even a point in any of this if he was this terrible? This whole session was wasted; all Tina had done was hurt Arthur. Perhaps his morals were so tightly knitted into him that he wouldn't even let himself protect his own body by hurting another?

'Arthur, the whole point of the pads is to protect you from the impact. By you doing that, you realise you're not hurting anyone, right?'

Arthur sat up, nodding.

'I don't think there's a point in us meeting tomorrow,' she said. There was no way he was going to be of any use against the Shadows of London. She turned around to leave the court but was startled by sweaty fingers holding her wrist.

'Please.' He stifled a cough. 'Don't give up on me just yet. We've just got started.'

'That's what I fear. Even the beginning looks like your end.'

Arthur shook his head. 'Tomorrow will be different, I promise.' He let go of her wrist.

She pursed her lips in doubt; she didn't want to waste even more time. But the determined eyes of the pacifist beckoned her for another chance.

'Fine, whatever.' She rolled her eyes. 'You better be able to walk to the shops. I'm hungry.'

***

Arthur

The next day, Arthur felt as if his arms would simply fall off his shoulders. He could hardly move his body as he dug holes at the dumpsite. He could have sworn the shovel weighed ten times its normal weight.

A nauseating feeling swept over him when he remembered he was standing only a few metres away from where he and

Lukas had discovered the first body. Lukas still hadn't turned up for his shift. In fact, there were even fewer people out here working than usual. Arthur spent the whole morning shovelling dirt out of the ground mostly by himself. Had more people gone missing or were they just finding work elsewhere?

The repeated mundane actions of thrusting, lifting and depositing dirt gave Arthur the opportunity to let his mind wander freely. He remembered the notes he had scribed a few days ago. Lillian, Amy, and Sylvia, those were the first three—and Arthur hoped the last three—of this new Jack the Ripper's prized murders. Each death killed in ritualistic fashion, their throats cut and their genital areas desecrated as if the killer was trying to recreate the exact murders of the 1800s—except he wasn't. The killer had taken a victim's heart instead of half a kidney. The heart was a better trophy than half a kidney. Was this new Jack trying to state that he was better than the old Jack? What if this killer was trying to compete with his historical counterpart?

Kingslee's words resurfaced in Arthur's mind.

The moment you step back, the moment you look away and try to ignore your problems. That isn't pacifism, its cowardice.

He needed to stop these killings from happening again, and he knew he couldn't do it without Tina's help. Today he would prove to her that he was capable of being her partner, of challenging whatever psychopathic killer or evil villainous group they would face, for the sake of justice. He wanted Whitechapel to be a town of peace again, just like when Mr Hudson was still alive, and Mr Murray was Mayor.

After a quick lunch, he found himself on the basketball court again. The assassin was waiting for him at the centre, her arms crossed and her lips curled disapprovingly. She seemed to be in a sullen mood, probably due to yesterday's disappointing show. Arthur promised her things would be different today, and he would make sure they were. He slipped his fingers through the pads and held them out, his knees bent, his eyes focused.

'You ready?' Tina asked.

He nodded.

He watched as she readied herself. After yesterday's session, he knew the assassin was surprisingly strong for someone with a small and skinny frame. Her movements were well marshalled and efficient, not letting herself exert any more energy than what was necessary. That in itself was a skill she must have learned in New India. She was diligent in every step she took and every blow she inflicted. Yet there was something different in her eyes today; she looked at him as if she had already concluded how this session would end.

Tina's body shifted to the right. The last time she did this she had struck him on his right arm. He quickly brought the pads up to his right. A loud crack resounded in the hall. Her eyes widened in surprise. He had blocked her.

She dropped her shoulder, just like yesterday. This time Arthur brought his pads lower to avoid getting hit in the stomach. Once again, he blocked her. Her eyes darted from his face to his pads. She continued to press, attacking him from a multitude of angles.

Each time she did, Arthur blocked her. After several more attempts, Tina paused.

'Take off the pads,' she ordered. 'This time there's nothing to cushion my attacks. You'll have to use your feet to avoid being hit.'

Arthur looked at her blankly.

She rolled her eyes. 'Get out of the way before I hit you.'

He nodded, throwing the pads to the floor. She threw a left hook first. Arthur had by now memorised how Tina moved. He shifted his body as he had seen her do yesterday. Her fist connected with his arm, sending shock waves of pain rippling through him.

'That could have been my dagger—I would have severed a tendon by now,' she scowled.

What happened? He was sure he'd done exactly what she had. He took a light step and shifted his shoulders. The confusion must have been easy to read on his face because she

123

laughed at him.

'Do you honestly think your body can move like mine? Don't try to just copy me. You need to be more calculated.' She made a fist towards his jaw. Arthur raised his arms to block it and winced as a sharp pain rang through his limbs. He had received her well but it still hurt.

Tina dropped her body and spun in a quick flash, sweeping a trailing leg under him. Arthur felt his legs give way, introducing him to the mercy of gravity. His body clattered to the floor, causing the familiar sound of defeat to echo through the hall.

'Is that all you got?' The assassin smirked. It seemed like she was in a better mood now.

***

Tina

She was surprised. No, even that would be an understatement. Arthur had made leaps of improvement since yesterday, even if it was because of his memory. His body was a lot more agile, and his movements seemed a bit more experienced. Something that would've taken most people weeks had taken him a day. He certainly had potential.

The sessions with Arthur made her feel quite nostalgic, like she was back in New India, training with the Ruh. Lars always had an unwavering spirit, always training harder than everyone and always looking as if he was going to collapse after every session. A warm feeling filled her gut. What was it?

They had agreed to train every other day from now on, giving him enough time to recover in between sessions.

'Tina. I'm going to use the shower here.' Arthur looked at her as if he was seeking her permission for using school facilities that she had no right over.

'Sure.'

Don't go red now, Tina.

16. The Weapon of Choice

The familiar feeling of nonchalance and ignorance filled the atmosphere in the bustling room. Moaning of the day's duties and other irrelevant chatter dimmed Arthur's focus. He had taken to the Wayward Tavern with the hopes that beer would fill the bellies of well-informed townsfolk and loosen their tongues. The afternoon sunlight crept in from the windows that were perched up close to the roof. It was an unusual design, almost as if the roof itself were decorated with glass patches of light and cloud. The wooden interior teased Arthur with the same magnificent look of Mr Murray's house; it made sense as he was heavily invested in this establishment. Very few people in Whitechapel lived as comfortably as Mr Murray did.

The corner of the warm tavern was occupied by a group of women who worked at the brothel, sitting in a cluster around the table and advertising themselves as if they were part of the brothel's marketing strategy. Arthur had already pestered them with questions a few days ago. Although they were wary of a killer on the loose, they weren't making their safety a priority over their midnight commissions. Money was more important. A group of men lingered towards the end of the bar, deep in conversation about which woman they wanted to pay visit to later in the evening. They kept peering over their shoulders, casting fickle looks at their targets and at times, licking their lips.

It was an unfair and cruel environment. Many of the women were widowed or cast out by their families. With no other qualifications or skills, they had to resort to this detestable way of making money. Sometimes life could hurt you by stripping you of options.

'What's with all those bruises, Arthur? The poor folk in the dumps beat you up or something?' Gareth laughed as he passed him.

Arthur shook his head slowly, caught off guard. He hadn't thought about the possibility of Gareth seeing him in this state. The two days of training with Tina had made him look like a beaten and bruised tomato now. Except, of course, he didn't resemble a shape of a tomato, but perhaps that of a cucumber.

'Or is Eve doing experiments on you at night? I thought I had given her enough work with those bodies,' Gareth muttered with a smirk.

Arthur blushed at the thought, before his eyes widened with a sense of realisation. This was his chance to find out more about these deaths. But he would need to ease it in without raising any suspicion.

Gareth sat down a few seats from him. He ordered his drink before passing Arthur a cool gaze, studying his face with all its decorations.

Arthur noticed the women in the corner shuffle, stretching their long necks higher than what Arthur thought physically possible, craning for the Peacekeeper's attention. Their eyes begged for reciprocation. His alpha male presence attracted all the attention he wanted from the corner.

'Must be tough dealing with the White Knights,' Arthur muttered loud enough for Gareth to hear.

The Peacekeeper indulged himself in his drink, gulping down every last drop, before turning to Arthur.

'Stupid townsfolk, always violating the rules. Look what it's come down to now.'

Gareth was by far one of the biggest offenders in Whitechapel with his dealings in the Dark Quarters, but Arthur made it a point to not bring that up now. He simply nodded along.

'So uh… did she mention that she was attacked last week?' Arthur asked casually.

Gareth nodded. 'Thanks for being around to scare him away.

But…' His eyes narrowed. 'She mentioned that you weren't alone.'

Panic rippled through Arthur's mind. This wasn't the direction he'd intended the conversation to take. He had to stay composed.

'Not alone? Are you sure?' Arthur raised his glass and took a gulp. Maybe talking to Gareth now would be a little too risky. 'I think she was in quite a panic when she was attacked. I know if I were attacked, my imagination would run wild too.' How stupid did he think Gareth really was? He knew exactly how shrewd and calculated Eve was; of course she wouldn't fabricate a crucial part of her statement.

Gareth stared at him stubbornly for a few seconds, glancing at the purple that now stained his jaw.

'Yeah, maybe,' he said slowly. 'For the record. From all the gory description of this mythical Jack the Ripper person you gave me, you said that Jack would slice the throats of his victims and then their bodies?'

Arthur nodded. Did Gareth finally believe him?

'Well, from what I saw and through Eve's post-mortems, the victims weren't killed with a knife. None of these victims were attacked by a knife at all. It had to have been a different object, since their necks weren't sliced…more like punctured and ripped.'

Arthur fell silent. His mind raced with questions that spiralled into further questions. He'd always had a feeling there was something wrong with the way the neck of each victim looked. Was it not a Jack the Ripper copycat but actions of another delusional character? Or simply an ordinary psychopath?

He wanted to stick with his gut feeling. The way the bodies had been left for dead, the way they had been mutilated, everything pointed towards this historical killer. Someone in Whitechapel had to be trying to resurrect his work. Perhaps not exactly in line with the stories, history surely couldn't repeat itself with perfect symmetry.

Arthur caught Gareth making flirtatious eye contact with a woman from across the room and used this opportunity to finish his drink and slip out of the tavern. Just as he reached the door, Mary-Anne entered. An apron in her hand, she looked like she was about to start her shift. She drew closer to him and whispered.

'My father wanted to invite you and your friend over for dinner tonight.'

Arthur nodded, before pushing the door open into the eerie streets of Whitechapel.

***

Arthur almost felt giddy at the thought of having dinner at Mr Murray's. Tina shot him a look that probably meant: *Stop fidgeting and sit still before I stab you with this fork.* Or maybe it didn't. She'd been giving him a lot of weird looks as of late. Maybe this was an assassin thing? Perhaps one day he could communicate with her like this.

Chicken, stew, different variants of bread, and even a rare spicy sauce were all laid out in front of them on the dinner table. Mr Murray's voice boomed in high spirit as he ushered them all to tuck in. He seemed to have recovered a little. He hadn't forgotten them since the last time they had come and from what Mary-Anne had mentioned, he enjoyed their company.

'You must enlighten me, Arthur. Why exactly do you look like you've been beaten to a pulp?' Mr Murray asked.

'Well, Mr Murray. With all the trouble Whitechapel is facing today, Tina has been teaching me the art of self-defence.'

'Ah, a wise choice indeed.' He winked at Tina. He then turned to his daughter and whispered something in her ear.

Mary-Anne stood up and walked to the end of the room, where she pushed open a door to her right. After a moment, she returned with a book in her hand.

'That there was my study, a room where most of my work as Mayor was done.' Mr Murray passed a longing gaze at the door before returning to the item in Mary-Anne's hand.

The book was worn, the paper crinkled and deteriorated near the edges. He took it from Mary-Anne gingerly. 'Anyway, I hear you and Tina saved Eve from a spot of bother.'

Arthur nodded.

'Well, for your troubles and as former Mayor, I insist on giving you this, as my token of appreciation.' He smiled and passed Arthur a browning journal. 'As you can see from my…condition, I don't have the ability to write much anymore. Perhaps it is better suited in your hands.'

Arthur accepted the journal with a slight frown. How did Mr Murray know he read books?

'Wait…you used to write? Isn't that illegal for even the Mayor?' Arthur asked.

'My dear boy, I was writing before all these laws came to be.' Mr Murray laughed. 'Back in my day, we used to post our thoughts through tablets and mobile phones onto the net.'

Mary-Anne rolled her eyes. 'Father, not another one of these ancient stories please, you'll bore them,' she pleaded.

Mr Murray chuckled. 'You youngsters don't know the half of it, and you won't know in this age, with everything old being wiped out—unless I write it down. God, even cameras have become too expensive.'

Arthur flicked through a few pages of the journal. His eyes widened. This was really old, and each entry had a heading. *The River Thames, The First Purge, The First Black Prime Minister, The Underground Cars, The First to Mars, The End of Democracy, Civil War.* There were so many interesting topics for Arthur to indulge in later. A flutter of excitement coursed through his stomach.

'But thank you for saving Eve,' Mr Murray continued. 'What would Whitechapel do without a nurse? We've already lost a doctor, the poor soul.'

'May Dr Dovedi rest in peace,' Mary-Anne said, raising her glass.

They all joined in, even Tina, who looked slightly confused.

'It's been nearly two months since he died, right?' Arthur asked Mary-Anne. It was around the same time Lucy had gone missing.

She nodded. 'His death was so sudden, even Eve couldn't determine what the cause was. But I haven't spoken to her about him since. Perhaps they figured it out?'

'It's worth asking Gareth about the details, he should be on top of it by now,' Mr Murray added, helping himself to some more roasted chicken.

'You don't think it was anything unnatural?' Arthur asked daringly.

'Murder, you mean?' Mary-Anne replied. 'Who would want to do such a thing to the good doctor?'

Tina finished chewing on her food. 'Wait…who exactly is Dr Dovedi?'

'He was the second in charge while my father was actively the Mayor. When Father became ill, Dr Dovedi took his place and continued the peace that Father had kept for so long. After he suddenly passed—and as my father was still bedridden—Gareth took the opportunity to take charge.'

Mr Murray frowned. 'Such a depressing conversation for the dinner table.' He turned to Tina. 'Any word from the Ruh, young Tina?'

She shook her head. 'I haven't heard from them in months.' If she was disappointed, she didn't show it on her face.

'Well, maybe you can invite them to Whitechapel. I'd love to meet this new generation of brave Peacekeepers that good old John invested his time into.'

Arthur still didn't really understand how Tina and Mr Murray were connected; there were too many names involved. This time it was Arthur's turn to question.

'If I may ask, who exactly *is* John?'

Mr Murray turned to Tina. 'You haven't told him much, have you?' She shook her head, ripping a piece of bread and dipping it into her stew.

'Have you heard of a man named Lennart Chance?' Mr

Murray asked. His attention undivided, as if what he was about to explain held considerable weight on him.

'Yeah, he's the Hero of the Slums, the man who led the Battle of the Bridges against the White Arrow four years ago.'

'Yes, but he's more than that. Lennart was the first to form a guild of strong warriors. John was their marksmen, Astal their technician, and Khalid their vanguard. All of them were fiercely strong Peacekeepers. They passed by Whitechapel a long time ago, dealing with all the bandits that used to occupy this place. They were like a beacon of hope, a shining light during a dark time. I'm sure Tina would know more about them as she trained with one of them.'

All eyes turned to the assassin, who seemed to be giving more attention to her chicken than to their conversation. She looked up with her mouth full of chicken.

'Mhmm.' She reached for some water and washed her food down.

Mary-Anne laughed. 'For someone so little in size, you seem to have a big appetite.'

Tina placed her cutlery down, before looking at each one of them. 'My guild was formed by Master John, a former member of Lennart's guild. We were all inspired by Lennart and his group. The King's Arm was his official guild name.'

'King? But there isn't a king,' Arthur interjected.

Tina shook her head. 'That's not what they believed. Lennart taught us that there was still hope, that one day someone would unite both Inner and Outer London. They would lead the city, then the country, as the King of New England.' She paused, taking another sip of water. 'But he didn't believe the slums were ready yet—it could take decades, he said.'

'Wait, let me get this straight. He believed this city, this country, is going to be united? Poor and rich? All races and religions?' Mary-Anne was clearly struggling to comprehend the idea.

'Why did he believe it had to be a man to unite the city?' Arthur asked. It was bad enough that Whitechapel had a poor attitude towards women.

'Who said anything about a man?' Tina snapped. 'Maybe it'll be a woman.'

'But you said a *king*. Not a queen.' Arthur wondered what went through Tina's mind sometimes.

'They're just names of positions. Throughout history, the word "King" has generally been favoured and respected more than "Queen." We're living in a new world now. Maybe a woman will take the title of King. It's not like anyone would object to the term now.'

Arthur rolled his eyes. None of this made sense. 'Okay, let's get back to the subject at hand. So Lennart truly believed that one day this country would be united again? That would mean defeating the White Arrow.'

'Yes. The Ruh will defeat the White Arrow.' She said this with ease, as if it were a matter of fact.

Silence filled the room as no one dared to speak. Did the Ruh really think they were capable of accomplishing such a feat? Arthur shifted uncomfortably in his seat, wondering what Mr Murray's stance would be on this open declaration of treason.

The old man's eyes flitted from Tina's to Arthur's, and his mouth widened into a grin. Mr Murray burst into a hearty laugh. 'Such spirit! I hope I get to live to see that day!'

'Don't be silly, Father.' Mary-Anne glanced at Tina as if she were truly observing the teenage girl, the Assassin of the Ruh. 'Of course you will. We all will,' She beamed.

Mr Murray raised his glass. 'To the Ru—' He stopped as if he were in mid-thought, his gaze fixed on nothing in particular.

His eyes widened and his glass fell to the floor with a shatter, shards spinning across the laminate. Arthur stood up; Mary-Anne rushed over to her father.

'Father, are you okay?' Her voice rippled with fear and anxiety.

'What? Yes, yes.' He looked around as if he couldn't recognise where he was. His bewildered gaze fell on Arthur and

Tina. 'Wh-who are you? What are you doing in my house?'

Tina and Arthur exchanged looks. The ageing figure was still suffering. Arthur wished he could give him some of the abilities he had, even an ounce of it would do him a world better. But things didn't work like that.

Tears started to spill from Mary-Anne's eyes.

17. The Punching Bag

Arthur

Arthur rhythmically turned the pages of Mr Murray's journal, his eyes shot from left to right like a madman frantically pouring his soul into the soft ink-filled parchments. The more he read, the more he was mesmerised by Mr Murray's experiences. No doubt he would not be able to recall much of it today though. The page that stood out to him the most was dated to 2071.

Dear Reader,

This is less so a journal entry as it is a short rant of history, but a necessary one. I hope you feel the same way as I after reading this.

It is absolutely shocking, disgusting and outrageous. London has never been so divided; The White Arrow Party and those that express views of a superior race, all live comfortably within the White Walls of London. The rest of us; anyone of a different colour, religion or race— more specifically; anyone that opposes the White Arrow's Aryan ideology, were forced into the slums. I can't help but feel useless in this political play. My father said it began years ago, when the voting had passed for a new wall to be constructed.

London had—by then—already succumbed to the effects of several global crises, after the fall of the internet and the scramble for resources. Everyone had suffered, we still suffer. But not only did the corrupt party get the vote to divide the land, but they also published the names of all the voters that voted for that decision. How treacherous; Neighbours, friends, and family all turned on each other, divided by their political views.

The cheek of them to then offer refuge to the same supporters, to offer protection and a home within the walls. A stark divide within the population of London led to these troubling times. During the confusion and conflict, the White Arrow began their purges, pushing people out of their homes and recouping more land for those who supported them. Thus, we have two wholly new societies living beside each other; the city-folk, those who lived within the walls; and the slum-folk, those that lived in the slums outside.

Over the years, the slums have been suffering from negligence and poverty. While the citizens of the city united under the political banner of the White Arrow, the slum-folk became divided amongst their diversity and differences, finding it hard to recoup the old times of unity.

Today, the White Arrow revealed a new unit of soldiers or warriors or whatever they were; the White Knights they were called. Ruthless and loyal to the Chancellor. I hope I never have to cross paths with one of them. I pray the rumours of purges never come to fruition.

Reader, this is how the White Arrow created the new London you see today.

Alan M.

A fire roared in Arthur's gut, a familiar feeling after reading such controversial and heartfelt material. It must have been tough for Mr Murray to maintain some level of peace in Whitechapel whilst still detesting the White Arrow, especially as this area was not too far from the walls and the influence of the party. Perhaps he simply *had* to rely on the White Arrow for their supplies. But things had changed in the past few years, New India, The Shamal, Greenlands and many other areas didn't rely on the White Arrow. If Whitechapel and other areas in the Hamlets could strike a deal with another area, they could surely stop relying on the party—that's if these areas could agree on something together and get along, which was certainly not a common thing. Diplomacy and collaboration could instil strength into this town, but it would need strong representation, and Mr Murray was currently not that in his current state.

One thing at a time.

He needed to focus on *his* task at hand. He needed to retrace his findings and untangle the complications that grew with every passing day. He leaned back against his desk chair and stretched his arms. He needed to let his bruises heal and his muscles rest; his body rippled with pain from the intense sessions at the school.

He still hadn't told Tina what Gareth had mentioned about the knife. He was struggling to answer several questions himself. If the killer didn't kill those women using a knife, then what had he used? Would it not have been simpler to use one? And what of the missing people? It wasn't part of Jack's story. Arthur pushed the latter thoughts out of his head. *One thing at a time.*

His mind raced back to both corpses he had engraved into his bank of memories, focusing on their necks. They were bloodied with different shades of red; he could make out a small hole from where the tearing of the flesh would have begun. A new train of thought blazed through Arthur. He quickly stood up and began his usual pacing. The tearing of skin had occurred from the right side, venturing all the way across to the left. Arthur imagined a knife in his right hand, he imagined the weight of it and the nauseating thought of blade meeting skin. It didn't make sense—no… it just didn't work like that. He tried again whilst still forcing the revulsion of this exercise down into his gut. He tried repeatedly to make sense of it, until—

'The ripper is left-handed.'

***

'So let me get this right, Gareth believes the weapon wasn't a blade and you think they're left-handed?' Tina swung the stick towards his shoulder, missing him by an inch as he leaned back on his pivot foot. 'I thought the killer was following the character of this ripper.'

'I still think it's something to do with Jack the Ripper—everything else fits his style of killing. From the type of victims to the time of night, and even to the mutilated parts of the body. Just because the throat wasn't sliced doesn't mean it isn't him.' Arthur felt like he was trying to convince himself more than anything. He leapt back, narrowly avoiding another flurry of jabs.

'Maybe it was a screwdriver? Maybe we check out the builders in town,' she said, applying pressure to her attacks and increasing her pace.

Arthur scanned his mind for his suspect list for all the people he knew were left-handed, but none seemed to fit the obvious profile.

'Do you think I can't tell when you're not paying attention?'

Arthur quickly refocused his attention on her. Her body moved like a dancer, left then right, then in circles, he struggled to keep up. Before he could even begin to find the correct defensive pattern of movements, he felt the wooden rod strike his body in three different positions and a sharp pain ring through his body. He quickly found himself back on his feet. He had become accustomed to the pain by now.

'Focus,' she said before moving towards him. 'Let me show you something.' The assassin was now almost within touching distance of Arthur.

'...Okay?'

'You can see me right now... right?'

'Well... obviously,' he replied.

She took a step back. 'And now?'

'Yep. Is this going anywhere?'

'Shut up and wait. I want you to continue looking in this direction as I move, just keep staring straight ahead.' She took a step back, then three steps to Arthur's left.

'Can you see m—'

'I can't see you. But... I know you're there.' It was as if her body had merged into the darkness that existed in the corner of his eyes, fading into the background like a wisp of smoke. She was there and not there at the same time; a ghost, almost.

'With your aura, you should eventually get to a point where you can see me or others that lurk in the shadows. Now try looking at me.'

Arthur did, he looked to his left—but Tina wasn't there.

'What are you doing? I said look at me.' Her voice came from his left, so he quickly swivelled his body to catch her in his sight.

Again, she was gone before his eyes could focus on her. It was as if she was taunting him; every time he got close to seeing her, all he would glimpse were the trailing ends of her wispy-curls. He would glimpse her for half-a-second at most, a petite woman wearing a sleeveless black frock. The skin she revealed was ghost-white like the moon, yet the colourful lioness behind her hazel eyes roared with an arid sun's glare.

'It's too late Arthur. You're already caught in my trap, you won't be able to see me until I let you now.' Her voice broke through the air to his right this time. She was moving with the direction of his own movement.

'Is that so?' Arthur stopped moving and waited for Tina's movements to stop. So long as his eyes were looking in a particular direction, she wouldn't move. That was the bane to her movement, she *had* to hide in the corners of one's vision, which meant—

Arthur leapt to his right without any warning, with nothing to indicate the direction of his movement, a clumsy move—but it worked. He could see the widening eyes of Tina as he drew closer. What he didn't realise was that he was only standing a few feet away from her.

To say he stumbled into her would be an understatement. Arthur didn't stumble, he tumbled over his own feet and fell off balance into her, bringing her victorious stand to an end. He watched as the seconds slowed down, and the descent of her body caught him by surprise. Her hair was soft; his fingers had passed through a few curls by accident, but again it was her startled eyes that stole his attention—

They clattered to the floor with a groan.

'FOR GOD'S SAKE, ARTHUR. AT LEAST HAVE SOME GRACE IN YOUR MOVEMENTS.'

***

Gareth

The dull-white circle in the blackened sky above, cast a weak light on the Dark Quarters, perhaps even the moon kept its distance from these roads. Gareth waited patiently, as if waiting for a friend. In the embodiment of this virtue, patience *had* served him best. It had elevated him to where he was today, and a little more of it would leave Whitechapel without a Mayor, and would see him crowned as ruler of the town. A smile broke on his face, only to quickly vanish at the sight of some burly men approaching from the darkness. He had decided to hire half-a-dozen bandits for some… less-than-pleasant covert operations.

'What news do you have?' Gareth asked one of the cloaked figures.

'You were right about Hudson's son, he's been making several trips up to the abandoned school, always travelling alone and returning late at night,' he whispered back, masking his voice with the gush of the wind.

Gareth raised a brow. 'The roads to the school are dangerous.'

The leader let out a chuckle. 'Dangerous indeed. Shall we move on to the next phase?'

'Yes, but…' Gareth let a thought simmer, considering everything that had been happening recently. 'Dispose of the body—you have a week to do it, let's do it patiently and thoroughly.'

'Consider it done.' With that, the bandits left, leaving Gareth to dwindle in his dark solitude.

It had been a few months since the boy had been left with neither his father nor sister. As much as he was a hard-working slave in this town, his meddling was growing ever so troublesome. He remembered the visit he'd had from Lucy Hudson, a few days before she had disappeared. The fierce look in her eyes was hard to forget. It was as if she had suddenly realised something of importance; her eyes portrayed a greater purpose.

'Pay no attention to my little brother,' she'd said. 'He's a simple person, wanting to live a simple life. He won't cause you any trouble.'

Had she known how much the boy would change? Or had he always been like this? Had she been lying to him? Questions stormed his mind. Ever since Arthur Hudson had spoken about this Jack the Ripper, there had been deaths. It was almost as if he spoke this killer into existence.

***

Arthur

Over the next few days, Arthur continued his training with Tina. He felt like he had made significant progress since he first entered the court. He had learned to avoid getting hit not only by an unarmed assassin but also one with a wooden stick. Of course, a real assassin wouldn't ever fight with a stick, but Tina didn't want to use a real weapon for training. Apparently, sharp weapons were only to be used on strong opponents, not the likes of Arthur. He had no objections of course.

She spent a lot of time working on his footwork, from the positioning of his toes to the weight on his heel to the bend of his knee. At first, he struggled to get used to all these new details but slowly everything became easier. He could remember how she moved, so all he had to do was adjust his legs to a similar pattern of movement.

After that, they moved on to using weapons. Arthur refused to use a sharp item and instead took to the stick, whilst Tina used one of her daggers. He learned to parry, to swing, and to strike. He found this easier to do than holding pads, probably from all the times he had seen others use weapons.

He had read somewhere that in the old age, people didn't

really use swords. They had guns and other electrical devices, weapons that were only found in Inner London today. But after the many wars and the end of munition production, guns were becoming a rarer item every year.

He fell back onto the familiar flooring once again.

No matter how much he tried to predict her and no matter how much experience he could gain, she was always so much faster than him. Her own experience outweighed his. At times he felt as if she was even using her aura to move with such ease.

His lungs worked furiously as he panted.

'So… hah… when are you… going to teach me… hah… how to Shadow-Step?' he dared to ask.

'Never. You only want to know how to defend yourself, right? Shadow-stepping is an assassin's technique.'

'Yeah bu—'

'No buts, you'll learn what I teach you. Nothing else.' Tina dropped the stick, letting the clatter reverberate around the court.

She was extremely restrictive of what she would teach him, as if she didn't want to teach him everything, or perhaps she didn't want to waste all her time teaching him something that he would never use.

'We'll go through the pieces to this puzzle later tonight, okay?' she said with a small warm smile.

He wiped the sweat off his brows and nodded, before exiting the building.

A few weeks ago, she was just a young girl with an ice-cold demeanour and an attitude of apathy that would have made even Mr Hudson turn away with a grimace. A polar opposite of Arthur. But now he had learned about her past, her worries, her intentions, and even her skills. Tina was certainly not the frosty figure of doom he had once believed her to be.

But something deep inside him posed a question, a thought. What if he was only seeing one side of her? After all, she was an assassin and yet she hadn't really been acting like one thus far. There would come a point in time when he would witness her violent streak, to see her commit to her duties of blood and blade. Would he still be able to look at her in the same way?

For now, he tried to ignore that worry. He picked up his satchel and thanked her for the day's session before making his way out of the school. It was time for him to get home.

Between working the streets, training in the school, and secretly trying to find the killer roaming the streets, Arthur had not left much time to work through and understand his new journals. He still had to read through the Emir Khalid's journal as well as the rest of Mr Murray's. The content of what he had read recently floated on the surface of his mind. At times he would piece together information, coming to a sudden realisation about what he'd read earlier. But he needed complete tranquillity to really absorb the meaning behind the words.

As Arthur walked past the school gates, he frowned and stopped a little way down the road. He felt something out of place. He scanned the dirt road and noticed the irregularity. A couple of cigarette butts littered the floor. Small and inconclusive as they might have seemed, they weren't there a few hours ago. Arthur could picture exactly how the road had looked earlier.

No one ever came down this road. But someone had been here—a group of people, by the looks of it.

He picked up one of the butts and smelled it. A strong bitter and burnt smell filled his nostrils. They weren't far, probably still here. He needed to warn Tina. He turned around to head back towards the school.

'You there.' A man stood between him and the school gate. It wasn't the same person who'd attacked Eve. This man wore clothes that looked worn out and dirty, a red bandanna was wrapped around his forehead, and a brown cloth covered his mouth. Bandits. 'I saw you coming out of this building. And here I was, thinking this place was abandoned.' Had they been waiting for him?

Arthur's eyes fell to the sword in the man's hand, before turning to see several other bandits slinking out of their hiding places. An ambush? All held a glint of murderous intent in their eyes. His heart began to race.

'Who...who are you?' Arthur asked. He didn't care what they called themselves—they'd probably lie anyway—he just wanted to buy some time. Buy time for what, though?

'We've been tasked with investigating this building.' A tall man from behind him spoke. His voice was hoarse, and his sword was pointed towards Arthur. 'There's some pretty spooky stories about this place. Tell us, were you alone in there?'

Arthur's eyes narrowed. 'Tasked by who?' Who would want to investigate this place? Gareth perhaps? Would he really hire a bunch of thugs to do such a task? He quickly counted seven men surrounding him.

'Kid, we're the ones doing the questioning here. Tell us what we want to know, and we won't hurt you,' Red Bandanna snarled back at him.

Arthur remained tight-lipped.

'Leave it, Boss. This chump is a waste of time. I say we see what's inside his satchel, might make this trip worthwhile.' A man with a mole on his face squeaked beside him before grinning at Arthur. His eyes were dark, and his skin shone with an Indian-brown complexion.

Red Bandanna nodded, signalling his men forward.

A black man behind him stepped forward and reached for Arthur's arm. Arthur leapt out of the way.

'Blud. Whadjoo think you're doin'?' The man spoke threateningly.

'I could ask you the same thing,' Arthur replied. Height was not an advantage he had over this man. He needed to get them away from the school and warn Tina at the same time. But he couldn't see a way out for himself, as the men were closing him in from all sides.

His eyes scanned for a gap but couldn't find one; he would have to wait for one of them to break the circle. But would he be fast enough to move his body? Especially after a long session of training with Tina. His muscles were already feeling cramped. His heart throbbed furiously. This was the first time he was

143

actually applying his training, and if he couldn't deal with simple bandits, how would he ever survive against the Shadows?

The men pounced one by one, swinging their sharp blades at him. Arthur avoided the first one with ease, swerving to his left before ducking an attempt from a second bandit. It took a lot of energy just to move at this pace.

The bandits exchanged shifty looks, like they sensed they weren't dealing with an ordinary man. One of the men nodded at something behind Arthur. He hadn't noticed one of the larger men creeping up on him, and before he could react, he felt an arm reach around his neck, tightening. He gasped, inhaling deeply for air that would not come. Pain slivered through his body, bypassing the areas that had become numb from Tina's handiwork earlier.

The men drew closer to him, and one began to pull his satchel off his body. They would discover his journals. He couldn't let them do that. He tried to flail, to kick out at the man holding him. A futile effort.

'Right, let's see what all this fuss was ab—' The Red Bandanna-man stopped and looked down, his eyes wide in shock. 'Where the hell did you come from?'

Tina's presence alone distracted the men. Arthur could feel the grip around him loosen. Without a moment's hesitation, he broke free, pushing the assailant away from him with a kick. He landed behind the man with his satchel, catching him unaware. He tore his satchel from Red Bandanna's hands and backed away with Tina. The bandits crept closer.

'Woah now, missy. I don't know who you think you are but playing with those weapons isn't something you should be doing.' All eyes fell to her daggers. Another man opened his palms as if expecting Tina to simply hand them over to him.

Are all bandits this stupid?

'Who are they?' Tina whispered to him, slowly backing away from them.

'Bandits hired to investigate the school,' Arthur replied.

'Well then...I can't have them go back and report anything.'

A dangerous tone rang in her voice.

Arthur looked at them, then back at Tina. 'Wait… you can't kill them.'

Tina scowled at him. 'And why not? They're threatening us and if I don't, who knows what other harm they might cause others.'

The bandits, who were now encircling both of them, began to laugh and let loose a barrage of taunts and remarks.

'Is this some sort of joke? You *do* realise that neither of you will be leaving here alive, right? Let's cut all this big talk about killing us.'

'Yeah, I mean seriously man. You're hiding behind a *girl*. Is she really supposed to protect you? Man up! Here I thought you were putting up a good fight.'

The laughter continued. Arthur didn't let their taunts harm his ego.

Tina looked at him with frustration. But Arthur didn't falter. 'No Tina. No deaths. There has to be a better way to deal with this.'

But even as he spoke the words, worry flooded through him. Just who was he to think he could control an assassin? Someone he had only met a few weeks ago? Someone who was protecting *him*. Teaching *him*. Helping *him* with catching the killer in Whitechapel. Someone who had probably killed dozens of people in the past. A friend maybe, but still a dangerous person. Her daggers spun on her fingers, moving as if the blades were as light as a pencil. A small string connected each dagger to her index finger to ensure it remained close to her touch.

After what seemed like an age, Tina's shoulders slumped. She rolled her eyes at him. 'Fine. No deaths.'

Her concession took Arthur by surprise. Since when did he hold so much of an influence over her?

'But, I need you to close your eyes,' she said.
'Why?'

'Because you don't like violence, right? I promise I won't kill anyone, but I don't see any other way of getting out of this without some violence. Understood?'

Had he really formed a compromise with her? The surprise on his face was nothing like that on the face of the bandits who had now grown furious with their conversation. But why did she want him to close his eyes? It wasn't as if he had never seen violence and all the horrors that came with it. Unlike her, he continued to remember every vivid detail of it. Or perhaps she simply didn't want him to see the violence *she* created and the pain she could inflict on others. Did she think he would see her differently or worse, judge her for it?

Arthur nodded at her, closing his eyes and putting his trust in the assassin.

A gush of wind recoiled from where she stood. Seconds passed, and the clattering of steel led to groans and gasps. The men shouted and shrieked in shock. Soon, the sounds of scuttling and footsteps overlapped everything else.

'You can open them.' Tina's voice came from the gates. She had already made her way back towards the school.

Arthur could see the bandits in the distance, some of them holding on to each other, clearly in pain. The Indian looked unconscious as the black man carried him away from the school. All of them were moving as if they had seen a demon. Not daring to turn back.

Arthur turned back to Tina to thank her, but she wasn't looking towards him at all.

'Tomorrow is the last day of training. I'll teach you one last thing. Meet me here in the morning. After that, we need to find Knox and this killer. My time here is almost up.'

That was all she said before she walked into the school. Leaving Arthur with a bitter feeling in his stomach. If the bandits reported her to Gareth, she would have to come out into the open. Did that really mean her time was up? Surely, she wouldn't be leaving?

***

Tina

Tina sidestepped a puddle of sweat that had started to build around a large punching bag. The chains holding the cylindrical leather cushion moaned with every forceful impact she inflicted. It swayed an inch, before resuming its centre point. She forced her body into a violent dance around the object, not letting it rest for more than a second. Her eyes pulsed with tears and bloodlust.

She wanted to kill them. Every single one of them.

The Red Bandanna, the dark man, the Indian, the one she'd stabbed in the leg, and the others—worthless sacks of bile. She let the anger course through her as if it were one with her blood. What she really wanted was to kill Knox. To avenge her family. That would fill the emptiness inside her. She hadn't killed in so long, and all this training with Arthur wasn't satisfying her.

She knew her own mind was being contaminated; she had been warned about this. Girls her age would start to feel things they had never felt before, and she'd been told to contain it, never to let it beat her. But she was so easily swayed by Arthur. His eyes were fierce. His ignorance annoyed her. She clenched her fist and began another thudding melee on the punching bag, imagining Arthur's sturdy body in its place. He annoyed her. How dare he order her around? He hadn't even fought a real battle before.

She stopped for breath, letting sweat trickle down her back and drip to the floor. She let out a deep sigh. She was an assassin. When society needed cleaning up quietly they would call for her. She was, in her own way, a street cleaner.

'You need to control your thirst for blood.'

This was what Sebastian had said to her. The reason he had advised her to leave the Ruh for a while, sending her on reconnaissance missions instead. She had objected at first but knew he was right; this was the only way for her to improve now. She needed to be able to control herself.

Sweat and tears trailed down the side of her face, she missed the Ruh so much. She still hadn't heard a response from them and Magnah the Merchant hadn't turned up as he usually would. It only added to her frustration.

She needed to find Knox and the Ripper and deal with them before things became too complicated. From now on, it would be *her* way, not Arthur's. She rested her body against the punching bag, bringing her arms around as if she were holding it in a warm embrace.

18. The Peacekeeper

Arthur

'If the Shadows are really here in Whitechapel then we'll definitely be fighting against those that use aura. Do you remember what I told you?' Tina's voice was cold and distant.

This was their last training session—and so far—it wasn't as physical as the previous ones, which Arthur had to admit he was grateful for.

He nodded. 'Aura isn't some fancy magical power but a human ability that can be explained by logic and science. It is the enhancement of our potential, making things occur which would normally require optimal physical conditions with years of training—something like that, right?'

Tina pursed her lips.

'Sometimes I think you just say complicated things to satisfy your own complicated mind.' She pointed to different parts of her body. Eyes, nose, ears, mouth, arms, legs, and then to her head. 'To use aura is to harness the energy within us, using it for our physical needs instead of just our spiritual. It enhances an individual's ability to use their body and mind. It can work in different ways and usually requires a great deal of skill to pull off.

'After the first discovery of aura, many people started to compile their own theories and research about it. They've named many of the feats that have been performed by great aura-users.' She began to list them off her fingers. 'The Lord's Ear, Brute Force, After-Image, Vision, King's Paralysis, and plenty more. Shadow-Stepping is more commonly used by those trained as assassins. It's simply the ability to move quickly without disturbing your surroundings as much, each step becoming so light it should be unnoticeable.'

Arthur nodded, scribbling all this down into one of his personal journals. He had heard of King's Paralysis before, in a journal from the Shamal about an ancient conqueror.

'Don't drift off into your memory bank now, Arthur.' Tina's sharp voice drew him back. 'I'm going to teach you something. Ordinarily, any of these skills would take years of practice, but I'm sure there's a way around it with you.'

***

After yesterday's attack, they decided to observe Gareth. Although it wasn't normal for Peacekeepers to work with bandits, Arthur knew Gareth wouldn't be the type to abstain from such a relationship if it benefited him. What he had said about the method of those poor women's deaths still clawed at Arthur's mind. What could the killer have used to kill them if it wasn't something like a knife?

After a week of speaking to people and observing their movements, Arthur found himself to believe that the townsfolk did not care—nor did they want any involvement—with the women's brutal murders. The butchers, the cooks, the barbers, the shopkeepers, the construction workers, and even the street cleaners, were either clueless about the murders or void of any interest towards them.

His mind wavered at the thought of Tina. She had reverted to her original cold self ever since the attack. He couldn't help but wonder if the bandits had reported back to Gareth yet. Judging by the way they had left, they would probably take more than a night to recover. But by nightfall, Gareth would surely know of Tina's existence.

Then there was the thought of the Shadows of London. Tina spoke of them with such caution; they were the ones who caused her so much pain and the reason why her family had perished. What troubled Arthur was that he couldn't tell whether Tina was fearful of meeting them or excited. He knew she wanted to meet

Knox again, but what good would come of it?

They picked up Gareth's trail after lunch. Tina scoured the rooftops and tracked him from above, whilst Arthur followed him on foot, creeping into the nooks of the road to avoid being seen. The clock perched on top of the bar indicated 4:30 pm by the time Arthur followed Gareth into The Wayward Inn. He sat at a round table for two behind Gareth; they were away from the bar, away from prying eyes and ears. Tina stayed outside— probably on the roof of the tavern—to watch all the exits for any suspicious behaviour.

Greg and Stu had joined Gareth, it seemed like a usual lad's evening. They complained about work, moaned about the weather, and teased each other about the women they were seeing. Gareth, on the other hand, was quiet. He fiddled with his drink as if he had better things to think about than work and women.

Arthur tuned in with better focus as their talk turned to a young group of musicians. In the corner of Arthur's eye, he spotted Mary-Anne lingering awfully close. She was well acquainted with Percy and his friends, after all, acting as their mentor for music at times.

'I hear they're planning a performance soon. You know how these rebellious kids can be,' Greg warned Gareth.

'There's more pressing matters at hand.' Gareth lowered his voice.

Arthur edged his chair closer, craning his neck as much as he could without looking suspicious.

'You mean the missing people?' Stu asked.

'One of their bodies turned up last night.'

'The same killer?' Greg leaned forward.

Gareth shook his head. 'I don't know. There wasn't the usual... you know... This time it looked as if the body was drained of all its blood. That's what Eve said anyway. But God, I don't know which method of death is worse.' Gareth frowned as if he were imagining it.

'Yeah, it sounds horrible. So was it another woman?' Greg

cast a quick look at Mary-Anne as she floated by.

'No, this time it was a man.'

'Then I guess the second death is worse. We need men alive, not dead. Whitechapel will become weak and vulnerable to attack if we don't have enough men.' Greg spoke the usual nonsense that fuelled Arthur's frustration.

The three men all nodded and continued to drink.

'So far, there've been four people reported missing, but those are four people who actually had someone notice they went missing, like Mrs Gower. I'm sure there are even more that haven't been reported yet.' Gareth cursed quietly, and banged his fist against the table. 'What on earth is going on here? First these murders, then these abductions, and now bodies are turning up with their blood drained.'

Arthur swallowed hard. He couldn't begin to fathom how a body with all its blood drained would look. It reminded him of one of the things Lukas had babbled about during his crazy dialogues with himself. *Vampires*. Arthur dismissed the idea quickly; there were no such things of course.

After a few minutes, a familiar figure walked in. A pointy nose stuck out of his face and his large belly hung a good way from his waist. His dark eyes had large circles around them, as if sleep avoided him or he had found nightmares for company. It was the man who had made Arthur do *his* work at the dump weeks ago. The man came over and sat on Gareth's table.

'Why, if it isn't Draga, where have you been lately?' Gareth asked.

The man grunted. 'I've been... busy.' He pressed a hand against his forearm, as if he were massaging an injury underneath his sleeve.

Gareth signalled Mary-Anne over and ordered another round of drinks. Mary-Anne smiled warmly as she passed Arthur, prompting him for another glass to drink, which he refused. He wanted to pay full attention to the people in front of him. Arthur found Draga staring a little too long at Mary-Anne, before Gareth pulled his attention away.

'I hear you've been bunking your duties, Draga. You know, as Peacekeeper, I could punish you for that.' Gareth cast him a sharp look. Arthur couldn't tell if he was genuinely threatening him or merely teasing him.

'Like I said Gareth, I've been busy,' Draga snapped in a hushed voice. 'I might even need your help soon.'

'Busy with what?' Greg murmured, so that even Arthur could barely hear him.

Arthur leaned forward, urging his ears to pick up their conversation again. In his earnestness, he didn't notice himself pulling down on the tablecloth. His glass tipped off the table and fell to the floor. It didn't smash against the wood but it did cause enough noise to attract Draga's attention.

His eyes narrowed at Arthur, as if he was surprised to see him of all people sitting near them. 'Listen, can we change the subject? I can't speak about it here.' He shot a look at Gareth, who in turn looked around.

All the men's eyes now fell on Arthur, who quickly restored his empty glass to the table. The only thing more suspicious than Draga, was Arthur sitting at a table by himself with an empty glass. How he wished he had some of Tina's innate ability to just blend into the background right now.

'Arthur! 'ow goes your search for this Jack person? I 'eard ee's been keeping you busy.' Greg, the Peacekeeper's deputy, held a crude smile on his sturdy face. His rough accent—as always—took Arthur a few seconds to understand.

'Yeah, seems like he's been giving you some trouble 'ey?' Stu sneered, his eyes lingering on Arthur's bruises.

'It's been going great,' he lied. 'But shouldn't you be asking Gareth? He's the Peacekeeper, after all.' His tone of voice surprised him; it was full of such defiance and pride.

Gareth's face scrunched up, his eyebrows furrowed and his teeth gritted together. The others exchanged looks. Arthur regretted saying anything now. The staunch man, with his large muscular arms, stood up and launched himself at Arthur, grabbing him by the scruff of his neck. 'What did you say?'

Arthur tried to answer him but found himself struggling to breathe. Gareth pinned him to the wall, lifting him with such ease to raise Arthur to his height.

He raised his hands in protest. 'Didn't mean to offend you, Gareth. You're doing fine, keep up the good work,' he choked.

Gareth glared at him before slowly letting him go. 'Don't come talking to me about any more of this Ripper rubbish. If you get in my way, I won't hold back.'

The other men chuckled, casting pitiful looks at Arthur.

He knew he was only going to stir up trouble if he stayed any longer. He could feel the heat from their glares burning into his back as he hurried out of the Wayward Inn. But a faint and hidden feeling of contentment burned inside him.

He had noticed something they could work with. A lead at last. The same eyes behind the masked man who'd attacked Eve, he felt like he'd just seen them again. He now had a suspect. Draga.

***

Arthur reported everything he had heard and felt in the tavern to Tina. Neither of them wanted to admit there were two killers on the prowl, but from what Gareth had mentioned, it certainly had them in deep thought. Two different types of killings... surely there couldn't be two psychopaths in Whitechapel?

They decided to leave that question for another time. One thing was for certain: Draga was up to no good. Arthur had promised Eve he would get to the bottom of this, and he would.

From his pointy nose, to his erupting belly, to his gruff voice, Arthur described Draga's appearance to Tina before they began their search for him. She didn't question him but simply followed his instincts. Did she trust him enough or was this the assassin way? Was a target all she needed?

By the time Arthur and Tina had returned to the Wayward Inn, he was already gone.

An hour passed, and Arthur's frustration began to grow.

They finally had some direction, and yet Draga was nowhere to be seen. They walked down several roads until a faint rhythmic drumming caught Arthur's ears. It came from Myrdle Street. As Arthur turned down the road he found a crowd of people stationed in the middle of the road. A group of teenagers had gathered. One was playing from a drum set, hitting his sticks against the steel and plastic to create a fast-paced beat. Another played the guitar, whilst a third played a flute. At the centre of them stood Percy with a new-tech microphone in his hand—a piece of technology from Inner London. It was probably worth more than everything Percy owned. Arthur saw Tina in the corner of his eye, watching from a nearby roof. A crowd began to gather around them.

His voice was projected loudly into the street. Arthur couldn't understand how that piece of technology worked.

'My name's Percy, and I wanna play you all a song. Please listen.'

The drumming stopped, and the others started playing their instruments slowly, creating a dark and ominous instrumental. Percy started to hum, then he rapped as the drumming began again:

Are you listening as I rip into this mic?
'Cos the ripper's gonna sin, and the prey is in sight.
Plenty women, kidney, and the venison.
Are you listening?
Will you let him feed off civilians?

This ain't how we planned it.
We wrote this for peace.
And the music we make,
Might tear us to pieces.

What's hanging by a thread?
What's alive? What's dead?
This world got us tainted.

Our past and our future, we made it.

Uh, forget about that now.
We can't even save our women,
What good is our future?
Our past, our present, our nature?
This story is ancient, but we won't forget.

We cannot SAY that we don't know jack.
We will make a STAND for the women in black.
We will raise our HANDS for a new Peacekeeper.
So hear my VOICE and wake up.

The beat changed, signalling the chorus as the other boys all joined in. Arthur felt admiration towards them for being brave enough to remember and speak out about these events. They were just like him, except they were kids, struggling to do their part, and holding their morals dear to them.

I will feed my soul,
I will feed my soul.
With remnants of honesty and hope,
Energy and freedom,
I'm bleeding and aching 'cos I will,
I will feed my soul.
I will feed my soul.
I will heed your call,
And pray you help me,
I'm just a sinner that's—

The music was interrupted by a sharp whistle; a Peacekeeper's whistle. Immediately the crowd dispersed; the boys packed their kit in a flash and darted in different directions. Gareth sped past Arthur, a sword in his hand.

'THIS IS NOT ACCEPTABLE. YOU KNOW THE RULES, NO MUSIC IN PUBLIC!' he shouted, chasing after

Percy.

Arthur found himself running after them both. They turned away from Myrdle Street onto a main road. He saw Percy weave past a crowd of people before turning into Hessel Street, an empty road. The falling sun had abandoned this road to darkness. A sinking feeling struck Arthur as he saw Percy slow down, tired of running. Gareth had caught up to him. He was probably twice the boy's size.

'I'll have you locked up for a month for this.' A malicious grin filled Gareth's face as he spoke.

The Peacekeeper's towering presence backed Percy towards a wall.

'Are you listening, kid?' Gareth struck him in the face. Percy staggered with the impact, then fell back against the bricks.

Arthur found his legs in motion again, moving automatically as if his morals were overriding his own safety. He darted between them with hands outstretched on either side. He didn't want to fight. If there was a way of resolving things through words then he would choose that, always.

'Enough, Gareth, you don't need to hurt him.'

'Huh? What do you think you're doing, Mr Fake-investigator? Do you think a man who can't even hold a sword properly can stand in my way? Move.' His eyes glared with a threatening pulse; he wasn't messing about.

'No,' Arthur replied, bracing himself.

As Gareth pulled back for a punch, Arthur noticed Tina standing right behind him. If Arthur avoided the blow, he was sure it would hit Percy instead. He needed to block it, but how? What was the best way to do it? Questions and scenarios flooded his mind.

But before he could move his hands, Gareth's fist came crashing against his cheeks. He fell to the floor. The pain stung as if he had been hit by a hammer. His mouth tasted of bloody saliva. Why hadn't Tina stopped him? Gareth raised his arm once again and both Arthur and Percy flinched. But this time there was no pain. Instead, there was a flurry of movement, and a thud, as Gareth fell to the floor.

'WHAT THE HELL IS GOING ON? WHO'S THERE?' His face contorted with a mixture of rage and bewilderment. He crawled in a circular motion, like he was trying to search for something. Just as Tina showed Arthur in training, she moved fast in the blurred line of sight, allowing her to phase in and out of sight with ease.

Arthur found his way to his feet, then helped Percy up and urged him to run away. The boy didn't need to be told twice.

'What is going on?' Gareth looked at Arthur with uncertainty, like he was doubting the reality of the situation. He simply couldn't fathom the idea of being on his knees in front of Arthur. 'I swear, Arthur...' He brandished his sword now. The sharp tip introduced itself in the faint light. The moon had begun its shift for the night.

A loud wailing scream caught them all unaware; it came from nearby. Was it the Ripper? Both Gareth and Arthur darted towards the sound. He caught Tina's eye in the shadows. This was it, their chance to catch the Ripper. They took a left turn. The road was dark, the end of it lost from sight.

'Are you behind this?' Gareth panted.

'Don't be ridiculous. Look!' Arthur pointed towards the movement of shadows, two of them. The road was scarce of lanterns and the moon was not so generous. He could barely make out the familiar form of a ginger-haired woman struggling against a figure that had grabbed her mouth with one hand and was carrying her with another—it was Mary-Anne. Arthur couldn't deduce if the dark figure was Draga.

He gritted his teeth. Mary-Anne would *not* be the next victim.

No more deaths.

Arthur continued to run, leaving the Peacekeeper in the shadows behind him. The wind gushed past his ears and he felt adrenaline rip through his insides. *I will catch you.* He repeated the words in his head. But this thought was followed by another—how exactly was he going to catch the killer? His gums were already aching from a simple punch from Gareth, let alone going toe-to-toe with a bloodthirsty psychopath.

He scanned the roofs, looking for Tina. He found her to his right, but she had stopped moving. An unfamiliar look painted her face. Arthur had never seen her like this before. He couldn't make out if she was nervous, or scared, or excited.

She wasn't alone. There was another woman on the roof, a woman who was staring down at Arthur, her eyes beetle-like, her lips purple. Everything about her indicated danger.

Tina was occupied; he needed to do what he could on his own. Blood and adrenaline pumped through his body. He would use everything he had learned from Tina to apprehend the Ripper. He drew closer and closer to Mary-Anne and her abductor. He watched as the two figures in front of him rushed into a familiar building. It was the same building Draga had escaped into after attacking Eve. Arthur rushed inside too. A part of him wished he had thought of a plan before going in, but the other part of him knew there wasn't a second to lose.

He wished he had listened to the former part, though, as a heavy blow struck the side of his face. Before his eyes lost all focus, he glimpsed a slim figure with long dark hair, a woman perhaps, standing by the door. Or maybe there were two of them, or four, or eight, or sixteen…

19. Purple Lips

Tina

Tina couldn't believe what she was seeing. Her fingers were cold and numb as they gripped her daggers. She wasn't holding them as she usually did—there was no fluidity or grace in her stance. No, she was holding on for the sake of the reality that unfolded before her. This woman had to be a figment of her imagination, or her nightmares. But why was she surprised? She knew this woman would be here. She had been warned about her, and she had longed to finally face her.

Knox passed a hand through her night-black hair as it danced in the wind. Her other hand rested on a black lance, her weapon of choice. Her dark beady insect-like eyes shifted from Arthur to Tina. Her lips were a deep purple. All five of the Shadows of London had purple lips, it was their call-sign. But it was the disgusting sneer on her face that displayed just how malicious her intention was. A few seconds passed before Tina realised she was frozen with fear. Was this how much of a demonic presence this woman possessed and what kind of effect it had on her?

Her blurring mind beckoned for rationale. No, she was falling for King's Paralysis. She remembered the time when the Ruh had faced a threat like this. What had Sebastian advised them to do in such a situation? And then she remembered.

Tina brought a dagger close to her face and lightly cut her own cheek. A sharp pain shot through her. The numb feeling slowly melted, and the icy fear in her was replaced by a burning sensation. She shifted her feet. She was able to move again.

Knox began to laugh, a shrill laugh that surely made

darkness itself hide.

'My, my, my, little Tina looks all grown up now. Sharp as always. Did the pain fight the shock away?'

'Why are you here, Knox?' Tina was focused on every part of Knox's body, from her tall slim figure to her long purple-painted fingernails that gripped the lance. The several inches of sharp blade at the tip welcomed her to attack.

'Why am I here? I've been here for a while. I was quite surprised when my follower reported to me about an assassin in Whitechapel, but of all the people in London, it had to be you. My, my, my, fate has served me well. Have you enjoyed my work here?'

'You've been killing people across Whitechapel?' Something didn't add up for Tina.

'Nope, not me, unfortunately. Though I hear some kids calling them Jack the Ripper, how archaic.' She spoke proudly, like a mother of a child that had won an award at school.

'How do you know about Jack the Ripper?'

'Do you think your blond friend is the only one who reads about the past? Yes, that's right, I know all about Arthur. In fact, I know more about him than you do. After all, he's just like the Master.'

Tina frowned. 'What do you mean, he's just like Shadow-Hat?'

'Hmm? You really don't know, do you?'

It was like every word Knox said portrayed just how superior she was to Tina. What did she know about Arthur?

'I guess there's no point in asking you to simply walk away from Whitechapel, is there?' Knox asked. Her pale skin was further brightened by the moonlight, causing her dark eyes to stand out menacingly. Her long hair completed the monstrous image.

'What are you scheming here?' spat Tina.

'The same as what we plan in any area. You should be familiar with it now as we did the same to your hometown.' Knox laughed.

A bitter taste found its way to Tina's mouth as she remembered how the Shadows of London had attacked her town in the Greenlands, burning their homes and leaving it in a desolate state. Their aim back then was to steal all the written information that had been kept hidden from the White Arrow. Every old newspaper, book, diary, journal, anything handwritten or printed from the old-age. Knowledge was everything to them.

'This time, Shadow-Hat sent us in advance. He said we could have our fun as long as the work was done at the same time.'

'You have a sickening interpretation of the word fun.'

Knox brought the lance close to her face and licked the side of her blade, her eyes not shifting from Tina's. 'By the way, how is young Lars doing? I'm sure you've all lost sleep over me, ever since—'

Tina didn't wait for her to finish. Memories of her and Lars' burning home, her brother's body, her father's screams, Lar's mother's tears, all rushed through her mind simultaneously.

If I don't kill you, Lars certainly will.

Her fury propelled her towards Knox. She crept low and attacked her from her left, but Knox simply sidestepped her. She continued with a relentless barrage of attacks, holding nothing back. Death was the last thing on her mind—revenge was the first. But Knox danced around her, slipping away at the last moment every time Tina's daggers came close to her. Teasing her with openings before gracefully weaving out of the way.

'What's the matter, Tina? Did you really think you could fight against me?' Her laughter whipped the eerie quiet of the night into submission. They both stepped back. 'Bow down, little girl. If you do, I might kill you before I drink your blood. Saves you some pain.'

Just how twisted was Knox? The thought ran through Tina's mind as she tried to gather her breath. She was one of the most feared women in the slums of London, and her reputation was certainly justified. Knox the Nightfire. She would only ever be seen at night time and just as the name suggested, she was a pyromaniac. But Tina didn't need to know her nickname to understand her love for fire.

Tina had only seen two people rival the powers of the Shadows, but neither Sebastian nor Lars was with her right now, nor did she need them. This was her fight, her vengeance.

'Oh, I do love the faces you make, Tina. But surely you know by now, you're no match for me. You're not a hero like the others. You're not a member of the King's Arm. You're not a superior aura-user like Sebastian, and you're not a complete warrior like Larsson. You're just a little girl who likes to hide in the dark.'

The words rang in Tina like an old church bell swinging in pendulum fashion. She shook her head. She wouldn't waver now, she couldn't. She had spent so many nights training for this. This was her opportunity to avenge her family; this was her time to end the nightmares she had been having ever since she was fourteen. A time when they were all weak and powerless children, with nothing but empty words and futile threats to hurl at the Shadows. But the Ruh had survived and grown over the last few years. A smile grew on Tina's face as she interpreted Knox's words. After four years, Knox had finally acknowledged them.

'You're right, I'm not Lars or Sebastian. I'm not even worth writing about. I'm just a faceless shadow of the Ruh.' She drew her memories back to her time in NIMAS, when she had learned to use aura. She focused her thoughts, her energies, her spiritual presence into the soul of her feet. She didn't have the eyes of Kisuke or the strength of Toby, but she certainly did have a small agile body.

'Oh my, aura is it?' Knox's eyes were glazed with curiosity.

Just then, another figure called out from below.

'MASTER! She's been delivered.' Draga's hoarse voice elevated to the rooftops.

'Looks like my time here is up, Tina! I'll have to kill you anoth—' Knox's eyes flickered as Tina pelted straight at her. She was fast, too fast for Knox to watch her Shadow-Step.

Tina released her first dagger, and it flew straight at Knox who—at the very last second—shifted her body, letting it graze her arm, ripping her silky black dress. Tina had already run past her to reclaim her weapon. She was able to keep up with the speed of her own daggers being thrown. She gritted her teeth; she could be faster. She needed to deal with both Jack and Knox right now.

She leapt off the building, allowing her feet to tease the ledges and windowsills as she tiptoed her way to the ground. She landed directly behind Draga. The large bulging belly Arthur had described could be seen at an angle. Draga turned to his left, letting the moonlight illuminate his crooked nose. Her assassin instincts rushed through her body like a powerful fever as she lifted back his hood and reached for his neck. Her dagger broke its several-months long fast from killing; she cut a gaping red smile before jumping back in time to avoid the spray of blood from soiling her clothes.

Draga's body slumped to the floor. She hoped he could now feel how those women had felt. But the idea of feeling was quickly erased from her mind as she found her way back to the roof.

A frustrated look cradled Knox's face as she tried to understand what had just happened. A small object dropped from her hand, making a crackling sound before blinding the roof with white light. Tina didn't cover her eyes in time and felt the full force of the flash. She made a defensive stance with one dagger in her hand, listening to the sounds around her. But there was nothing. A minute passed in blinding white. She couldn't tell whether her eyes were open or closed—everything she saw hurt, even behind her eyelids.

After a few minutes, she peeked to find herself alone on the roof. Knox had become a shadow in the shadows.

The darkness overwhelmed the light in Tina's eyes. Blood dripped down from somewhere, Tina couldn't tell where. Her body staggered forward, and her eyes blurred, darkness bled into her peripheral. Using her aura was draining. If only she could master it better.

Her breath escaped her as did her chance for vengeance, everything went dark as she slumped to the floor.

20. The Letter

Tina

A familiar warmth comforted her as she slept. She felt as if she was laying by the crackling fireplace of the Soulhaven, listening to the voices in the pub. Like the warmth of the food her father cooked had wafted into her nostrils. But the smell was different, it didn't smell of dough, and fresh herbs and spices—Wait, where was she? Her body ached. Why did it ache? Her eyes shot open.

'KNOX!' she yelled, her eyes frantically scanning around.

She was back in Arthur's room. Her voice caught the attention of a woman. Her long wavy hair was tied in a neat bun, and her skin looked smooth. Eve.

'Arthur,' she called out behind her. Her eyes quickly and methodically scanned over Tina's body. Tina had forgotten she was also a nurse. 'Your friend is awake!'

Tina could hear his fast footsteps across the corridor, thumping his way up the stairs before bursting in and offering her a warm smile. He then turned to Eve.

'Remember what I told you about Mr Murray. I don't know how he'll function without someone being there with him.'

'Don't worry! The nurse of Whitechapel is on the case. I'll be in my room getting ready now.' Her voice was too excited for Tina's liking.

Arthur nodded his gratitude, before closing the door behind Eve after she left.

'How are you feeling?'

'I'm okay. We need to find Mary-Anne.' She tried to make her best *okay*-face, which Arthur saw right through.

'We do need to find Mary-Anne, but not without a plan and

not without you getting some rest first.'

The main thing on Tina's mind was finding Mary-Anne and killing Knox. But she let his words settle her restlessness. He was right. They needed to figure things out first.

'Why am I back here?' she asked.

Arthur shrugged. 'Well, where else was I gonna carry you? We could barely manage to get you off the roof when you were unconscious, let alone all the way to the scho—'

'What do you mean, *we?*' She frowned.

'I mean me and Percy. The kid came back after he saw the light on the roof. Helped me carry you here, said it was the least he could've done. We found the body of Draga though.' Arthur looked away from her, as if he was wrestling with himself to say something to her. A look of disapproval faintly traced his face. 'I'm guessing that was your work?'

She nodded. Did he think of her as some monster? She brushed the thought away; she was not to be judged by him. Her attention shifted to a bruise on his cheek, one that she didn't inflict.

'What happened to you?' She frowned.

He smiled sheepishly and started to rub the back of his head. 'I got caught off guard. Seems like Draga wasn't working alone. What about you?'

Her fingers crept to the self-inflicted cut on her cheek. She quickly moved her hand away.

Arthur raised a brow.

'It's called King's Paralysis.' How would she explain this without getting into one of Master John's lectures? 'Most people think of it like the feeling of being so intimidated that your body doesn't react to your will. Just imagine a time when you felt so scared that you were frozen stiff.'

'I didn't think you were scared of anything,' he said with a teasing smile.

Tina ignored him. She took a sip of water from a cup by his bedside before continuing. 'It eventually wears off, and it can't be used on the same person twice as their mind has already adjusted to the aura.'

'But the quickest way out of the paralysis is pain?' A peculiar look glazed Arthur's face, as if he hated the sound of it.

Tina nodded. 'Anyway, I'm glad we got our Ripper at least.'

Arthur shifted in his seat. 'About that…I don't think we did.' He walked over to his desk and picked up a piece of withering paper. 'I didn't really notice it until now, but I think someone else has been in my room, a few times. I'm not sure when exactly, but it was probably how they ripped my sister's journal entry from the book. I didn't think it was possible, but after last night, it's certain.'

'What happened last night?'

'Last night they took all the journals on my desk, and they left me this.' The tone in his voice grew with concern.

She took the piece of paper in her own hands and began to read.

Dear Arthur,

Things are probably not looking so great for you, and if anything, they're about to get worse. Your meddling did not go down kindly, so I'll be sure to repay you in full. But first, let me tell you about your oh-so-beloved women.

Lillian, Amy, Sylvia. These are the three women I have killed so far. The first one was a victim of rape. I liked her. When I found out she had been raped I tried to convince her to confront the rapist, but she refused, saying that she didn't want everyone in town to know. That it would bring shame to her family. It infuriated me, God, it made me so angry. She cared more for her already-tarnished dignity than for justice. The second woman was beaten and bruised before I found her, thanks to her husband's rage. I gave her a chance to confront him too, but she trembled at the thought of justice. The last one was easy—I found her wandering the streets as she left the whore house, probably looking for extra commission. That isn't acceptable for women. I made sure to take my time on her.

I do love the feel of the soft coating of skin around us, but I

168

*love it more when the coat comes off. Do you get what I mean?
Oh, the smell of sweet blood. Have you figured it out yet? Haha.*

*I'm almost done toying with you. I've got the singer. You've
got nothing but three solid walls and iron bars. Sucks, right?*

*See you soon.
Jack The Ripper.*

The words were spelled correctly and written in a fancy yet
formal way, so whoever wrote it must have been someone well-
practised and educated.

'It's definitely the work of the Shadows of London,' Tina
concluded. 'But how would they know so much about you?'

'I'm not sure, but whoever these people are, they know
where I live. I think they've known for a long time, maybe
they've been watching me. Watching us. This handwriting just
looks so familiar too, but I can't figure out who it belongs to.'
He stared at the letter in front of him. 'It seems like Jack went
after each woman for a specific reason. But who wrote this
letter?'

Silence reigned down in Arthur's room, like a solemn cloud
waiting to burst with rain.

Arthur put a hand to his chin. He looked quite charming
whenever he had his thinking face on. Tina brushed the thought
aside.

'We've gone from searching for one killer to fighting a
group of killers,' Tina muttered. 'The more pressing question is,
why would the Shadows of London abduct Mary-Anne?' Even
forking out questions hurt Tina's head. She closed her eyes for a
few seconds and let her head stop ringing.

'I'm not sure. But this letter doesn't mention why Mary-
Anne was abducted at all, nor does it mention any of the people
that had started to go missing either…' Arthur made a fair point.

'Jack's victims weren't killed on the spot, were they?
Although when I first met you, there was someone mutilating a
victim's body in the alleyway.'

Arthur nodded, and she could see in his eyes he was searching back into his memory. 'The first body I found didn't look like a fresh kill. If anything, Jack must have killed her a few days earlier and then got rid of the body at the dumpsite. The second body had bruises on her that didn't look fresh at all. Perhaps those were the beatings she received from her husband, as Jack wrote.' It was as if they finally had the pieces to the puzzle, all scrambled across the desk, waiting to be pieced together. 'By the way, you still haven't told me—was that woman Knox?'

She squeezed her eyes, her palms, and sat up.

'Have you got anything to eat?' She needed to regain her strength after her use of aura yesterday.

Arthur handed her a sandwich. Tuna. She groaned quietly. She didn't usually like eating fish, but she was too hungry to protest.

'That was Knox.'

She told Arthur everything Knox said in their brief conversation. Perhaps his head would be better suited for finding clues in words. Arthur stroked his stubble as if he was trying to remember something.

'You said she would drink your blood? I don't think that's just what evil people say...I think she meant literally.'

'What...wait, what? Like a vampire?'

'Mmm, I've been thinking about it ever since the recent body was found. Are you ready for another story?'

'If you must.'

Arthur leaned back, closed his eyes for a second. Was he entering his memory bank of stories again?

'In the year 2020, almost a century ago.'

Tina rolled her eyes. A story so far back.

Arthur either didn't notice or chose to ignore it. 'Science had breached into a new phase of development. Genetic modification and gene splicing led to the first ever edited embryo, so humans were born with favourable qualities. This led to a global crisis almost thirty years later. Radiation from a

170

multitude of waves and frequencies was being absorbed by the human body, leading to a new form of evolution that you call aura. But the worst one of these developments was the idea of sustaining your body for longer, delaying the ageing process by drinking the blood of other people.'

Tina, who had taken a bite out of her sandwich, started to choke. What was she listening to? All of this sounded like a joke.

'Are you okay?' Arthur asked. She nodded, beckoning him to continue. 'At first, this research came to nothing. But something happened in 2025 that made this theory work. Dr Bathory, a scientist, living in a scientific golden age, had developed this theory and made it work. But something went wrong for him, there were reports that he had started to drink human blood himself. Skip forward a few decades, and he was put to death for the murders of around sixty people. He would drink their blood whilst they were still alive, until—'

'Until they died, I get it.' Tina shuddered at the thought. Even though she was an assassin, there was a line of morality she never crossed. 'Knox really is a sadistic evil b—'

'Is it spelled with a K?'

'Yeah…K-N-O-X. Why?'

He stood up and pulled out his box of journals from under the floorboards.

'It's a good thing I hide some of my journals. Imagine all of this in the hands of the Shadows.'

After a minute of rummaging through the box, he carefully placed it back after he had fished out a fairly new-looking blue journal. He flicked through the pages before turning to Tina.

'I did some research of my own after Mind spoke about the Shadows of London. They've been written about briefly.'

She raised a brow curiously. 'Who exactly wrote about the Shadows? Not many people know about them.'

'Umm…it was written a couple years ago, by a Benjamin?'

Tina rolled her eyes. Arthur frowned.

'Do you know him?'

'Something like that. Benjamin Balfour, he was at NIMAS with us.' She remembered the times when Benjamin would pick on Lars. A sudden realisation dawned on her. 'The Shadows thrive for knowledge...'

'Yes...'

'So, who do you know that has more journals than you in this town?'

Arthur's eyes widened. 'They're targeting the Murrays!'

A loud crash from downstairs suddenly shook everything around them. Doors could be heard crashing against walls as they were flung open, followed by the trudging of heavy boots.

'Wait, what are you doing Gareth?' Eve's distant voice squealed. 'Where are you going?'

'Why hasn't Eve left yet?' Arthur snapped. 'Tina, what do we do?'

His mind—like Tina's—was probably in a frenzy. Could she hide? Did she have enough energy to climb out of the window? Why was Gareth even here? But there wasn't enough time to do anything. Three burly men pushed the door open and walked in, followed by Gareth.

'Arthur, you and this assassin are under arrest for the murder of Draga Romanov.' He spoke formally, but his presence resonated with something more than just formality.

Tina's eyes met Arthur's before he was blindfolded and dragged away. Jack's words suddenly made a lot more sense.

I'm almost done toying with you. I've got the singer. You've got nothing but three solid walls and iron bars. Sucks, right?

21. Tina of the Ruh

Tina

Several hours passed in darkness before the large steel doors swung open. A man with a lantern held to his head entered. Gareth. She could hear the jingling of keys, the turn of a lock, and her own cell doors opening as he walked through and stood over her weary figure.

'You've been arrested for the murder of Draga Romanov and on suspicion of abducting Mary-Anne Murray.' He narrowed his eyes at her. 'So, what's a murderous street urchin like you doing here in my town?' he sneered.

His eyes passed over her frazzled hair and dirty face, casting silent judgements perhaps. None of that mattered to Tina. What mattered to her was that he was able to see her. At this point, she needed to be as visible as possible. She couldn't let him feel threatened by her; it was dangerous for him to know the extent to her abilities.

Without any warning, he swung his foot at her stomach. Pain wrung across her body, and she let out a groan before spitting saliva.

'I asked you a question.' His tone was malicious. This man was clearly derailed. 'Who are you and what are you doing in Whitechapel? You're not a registered citizen and I *know* you've been staying at that abandoned school up the road.' The bandits must have reported her. She should have killed them when she had the chance. *God damn, Arthur.*

'My name is Christie. I'm… just passing through Whitechapel.' She struggled to speak.

Another jolt of pain swept her body as Gareth kicked her again. His large leather boots clearly weren't just for wearing.

Was this how he questioned everyone?

'Don't lie to me, child. I know your name is Tina and I know you're an assassin,' he snarled. Eve must have told him. Did Tina detect a small smile on his face? Was he genuinely enjoying this?

'Fine. My name is Tina, I'm the Assassin of the Ruh, a guild of New India.' She gave him a furious stare. If he knew this much, then maybe him knowing the true extent of her identity would relieve her of this treatment.

'Assassin of the Ruh? I've heard of them. A bunch of kids who think they're some hotshots in New India after some big battle?' His laugh turned to echoes in the stone-walled cell. 'Either way, I don't recall them ever having an assassin. You're still lying.' He bent down and grabbed her by her hair. Tina let out a sharp gasp. 'Do you know what would happen to you if I let the boys come in to interrogate you? You better not mess about with me.' His malicious eyes shone in the light of the fire as he held her face closer to the lantern.

She gritted her teeth. *Do you know what would happen to you if the Ruh saw you doing this to me?* She wanted to say.

'You know what's worse than having a killer on the loose?' she groaned instead. His eyes narrowed. 'Having someone like you protecting the people. They're doomed from the start.'

Her face hit the floor before Gareth began to kick her over and over. Pain ripped through her body before it all turned numb to her.

'You're not so much of an assassin without your daggers, are you? Seems like you were already beaten up before I even got to you. Who do you really work for? Where is Mary-Anne?'

Tina couldn't even bring herself to reply. Gareth must have sensed this too as he turned away from her.

'I've got some kids to arrest, but before that, I'll pay Arthur a quick visit. We'll *talk* again later. Don't go anywhere now, assassin.' He locked the cell and burst into another fit of dark laughter.

***

Mary-Anne

The sound of something dripping brought a refreshing difference to the hour-long constant drumming that filled her head. Pain. Every now and then she would hear the rustling of movement around her. Her eyes had given in to the darkness. Pain. Her arms felt heavy, as if someone was holding them down with all their strength. Or was she simply not trying to move them? She couldn't tell at this point. Pain. Mary-Anne's head throbbed with a slow dizzying pain. She tried to fight it, tried to bring herself to consciousness, tried to question the past few hours.

She could remember being snatched up, tackled into an alleyway. She could remember the vulgar smell of someone she knew covering her mouth to stop her from screaming. God, her father. What would her father do at this moment? He needed her. She stirred, trying to open her mouth for words but a slurred sound slipped off her tongue.

'What was that, Miss Murray?' a voice called out. A voice she couldn't recognise, a woman. 'Here, let me take this blindfold off you.' The voice drew closer.

Someone lifted a black cloth from her eyes. It didn't make much of a difference; she was being held in a dark room. A shadow of a figure walked away from her.

'Whooooo…?' She tried to produce some meaningful sounds.

'Who am I?' the shadow whispered. 'I have many names, but I believe my enemies call me Knox the Nightfire.'

Her voice chilled Mary-Anne's insides, making the hair on her arms stand tall.

Mary-Anne's eyes widened as she looked down. Tubes of red protruded from her forearms, leading away from her line of blurring vision. What were they doing to her?

She could hear a door open.

'Ah you've come,' Knox said. 'How goes your hunt?'

'Well, I think I've done my part as Jack the Ripper. The

show is all yours now, Knox,' the voice replied.

The strangest thing is, Mary-Anne couldn't tell whether the voice belonged to a man or a woman. The sound was as unclear as her vision; she was slipping out of consciousness.

She forced her eyes towards the sound, hoping to catch even a blurred outline of the monster who had been killing the women in Whitechapel.

'But… but I…' She couldn't even finish her sentence as she felt her energy drain from her body.

But I know you.

22. The Ripper

Arthur

The smell of damp filled Arthur's nostrils. It was about the only clear thing his senses could pick up in the dark cell they had locked him in. He tried to feel his way around the square block, his fingers pressing against the jagged edge of a rough brick wall. He was alone. He had been blindfolded as he left his home. He could have been anywhere in Whitechapel right now—or perhaps he wasn't even in Whitechapel anymore. Arthur always wondered where Gareth locked up his prisoners.

Another thought snapped at his attention. Mr Murray. The Shadows would come for him, for his stash of journals. He was in danger and the only person who was around was Eve. Arthur felt sick; he had put Eve in harm's way.

He could hear the jingle of keys draw closer and closer. The door swung open. *Speak of the devil.*

'You once said that if you were ever attacked, your imagination would run wild. Perhaps it wasn't Eve's imagination that was running wild now, 'ey?'

A lantern in his hand illuminated his brutish facial features. The only thing separating the two men were iron bars. The same bars that Jack had written to him about. Had Jack predicted that Gareth would arrest them? Or was Gareth the real Jack? He didn't want to say anything about Mr Murray or Eve if he was. But that accusation didn't sit well with him. Gareth had genuinely believed *he* was on the right track to catch the Ripper. Unless it was an act all along?

'So, you've been lying to me, Arthur. Hiding a fugitive assassin in Whitechapel is punishable.'

Arthur gritted his teeth. 'She's not a fugitive! She's the

assassin of the Ru—'

'Blah blah blah, I've heard it all already. I couldn't care if she was the daughter of the Chancellor himself. Everyone in Whitechapel is under my protection and with your careless actions, you've allowed someone like her to endanger the lives of people here.'

Arthur couldn't believe what he was saying. Was there any point in trying to defend himself? In trying to convince Gareth that Tina wasn't a threat to anyone here?

'Tina has been helping me try to find the k—'

'Yes, this so-called Jack the Ripper you keep going on about. Have you never thought about the fact that maybe she's been using you? She probably killed Dr Dovedi too.' A smile crept on his face as he saw the shock on Arthur's face. 'That's right, Dr Dovedi was poisoned. The man who was leading Whitechapel, the substitute Mayor. The one who kept the peace before me. Maybe she *is* Jack the Ripper, even if she is a little girl. *She* killed Draga, after all. Eve confirmed it as an eyewitness!'

'Draga kidnapped Mary-Anne!' Arthur snapped at him. But the information he spoke was still relaying through his mind. Dr Dovedi really was murdered? Who would do such a thing?

'I didn't see that. All I saw was someone running away with Mary-Anne. Now I'm going to get to the bottom of this. I've got limited men, and even Eve is busy looking after Murray—'

'They're in danger. They're targeting Mr Murray next. You need to do something—'

Gareth's boot met Arthur's stomach. He groaned in pain, curling himself into a ball.

'Quit your babbling and don't tell me what to do. You need to worry about yourself.' Gareth's teeth were gritted and his fury surreal. 'I'll be handing you over to the White Knights tomorrow. They'll be interested in the book we found in your possession when we arrested you.'

'Book?' Arthur whispered, before he remembered he'd been showing Tina something from a journal before they had stormed in. But the thought of his own safety didn't occupy his mind long. He tried to find his way to his feet again. 'Mary-Ann—'

'I'll find Mary-Anne… eventually. You're going to sit here and not get in my way.' Gareth left quickly, locking the door shut.

What did he mean, *eventually*? Arthur cursed at the walls around him. How did things come to this? He leaned against the wall and slowly slid to the stone floor, his knees tucked in by his side. He closed his eyes, as if it was supposed to make any difference to the pitch dark that engulfed him when they were open.

He could assume Knox was masterminding this scheme, but it still didn't answer his question. Who was the Ripper who had killed three women? And why were they working with the Shadows of London? He had to think this through; he had to complete the puzzle.

He had asked a ton of questions to more than a couple of dozen people in Whitechapel. He was certain he'd targeted those who strongly believed women were inferior. But Jack spoke as if he were an advocate of women's rights, a feminist in his own twisted way. Something else in Jack's letter didn't make sense. Arthur scanned his memory for the hundreds of journal entries and pieces of writing, searching for a clue or a pattern. He had read writing from all sorts of people, but the way this note was written was especially odd.

A squirming feeling erupted in his stomach. How many times had he doubted himself? It felt like someone was playing a game with him, pulling him towards Jack the Ripper before dumping on the whole idea. Making him twist and turn and bend to their sick conundrum.

He squinted, letting another thought creep in. What if that was the first step? Acceptance. Knowing that the Shadows of London were smarter than him, that he had been playing into their games all along. Arthur let this thought entertain him for a minute. He recited Jack's note back to himself.

'Let me tell you about your oh-so-beloved women…'

It had to be someone who knew him well enough. He retraced the events of last night. Draga was dead. He had chased them to the same building that the big-bellied thug had escaped in after he had attacked Eve. How convenient was it that he was standing right next to a door? He retraced his mind to the evening of Eve's attack. Her face under the threat of Draga's blade was cool and collected. She barely had a scratch on her. The Shadows of London were smarter than him; he was a player in their game.

'I was so rudely interrupted by your friend.'

Someone who knew of his bond with Tina? Arthur's face grew pale. Sweat started to build at his temples, and a throbbing headache dealt the final blow, as he realised the answer was so close to him. He repeated his conversation with Gareth in his head. Since when was Eve an eyewitness? She wasn't even there. His mind raced back to the letter, spinning and turning around with all the information he was trying to piece together.

Goddamn Sherlock Holmes. How did he do this?

It was under his roof the entire time. He had read enough to know—the handwriting had given it away, the looped and rounded letters—the note was written by a woman. Jack the Ripper was not a man. The only person who would have had the time and opportunity to write him the letter, who know where he lived, who had the knowledge to deal with the human body—

Arthur puked.

***

Eve

Eve found her way down to the cellar that held both Arthur and the assassin. It was a dingy house that not many people noticed on the outskirts of Whitechapel. She had waited for Gareth to occupy himself with a meaningless task before slipping into the cellar. She tried to weigh up who was the bigger fool—Arthur or Gareth?

The staircase was dimly lit, light enough for her to walk

down and dark enough for the prisoners to struggle to see anyone else. She tiptoed her way across a narrow stone corridor, her fashionable boots lightly caressing the floor as she stepped. The high collars of her black overcoat apparently made her look like a detective, Arthur had told her that a long time ago. How ironic. She held a paper bag in one hand. The bottom of it was wet and sticky.

She approached a narrow corridor. She could hear the shuffling of a few prisoners in the cells beyond her. Arthur's cell was on the left; she could hear him groaning, probably sick from the stench that stung the air. She ignored her duty as a nurse and turned right instead. When she reached the end of the corridor, she twisted a latch and swung open a steel door. They had placed the assassin in a more secure cell than the others. She took a lantern off the wall and brought it inside with her, closing the large steel door behind her. The flame illuminated the dark cell. There was now nothing but iron bars separating her and the assassin.

She smiled and threw the bag into the cell. It fell to the floor with a small thud.

'Have you figured it out yet?' she whispered. A sense of giddy euphoria filled her insides. After all this planning and devotion to her art, this moment would be the most satisfying, the sweet taste of despair.

Silence entertained her question.

'Earth to assassin, are you listening?'

Still no answer. Frustration grew in her like a wild dog, except she wasn't hungry for food, but for attention.

Eve brought the candle closer to the bars, illuminating the corners of the cell. It was empty. How could it possibly be empty? The alarming thoughts swept over her like a blanket of ice. She leaned in closer; her nose was now in between the bars. It was dark, the walls were bare. Her eyes did a scan from corner to corner. Where the hell did this little girl go?

'Where are you looking, Jack?' The voice sent shivers down her spine.

One second she was staring into pitch-black, the next she was staring into the dangerous hazel eyes of the assassin. The icy-lake inside her broke, and Eve leapt back in fright. The girl was standing right in front of her, as if she had always been there. How had she not noticed her? Was this what Knox had warned her about? She had reduced her presence by stifling her aura, that and the fact she was a slight figure, small and skinny. It was as if Eve's eyes had neglected her presence. She quickly regained her composure.

'What a fitting power for an assassin. Too bad you're stuck here. Does this feel like hell?' Eve looked at her with a newfound sense of admiration. 'I must say, I was surprised when I first met you in that alley next to the school.' The girl didn't respond. 'But I think from here on out, there is no underestimating you, Tina of the Ruh.'

'Where's Mary-Anne?'

'Don't worry about her, we need her alive for... our own purposes. But let's see how long she lasts. I think *you* have more pressing issues at hand, no?'

'What do you want, Jack?' The assassin clearly wasn't in a mood to entertain her. But it irritated her, the way she called her Jack. It annoyed her every time Arthur referred to her beautiful work as the work of Jack the Ripper.

'I'm here to deliver a message from Knox.' Eve waited, but again she was met with silence. 'She said to let you know...' She paused to give her next few words an added effect, it was all part of the dramatic scene she had imagined up in her head. '...that it satisfies her at night, when she remembers the way your father screamed before the soul in his eyes evaporated and his broken body burned to ash.'

Eve started to giggle. She could imagine the young orphan writhing in agony deep down, how terrible. Aunt Knox must have scarred her with the death of her family, but to also end up in a position like this was surely beyond the mental capabilities of a young girl. She hoped Tina would sink back into the dark, like a broken doll forgotten by a child, or a widow sinking into a terrible abyss of dark solitude. *Be broken.*

There was a sudden gush of air as the assassin moved lightning-quick. Eve blinked and felt something cold and wet hit her hard in the face. She staggered backwards and crashed into the wall. The muscular piece of meat—Sylvia's heart—had hit her own face.

She wiped the cold red substance away from her eyes. She had brought the little souvenir of her last body to rub salt into Tina's wounds, to instil a deeper fear in the child.

'Did you think your words and actions could really break me?' The voice was cold and harsh. It was difficult to believe it was coming from a girl who was probably a decade younger than her. 'I've fought in wars you've only heard about, killed people that were more blood-thirsty and dangerous than anything you could ever fathom, endured the depths of darkness like you could only imagine. This is nothing. Hell isn't the idea of going to a place of punishment. It's the idea of having your most treasured things stripped away from you. I *know* what hell is. What use are your petty games to me? Run along Jack, back to your mistress, let her know I'm coming.'

The threat felt real; Eve didn't want to stay here any longer. This wasn't how she had planned things to go. *She* was supposed to strike the final mental blow. She had heard about the Ruh, the struggles they had gone through, the people they had lost during the Battle of the Bridge, but she had never expected someone so young to be so mentally strong.

She dropped Sylvia's heart and swiftly swung the door behind her, making sure the latch was tightly fixed in place. This monster needed to stay far away from her. Eve swiftly climbed up the dark stairs and into the light of the world above them.

She needed to pay Mr Murray a visit.

23. I Want You to Live

Tina

For the first time in a very long time, Tina felt liberated. Sitting in a dark cell in some basement did not for any second dampen her spirits. She finally had the chance to find some closure—after all, she had met with Knox. All those sleepless nights, all those troublesome times with Lars, they were meant for this. At first, she'd thought she was running away from her problems by coming to Whitechapel, but fate had a twisted way of revealing answers. Her fingers brushed the cut on her cheek.

Now all she had to do was wait. Her gaze fell on the piece of meat across the room.

She sunk into the shadows and steadied her breathing. She had seen Eve's face when they were arrested, seen her smile as they were blindfolded. Eve had lived next door to the man trying to catch her; she would easily be up-to-date with his progress. Her mind fluttered back to when they found her being attacked. Eve knew she was going to be questioned, so being attacked by a look-alike Ripper was a perfect way to cross her off the list. It made sense—the nurse of Whitechapel was behind the mutilated bodies. But did she really have such hatred towards weaker women? Tina hoped Arthur had figured it out by now too, hoped that he wasn't broken by Eve's betrayal. But it had to have been a two-person job; she must have used Draga to move the bodies.

Tina's tongue stretched across her lips, wetting them. Hours passed in sombre silence before she heard movement behind the door. It was time. The latch clicked open and a man with a tray of food walked in. He opened a small hatch by the floor and slid the tray inside, before banging a baton against the bars.

'Lunch time.' His voice was deep. It was probably Stu…or

Greg. It didn't matter who it was. They were simply the way out. She stood silently, camouflaging in the darkness. 'Hey. I said it's lunch time. Take your food.' He hit the bars a few more times but received no reaction. 'What the hell?'

He stepped outside to retrieve a lantern and came back to investigate the cell. The light passed from corner to corner. *Please let him be one of the stupid ones.*

The frustrated man started to show signs of panic; a bead of sweat dripped across his forehead. 'Damnit, WHERE ARE YOU?' He reached for his keys and unlocked the door. First mistake. He entered the cell, her territory. Second mistake. A baton in one hand, the lantern in the other. He moved from the left, in a clockwise fashion, trying to find her. Third mistake, as she reached for his keys with trained subtlety, and slid out of the cell. She closed the cell door behind her.

Greg, or Stu, swivelled around and lunged for the door. His eyes wide with shock and panic. Too late.

'It's lunch time,' she whispered. 'Eat up.'

'NO. NO, YOU CAN'T DO THIS. I'LL HAVE YOUR HEAD FOR THIS, YOU BITCH.'

'Yeah? Well, why don't you start with a heart?' She picked up the heart that Eve had dropped and lumped it inside the cell. The man's outrage was stifled by the closing door. She turned the latch and entered the narrow passage of the cellar.

The walls were lined with lanterns that made little difference to the darkness that overwhelmed the foul corridor. She scuffled through the dark, fiddling with the sheer number of keys. One of them would be the key to Arthur's cell, but which one? She counted the steps in the dark, and eventually met with a fork in her path. She listened carefully. A series of voices could be heard from her left, but none of them sounded like Arthur. A groan sounded ahead of her—that would be him.

She reached a large steel door, identical to the one that decorated her cell, twisted the latch and entered. Her hand came to her nose immediately as the smell of vomit wafted out. She reached for a lantern and stepped inside.

'God, Arthur. You really are a weakling,' she muttered.

She heard Arthur stirring in the cell.

'Whooz der?' he groaned.

Tina rolled her eyes and brought the lantern closer to her face. 'Your worst nightmare,' she said in the deepest, huskiest voice she could make.

'What?' He whimpered as he got a glimpse of Tina's best attempt at a spooky face. 'Tina? That's not even funny. Why are you in such a good mood? How did you get out?'

'Simple,' she replied. 'By not moping about like you.'

Arthur's face changed from surprise to stress. 'It's Eve! She's the killer—'

'I know, I know. Jesus, calm down and breathe.' Tina scowled. 'Actually, sitting in this stench, don't breathe.'

'Make your mind up.' He coughed. 'Are you gonna let me out now or are we going to just sit here and talk?'

'Well, actually…' Her face mirrored the cold hard surface; her mood changed. 'We're going to sit here and talk.'

'We don't have time to waste, we need to save Mary-Anne.' His frustration was growing.

'*You* are not going to be much help in the state that you're in. I need you to understand something before I let you out.' She paused, waiting for his undivided attention.

'Okay…? I'm guessing you're not going to confess your undying love for me,' he joked. Tina made sure to not react in any way to this. Besides, it wasn't like Arthur liked *her*. He just wanted someone to help him solve these murders. That's all.

'This isn't a joke, Arthur. I need to know you're with me on this.'

'Of course, I'm with you. I've been with you all alon—'

'No, you haven't. What exactly would you do if you came face-to-face with Eve? Disarm her with your eloquent choice of words?'

A look of realisation suddenly crossed Arthur's face. He knew where she was going with this. He bit his lip.

'No Arthur, stop thinking. This is the problem. A thousand

thoughts cross your mind, and before you know it, another person will die. You need to—'

'You don't understand. The idea of violence and killing being socially acceptable is the very reason why the population of the world today is around four billion. Can you imagine that in the last eighty years the population of the world was halved! I don't want any part in that. I don't want to kill peop—'

'GOD DAMN, I'M NOT ASKING YOU TO KILL ANYONE.' Her voice echoed around the stone walls. 'Why do you think I let Gareth hit you? I wanted to see if you would at least defend yourself. There's one thing to be against killing someone, but it's another thing to save your own life. If I bring you with me, I need to know that I don't have to constantly look over my shoulder. I don't want you to die because you're too up your own arse with your pacifistic morals.' Her voice broke as she said this, and tears started to build up. Her hands were now gripping the iron bars, almost willing them to break apart. 'I don't want anyone else I care about to die.'

Silence, a different kind of silence than she had given Eve earlier. A strange type of raw silence that felt awkward. Did she go too far? A tear dropped from her eyelids. Of all the times she wanted to seem invisible, now would be a good time; she hoped Arthur couldn't see her right now.

Her worries were answered as her hands were enveloped by his. He leaned closer into the light. His blond hair ruffled, his eyes only focused on her. He smiled, a smile that made her feel warm, a new type of warmth altogether.

'I won't burden you anymore. I promise.' His voice had stopped trembling, matching his demeanour.

A few seconds passed before Tina drew back from the bars. She started to fiddle with the keys.

'Yeah…well. I just hope your hands were clean.' She wiped the back of her hands on her trousers and unlocked his cell.

Just then, the door swung open and several boys bustled their way in. One had a set of keys in his hand. 'The mandem are here to save you, Arthur!' They were the same boys who had been caught playing music in public. Everyone except Percy.

'Does it look like we need saving?' Tina said, an eyebrow raised.

They looked at each other in confusion.

'Sorry guys, but the girl beat you to it.' Arthur put a hand on their shoulders, expressing his gratitude. There was something heart-warming about his mannerism. 'Where's Percy?'

'He's on the other side of Whitechapel, playing his tunes as loud as he can. We needed a way to distract Gareth, init.' A small, timid-looking figure piped up.

One of them, the drummer as Tina remembered him, a short chubby black teenager, held a lantern close to their faces as if he was checking they had the right cell and were letting out the right prisoners.

'There's word out that some really shady figures are gathering in the Dark Quarters tonight. Certain bruddas in the Wayward Inn were talking about it.' His voice squeaked with adolescence. These boys were probably younger than her.

He fiddled with the inside pocket of his jacket and brought out two sharp steel blades, gingerly passing them carefully to Tina. Her daggers, beautifully handcrafted by Astal, Sebastian's older brother.

'Thanks for the info, Jerome.' Arthur nodded.

'My name's not Jerome my G, call me Wreckless.'

'Er… sure.'

Two of the boys started nudging each other and whispering. 'Is this the ting that lives by herself in the haunted school?'

'Yeah man, she fine as well.'

Tina scowled.

Arthur turned to her. 'We need to go and check on Mr Murray.'

24. The Book Thief

Arthur

Having spent almost a full day in the dark, Arthur had to squint to adjust to the blinding light of the sun. He asked Wreckless for the time. *3:30 pm*. The afternoon had crept up on them; what felt like forever in the cells had really only been seven hours. They were in one of the abandoned buildings at the edge of town, an area that Gareth frequented often, close to the Dark Quarters. It took them twenty minutes to make their way back to town.

'I have *always* wanted to check out Miss Murray's home, I heard it's one of the nicest houses in Whitechapel,' one of the boys muttered.

'It is,' Arthur said.

He walked up to their door and was about to knock when he noticed the door was ajar. Either someone had left it open or someone had broken in; either deduction sent a chill down Arthur's spine. If Mr Murray had left the house, he could have gotten lost and hurt himself, and if he hadn't then—

Tina shoved past him in a hurry.

'MR MURRAY!' she shouted. She pelted down the corridor towards his room.

Arthur raced to keep up with her. Nothing looked out of the ordinary, not according to his memory anyway. Tina pushed open the door to Mr Murray's study. She gasped as Arthur followed her in.

Mr Murray had mentioned this room was used during his time as Mayor. A large mahogany desk was positioned at the back by the windows. A dark yet colourful pattern decorated the wallpaper, and the smell of dust and paper stung the air.

Mr Murray sat in the chair by the desk, his eyes closed. Tina rushed to him and checked his pulse. Arthur felt an anchor sink into his stomach, pressing down against the very flicker of hope he had in his optimistic self.

Tina smiled. 'He's asleep. Doesn't seem like he's hurt at all.'

The anchor lifted. 'Wreckless,' Arthur addressed Jerome, who stood outside the room, 'I need you to go get Bart the Barber, tell him Arthur needs him here.' Wreckless left in a hurry.

This was the last person Arthur could trust in Whitechapel. Guilt gnawed at him for telling Eve to take care of Mr Murray in the first place.

Arthur peered around the room. Someone had clearly been here and left in a hurry. Paper and other forms of parchment scattered the desk and the floor around it. In the corner of his eye, he noticed part of the wallpaper peeled off. Behind it was a large metal safe, the door of it unhinged and open, revealing the emptiness inside.

'What do you think they took?' Tina asked him, raising an eyebrow, but they both knew the answer to that.

Arthur clenched his fist. He remembered what Mind had said about the Shadows of London.

'They took the most valuable thing you could take from an old man who lived in the previous era. They took his knowledge and his memories. They've taken all his journals.'

Wreckless had returned with Bart. Arthur quickly explained the situation to him and Bart agreed to stay and look after Mr Murray.

'Boys, I need you all to keep Gareth busy for a while longer. Can you do that?'

'Leave it with us, G,' one of them said.

Tina snatched up one of the leaflets on Mr Murray's desk before they left the house.

Outside, the road was empty, little daylight remained, yet no one busied the streets with their usual activities. Most of the shops were closed and an unusual silence pierced the heart of

Whitechapel.

'What's going on here?' Tina asked.

Arthur looked around, studying the homes and shops. The sound of a window swinging shut caught Arthur's attention, the lady behind it gave them a cold stare.

'I think the town finally understands that someone's been killing people.' Arthur suggested.

Tina shook her head. 'They think it's me…'

'They probably can't even see you.' Arthur tried to sound reassuring but the look on Tina's face didn't seem to show any signs of Arthur succeeding.

He stepped in front of her and placed his hands on her bare shoulders, her skin felt soft, and her hazel eyes were fixed on his. 'We're going to fix this.'

'It doesn't matter to me, I'm just a ghost here.' She shifted away from him. 'Now pay attention. I think I know where they may have been hiding all this time.'

She passed him the leaflet as they continued their walk down the cobblestone road.

Arthur eyed the leaflet, it displayed the old underground system of London.

'But Whitechapel Station has been closed off for decades—they couldn't possibly enter through there.'

'No. They entered through another building.'

'Where?' Arthur asked her, as he patted the dirt off his clothes.

'Do you remember that building where Draga slipped away from us? I mentioned that I didn't see him leave, right? If you consider that the whole thing was staged, then what if there was an escape route ready for him? What if instead of coming back out onto the streets, he went underground?'

Arthur had wondered about this in his solitary confinement too, it couldn't be a coincidence that the ordinary looking building that Draga had run into during his attack on Eve, was the same building he had chased Draga into before being knocked unconscious.

Just then, a tall shadow cast over them. With all the attention on the leaflet, neither Tina nor Arthur had noticed the bulky figure of Greg sneaking around them. He grabbed Tina, locking her arms to stop her from reaching her daggers.

'How did you get out? And what did you do with Stu?' he snarled, veins on his forehead drawn vividly like lightning in the sky.

'To be fair…' Tina struggled to find her way out of his grip. 'I thought *you* were Stu.'

'You fink this funny? Wha'd you think you're doing Arthur? Come any closer and I'll snap 'er neck.'

Arthur stopped moving. 'Oh, I don't think I need to come any closer.' He rooted his feet.

In a quick motion, Tina kicked her legs against Arthur's body. This gave her enough of a footing to flip out of Greg's grip.

He snarled and moved towards her. 'I swear when you're back in your cell and I'm done punishin' you, you're going to wish you were born a lad.'

Some of the townsfolk were coming out of their houses to see what the commotion was. Eyes peered out of windows, eyes full of judgement. None of that meant anything to Arthur right now. He felt a blackening rage seep up from his gut, an unfamiliar feeling. His body shook with fury at Greg's words.

He found himself walking towards him, his fist clenched. He tapped the hardened shoulder of the broad figure who matched Gareth in bulk and was an inch or two taller than Arthur. Greg turned around, his lips extended and formed a smug grin. He knew Arthur would never attack him.

'I just wanted to ask, did something other than a woman give birth to you?'

Before Greg could even begin to rack his brain around the question, Arthur's anger reached its zenith. A strange feeling travelled through his body, reaching his arms, his fist. His body shifted, and in one quick motion, he let the fury travel from his fist to Greg's chin.

A look of surprise courted his face before his body crashed to the floor, forcing dust to unsettle from the broken tarmac. Someone let out a squeal. A few of the townsfolk *oooh'd*. Greg was out cold.

Tina walked up to him, her brows raised.

'I didn't know I was that strong,' Arthur said, breathing hard.

'You didn't notice, did you?' she asked, shaking her head.

'Notice what?'

'You just used your aura in the same way Toby does. It's called Brute Force.'

Toby Welder, the giant-like warrior from the Ruh he had read about. Arthur frowned. But how could he have used aura like that?

'I guess you were serious after all,' Tina muttered. 'Come, we need to prepare ourselves. Oh, and you need a shower. Not sure if Mary-Anne would appreciate you saving her smelling like that.' She smirked.

Arthur rolled his eyes.

As they hurried back to the school, the realisation slowly hit him. He had hurt someone, thrown them off their feet, in public too. But he didn't feel like it was unjust, he didn't feel overly terrible for it. Greg deserved it.

Right?

25. King's Paralysis

Arthur

The building that Draga had twice retreated in to, stood as ordinary as the rest. Not much could be seen through the dirt that clung tightly to the cracks of the windows. The sign above had been blacked out to conceal the original purpose of the building, but from what Arthur could tell from the design of the door and the silhouettes of desks and chairs inside, it looked like an old redundant office.

Arthur took a glance at his partner. After a quick trip to the school, Tina had changed into a leather black outfit; it was tightly fitted to her small frame. Dark grey elbow and shoulders pads decorated her attire, whilst numerous buckles and buttons lined her abdomen area. Her two daggers were holstered on either side of her waist. A quiver—which hosted a dozen or more arrows—accompanied the bow she had bought from the circus, the weapon rested on her back. A black cloth covered her mouth, only revealing her hazel eyes. A strange and untimely thought struck Arthur about Tina, but he pushed it aside. Now certainly wasn't the time to think of such thoughts.

Tina broke open the door with a kick and waited for the dust to clear from inside.

'Are you ready?' Arthur asked, his own grey trench coat wrapped around him like a White Knight's uniform.

'Almost,' she said, looking around the building as if she had misplaced something. She slipped out of sight before re-emerging with an old rusty-looking pipe. She held out the piece of lead for Arthur, who took the weighty item in his grasp. 'Now I'm ready,' she said, the end of her lips curling slightly.

'The pacifist's sword.' Arthur mused.

They entered the building cautiously, scanning the inside for anything that looked like a hidden door or passage towards an underground space. To their left were a couple of empty desks, only accompanied by chairs that were toppled, and missing a leg or two. To their right were large machines that looked as if they hadn't been operated in decades. This must have been an old printing shop. A shop that would have been in use before the ban on written produce. They walked over to the back, passing a dingy kitchen as they crept through a narrow corridor.

'Here,' Tina called out, pointing to several large empty canvases that were posted on a large wall. 'What do you notice?'

Arthur surveyed the walls. Nothing really looked out of place, except—

'The lines of dust stop here.' He swiped a finger across the frame of the canvas. It was clean, where everything else had dust building upon dust. 'There's more...' Arthur dropped to his knees and studied the floor; his eyes trailed an almost invisible line. 'Drops of dried blood. I'd be willing to bet it's Draga's blood from the time you injured him.'

She nodded, looking impressed with Arthur's deductions. They put down their weapons and lifted the canvas off the wall. Arthur whistled. There was a large gaping hole in the wall. This must have been how Draga had escaped after attacking Eve. Tina crouched inside and motioned for something, making an L shape with her fingers. Why she didn't just ask for a lantern was beyond him. He wondered if all assassins acted like this when they were focusing. He rummaged through his bag and brought out a lantern. Quickly lighting the flame, he passed the item to her.

'It looks like we'll be going down from heeeeee—' as she said this, she slipped through the hole and out of sight.

'For God's sake,' Arthur muttered, reaching for his make-shift pipe-sword-baton-weapon.

He hoisted himself through the hole. He reached for a steady step in vain. Before he knew it, he was plummeting into the darkness. He couldn't tell whether he had his eyes open or not at this point. His heart reached for his throat as he felt the damp air pass by his descent. He landed on his back with a great thump.

When he opened his eyes, he was greeted with the light from his lantern. A cold hand helped him to his feet.

'We'll need to be quiet from here on out. Take this.' Tina handed back the lantern. 'Don't worry about me. I'll be nearby.' She stepped back, letting her face fade into the shadows.

Arthur translated everything she said to: *You're on your own for a while.* He had spent enough time to know that she did her work best in the dark. He needed to focus on finding a way through this tunnel. He needed to save Mary-Anne.

The natural and pungent smell of bodies decomposing filled his nostrils. The image of the Ripper's first victim flashed across his mind. He stowed his pipe in his bag and covered his nose using the back of his hand. The sound of dripping could be heard from his left, its constant rhythm echoing against the narrow tunnels. The walls were arched and cemented with bricks that looked strangely new. Someone must have dug this recently, at least in the past year.

Something scurried to his left, and he stifled a yelp. His heart pace doubled.

And then nothing.

Just a rat, or a mouse, or something, he convinced himself. Tina was probably laughing at him.

The light was attracting insects now. He marched forward, holding the lantern in front of him, taking caution with every step he took and waving away the flies that intruded his personal space. The ground started to feel soft, as if he were treading through a dampened field. He shivered at the thought of stepping on a body. Was the flickering light playing with his imagination? A face suddenly flashed through his mind, her dark beetle-like eyes and her stark plum-purple lips. Knox. Arthur shook his head.

At this point, all earlier interest in the old Jack the Ripper story had subsided. After all, this murderer had made too many uncharacteristic mistakes, they had strayed from the original profile of the ripper and therefore there was a chance. A chance for history to not repeat itself, this time they could actually catch the ripper. He wouldn't let himself be blindsided by the past anymore.

He felt like he had been walking for half an hour, but it may have been an hour. The dripping had finally subsided, and his eyes had become accustomed to the dark once again. Ahead of him, he could make out a small crack of light. He trusted his instincts and walked towards it. He had no idea where Tina was at this moment; whether she had already breached the light ahead of him, or whether she was behind him. Her footsteps were impossible to hear. As he approached what seemed to be the end of the tunnel he slowed down, reached into his bag and grabbed his weapon. He pushed past the rotting air and climbed down from the tunnel.

The moonlight stunned him for a few seconds, holding his eyes at mercy. He didn't recognise where he was. A dome-like glass structure formed the roof, letting natural light seep into the unfamiliar pebble-filled site. He almost stumbled on a long line of metal and wood. Were these train-tracks? The area was closed off by high walls, and farther along he could make out four other entrances to tunnels, branching into different directions. He had never seen infrastructure like this before. Perhaps he was in the tunnels that the old trains used to travel through, which meant they were close to Whitechapel Station.

A few metres away, he could make out a large broken snake-like machine, or perhaps it was a vehicle. Arthur had never seen a train before, but he could imagine this was what it looked like. He had read about them in several journals. Back in the age when London was fully functioning, trains would take hundreds of people all across the city, from the Greenlands in the East to the Great West, cutting across the Hamlets, Kingsland, and even the Churchlands. One person wrote about a time when they travelled from southern areas, before the times of the United Slum Associations, to the Shamal in the north. Arthur was always fascinated by this. What was even more fascinating was the idea of how these modes of transport were brought to ruin after the electricity was shut off several decades ago. Perhaps transports like this were only available in Inner London now, behind the walls.

His thoughts were cut short as he heard a sound ahead of him. Voices. He strode over and crouched behind the nearest train, doing his best to make sure he wasn't heard or seen. Tina was still nowhere in sight. He peered through the empty shell of the train, past the broken seats and poles that looked like people would hang on to them for their dear lives. In the distance, he could make out a few figures dressed in dark cloaks. One was a tall woman dressed in black. The woman who had fought with Tina. Knox. The other was Eve.

Arthur couldn't make out what they were saying. But his focus quickly turned to a group of bodies huddled by Knox's feet. Mary-Anne was one of them. Her clothes were dirtied, and patches of blood stained her arms. His heart raced, and his stomach sank at the sight. Surely she wasn't—no, she was alive; she was struggling to move. Something was wrong. He needed to get closer. He tucked the metal pipe into his jacket, making sure it wouldn't drop and give away his presence. He abandoned his bag, as it would only weigh him down.

As he tiptoed towards them the smell of decaying bodies and rusted metal grew stronger. A crow squawked and flew over Arthur's head, making him jump. This time he couldn't stifle the sound that erupted from his lips. He quickly put his hands over his mouth; his eyes bulged in surprise and his heart throbbed painfully.

Stupid distrustful creatures.

Eve looked in his direction, her face full of surprise.

Where was Knox? He had just seen her a few seconds ago bu—

Something wet caressed his cheek, a tongue. He turned to find Knox facing him, her tongue trailing her purple lips. Nothing Arthur had experienced—not the mutilated bodies, nor the dark streets of Whitechapel, nor the idea of killing someone—nothing compared to the fear he felt now. A thousand questions raced through his mind. How had she moved so fast? And to come so close to him without him seeing her? Did she just lick him? Her teeth were stained with red, almost as if her mouth was bleeding. His body was frozen stiff. His mind urged his legs to move, but an unnatural fear had swept over him.

Knox leapt away from him, just as two arrows landed in the spot where she was just standing.

Tina.

Where had she been all this time? God damn assassin. Arthur could now hear her slowly walking somewhere behind him.

'Are you okay?' Tina asked. Her voice sounded the polar opposite of how he felt—calm.

Arthur still couldn't move, what was going on with his body? It was as if he was frozen with fright. Knox watched them with gleeful eyes. She must have known what was happening to him.

'Here, let me give you a hand,' Tina said, taking one of her leather gloves off. Her eyes bore into his, inducing him with her calm demeanour. He was almost lost in the moment, staring into the hazel brown, before pain stung his mind, body, and soul. Tina had struck him across the face. The slap propelled his body forward. His mind raced for understanding and soon realisation sunk in—King's Paralysis.

One of the oldest techniques of aura, an ancient technique that had been around for thousands of years but that was never really understood until this age. He had read about fearsome and frightening men from the ancient ages who had used King's Paralysis on their enemies, men like Genghis Khan and Alexander the Great.

Arthur's body was moving at last.

Just as he was about to fall, Tina's arm wrapped around him, holding him in a soft embrace. He was surprised she could hold his body weight with just one arm. Her cheek pressed against his and her lips drew close to his ear.

'Sorry, this was just the fastest way to get you out of it,' she whispered.

A loud cackle filled the air as Knox clutched her stomach.

'I do love your methods, little Tina of the Ruh. You broke my aura on the roof by cutting yourself, and you broke your pet's paralysis by slapping him.' Shivers ran down Arthur's spine as her voice turned from sounding amused to annoyed. 'How romantic.'

'This ends tonight, Knox.' Tina picked up her arrows and restored them to her quiver.

'You're right about it ending tonight. But not just yet.' Knox walked back towards Eve, taking a seat on a wooden chair besides the pile of bodies. Every movement she made was elegant and calm, as if she was under no threat whatsoever.

Tina and Arthur stepped closer to the pair of them. A strange feeling crept through Arthur's mind. Something in his visual focus looked familiar, but he couldn't quite put a finger on it. He glanced from Knox, to Eve, to the large heap of bodies that surrounded them like an immobile audience. Why were they here? He stumbled as someone's hand almost grabbed his foot. He gasped and jumped back into Tina.

He was wrong; he had almost tripped over a corpse, their hand outstretched as if they were reaching for salvation in their dying moments. The body was pale, for Arthur to describe it as malnourished would've been an understatement. The corpse's eyes stared back him, filling his memory with those shrivelled sockets and withered skin.

'Look away Arthur,' Tina whispered.

Were these the bodies that Gareth had described? The remains of the people who had gone missing. It was like the blood in their body had been drained.

He turned back to Knox, finally understanding what looked familiar. Beside the pair of them was a body he recognised, the body of Mrs Gower, dressed in the same white and pink floral dress that she usually wore.

Poor Mrs Gower.

Arthur caught Tina's eye and nodded towards Mary-Anne. They edged closer. He noticed a long red tube protruding from her arm. From where he stood, he instantly realised it was one of the clear tubes he had seen in Eve's room, stained red with blood. Eve was kneeling beside the frail form of Mary-Anne. Her ginger hair wet and dirtied, and her clothes a mixed shade of dull-grey and brown.

'What are you doing to her?' Anger flushed through Arthur's body now that he was able to move freely.

'What do you think, Mr Historian?' This was the first time Eve had spoken to him since their arrest. Since he had discovered her betrayal. 'We're draining her blood.' She held up a medical bag full of blood. 'Mary-Anne will give us the last of the good batch of blood. Our time here is almost up.'

A swarm of memories cascaded through Arthur's mind.

'This… you're… you're not serious?' A bead of sweat started to drip down the side of his face. 'You're actually trying to revive the work of Dr Bathory?'

Knox laughed, reaching for a bag of blood. She ripped it open and began to drink. The sight made his stomach twist. Now of all times, he didn't want to vomit. She licked her lips. 'As clued up as you are, Arthur, you are pretty naive, aren't you? I don't need to *revive* Dr Bathory's work at all. I'm just continuing it. As mad as he was, his theory worked. He lived longer than most people before he was executed, and his children all had the genes to live longer too.' She let out a small giggle that made her sound as psychotic as she looked.

'What do you mean?' Arthur asked. There was something more to all of this. He felt like he was just scratching the surface of Knox's great scheme.

Knox's fingers trailed the side of her face, her eyes narrowed at Arthur. 'And why would I be so naïve as to reveal my plans to you?'

'Because you're one of the Shadows, you guys would do anything for buried knowledge.'

'What's your point?'

'I've read things that you haven'—'

'Don't mock me, child! You're decades too young to have any serious information for us.'

'Oh yeah? Are you sure you don't want to know more about the Great Cyber War? The end of nuke warfare? The fall of the internet and the end of borders? The rise of Anonymous? The return of the King?'

As much as she tried to quell her surprise, Knox's eyes lit up as Arthur spoke. She *was* interested. A long silence breached the conversation, each side weighed the other up with both doubt and intrigue. Knox took another swig of blood.

'Very well. But first…' She shot a look at Tina. 'I wouldn't move if I were you. I know how you like to shy away from the attention. I'm well aware of how you fight, Tina. That's why Arthur is taking the centre of attention right now. But it would annoy me if you do try anything. You see, Mary-Anne's blood is a nice blend of sweet and bitter. If you move, I'll have Eve kill her, and her blood won't be as fresh as it is now.'

Knox was surely the epitome of all evil. Arthur turned to Eve, his fist clenched to subdue his rising rage. This was the woman he had been friends with for years, a woman who had won his trust, who knew of his illegal activities. A woman who had killed three other women and been involved with the abduction of several townsfolk. Arthur still couldn't begin to fathom how she'd turned from the town's saviour as a nurse, to the town's Ripper.

'I can't believe you, Eve. I trusted you. But to kill those women like you did…' Arthur gritted his teeth.

Eve rolled her eyes. 'Ah yes, about that. You see Arthur, I did see you as a friend, before you got involved in my business. But…' Her eyes flitted to Tina, then to Arthur. 'I didn't kill anyone. I'm not Jack the Ripper.' Her voice was flat and emotionless.

'I think we're past the point of denial now.'

'No. I'm not the killer—okay, well, I might have poisoned Dr Dovedi to take over his labs. And I do admit to cutting the women up. Of course I get a thrill out of learning the inner workings of the human body. Come on, it's not like I can read about it anymore. Besides, seeing it for real is better than reading about it.' She brushed over this like it wasn't a horrifying act but one of pure science and rationale for the sane mind. 'I mean, it *was* such a chore to delve into their bodies and then to pretend to do it all over again for their post-mortem. But really, *I* didn't kill any of those wome—'

'THEN WHO DID?' This godforsaken mystery was stretching far longer than he could take now.

Her beauty was sullen in his eyes, there was nothing left in her for him to see her that way. She simply smiled back at him, her eyes falling over his shoulders, at someone else.

'I did,' a voice spoke from behind him.

26. Nightmare

Tina

Tina turned around to see where the voice was coming from. A frail-looking man walked towards them, with a pale complexion that made him look ill. A fisherman's hat clung to his head, creating a shade over his eyes. Tina had picked up on a strong Eastern-European accent. As he drew closer, she noticed he had an arm in a sling. His other hand held the same mask that she had seen both Eve and Draga wear. It made sense now; the mask had a voice distorter attached to it. A perfect way to disguise your gender. Jack the Ripper could then be a multitude of people, unidentifiable by face or voice.

'L-Lukas?' Arthur's voice trembled in bewilderment.

'Hey, Blondy!' he said, walking closer to them. He bowed towards Tina. 'Miss Tina, glad to see you doing well.'

There was something odd about this man; he triggered a sense of nostalgia in her. As if she had met him years ago. Her eyes narrowed.

'It seems like you don't remember me,' he said, as he unwrapped his arm. He let the browning bandages twist from his limb and fall to the floor, like a snake shedding its skin.

'I don't understand, Lukas, where have you been? What are you doing here?' Arthur continued to babble.

'Oh chill out, Arthur. I thought you wanted to know who killed all the women.' He finished unwrapping his hand and revealed a silver hook in place of where his hand would have been. He lifted it up. 'My little buddy here killed them. Take a look, I just polished it earlier.'

It wasn't a knife—it was a hook. The same realisation painted itself on Arthur's face. His eyes widened, and his hands shook.

Keep it together, Arthur.

Suddenly Tina remembered who was standing in front of her. She reached for her daggers.

'You…but you look different.'

'Yes, well the Master of Disguises and all. What can I say?' He shrugged.

She turned to Arthur, who was still confused.

'This isn't Lukas, Arthur. There never was a Lukas. This is another one of the Shadows. Mare, the imposter.'

'Well done, assassin. Although can we please go with Mare, the Master of Disguises.' He chuckled. 'You know, I was surprised when you first spouted all those Jack the Ripper theories, Arthur. He sounded like such a fascinating character. I longed to become him so, so much.'

'Wait, let me get this straight. So, all these brutal deaths were all your doing, Lukas?' Arthur shook his head, clearly struggling to comprehend the recent revelation.

'My name is Mare!' A toothy grin stained his face. 'But that's right. I killed those women. Eve over here wanted to use their bodies for other purposes, so I let her do that. She's quite a scientific talent.' His overly excited face beamed at her before it turned back to curiosity. This man had issues. 'But isn't Jack such a fascinating character? You believe he was too, right? I could tell by the way you spoke about him! My Master even told me more about him—in fact, I know more about him than you do now.'

'Your Master? Shadow-Hat is here?' Tina asked. A cold, distant fear began to grow in her. It was bad enough to be up against two members of the Dark Guild, but she would have no chance against their leader, Shadow-Hat.

'Isn't Shadow-Hat everywhere? Always?' Knox spoke out a riddle. 'Thanks for joining us, brother.' She nodded towards Mare. 'So, let me continue from where I left off.'

She stood up and walked over to one of the corpses by Mary-Anne, giving it a little kick, almost as if she was checking if it were still alive. The barmaid looked too weak to move, slipping in and out of consciousness.

'After I heard brother Mare was up to his usual mischief, I couldn't help myself. I had to come to Whitechapel. I knew I could rely on my niece Eve to help me out.'

'Wait. Wait, your *niece?* Just how old are you?' Arthur blurted out. This played down on Tina's mind too. Eve was easily close to her thirties now.

'I'll let you in on my secret now.' She let her fingers course through her long dark hair. 'I'm easily more than double your age. Possibly close to the Mayor's age, in fact. But the blood helps me look and feel younger. You see, my grandfather Dr Bathory developed a unique way of consuming blood, something that worked with our own blood specifically. Like I said earlier, his children all lived long lives.' She turned to Arthur now. 'You know what I find most interesting?' She wasn't asking for a response. 'You, Arthur.' She walked over to a stone pillar where her lance rested.

'Me?' He took a step back.

'You, and all those who study the past—that was so efficiently deleted by the White Arrow—have the potential to become the most powerful amongst us. But I'm afraid you're too far behind us. We've got all of Murray's journals and every other book he's been hiding away all these years, and Master is reading them right now.'

So, Shadow-Hat was nearby. *One problem at a time*, Tina told herself. Saving Mary-Anne was the priority; the books could wait.

Knox continued, 'Like you said Arthur, the Shadows of London are hungry for knowledge, we seek it in ways others don't. We're not afraid of anyone or any law. We see things repeating that others are oblivious to, and thus we can act better, quicker, stronger.'

Knox took her place back in her wooden chair, sitting as if she were a queen on her throne in a royal courtyard. Her long black dress trailed to the floor, and her purple lips embellished the tense atmosphere.

'Now tell me about this King that is to return.'

Arthur locked eyes with Tina before turning back to Knox.

'Yeah…I may have got a little too carried away earlier. I haven't actually read anything about any King returning.'

'You're a liar,' Eve snarled at him.

'And you're no better,' Arthur replied.

Knox remained calm, yet somewhere beneath her composed figure, Tina could tell she was growing with frustration. Knox put her hands between her breasts and retrieved a folded piece of paper. It looked like a page from one of his journals. 'Recognise this?'

The sound of Mary-Anne's moan was the only thing that accommodated the unfolding silence. Tina watched as Arthur's body went limp, as if the very soul in him was being drained. His entire demeanour changed. A smile grew on Knox's face.

'Give that to me.' His voice was dark and dangerous, as if the softness in him was evaporating by the second.

'Arthur, what is that?' Tina asked.

'This?' Knox said as she folded the paper up once more. 'The last words of Lucy Hudson.'

Tina watched Arthur clench his fists; his arms shook. She watched him make one of the biggest mistakes she had been taught to never make. She wanted to reach out to him, to say or do something before he acted rashly. Knox was taunting him the way she always taunted her, and Arthur was a fresh new guinea pig in her cage.

'You shouldn't go back on your word Arthur, but I knew you were full of yourself. Now you won't ever know what your sister left for you, why she left you.'

So Lucy had left on her own accord.

'I had Eve acquire this for me.' Knox turned back to Arthur. 'Like I said, we love information. What Lucy had written here was simply ground-breaking. Of course, it was an emotional read too, what a clever girl she was. She even learned the truth about you. Something even *you* don't know. Information that could make the slums wake from their slumber. Dangerous writing.'

'Give it to me.' Arthur stepped forward.

'Don't move!' Eve shouted as she held the short blade to Mary-Anne's neck.

Tina kept an eye on Mare, making sure he didn't make any sudden movements. Even if she were to Shadow-Step towards Eve, Mare would intervene. They were easily at a disadvantage, the way things stood.

Knox giggled. 'Oh, we're not done yet. You peasants still haven't acknowledged my meticulous work. If only you knew enough of history, you would've stopped focusing on Jack the Ripper and started to actually understand the real historical mastermind behind these deaths. Unfortunately, you won't get to look it up in your journals, but if Mare over here is Jack the Ripper…' She spun her lance around her fingers, unsettling the dust around her. 'That makes me one of the vilest and ruthless killers of all time, Eli—'

'Elizabeth Bathory, the blood countess of the 1500s. That was obvious the moment you said your grandfather was Dr Bathory,' Arthur finished her sentence. His voice was stoic, unimpressed.

Tina always knew the Shadows were a dangerous group of people, but to think they were learning the history of dangerous killers of the past and attempting to repeat their work was unimaginable.

Knox dipped the paper she was holding into a plastic bag of blood, marinating it with her red fingers.

'NO!' Arthur shouted. 'DON'T DO THAT.'

Keep it together, Arthur. I need you to keep it together.

It pained Tina to see Arthur like this, to see him crumble in front of Knox the way she had once done. Knox threw the blood-soaked words of Lucy's into her mouth and let the paper slowly worm its way down her throat.

Silence stunned the desolate steel site. Arthur fell to his knees.

Tina added this on to the list of things she would never forgive Knox for.

A brisk rush of air followed by a blur of movement stole their attention. Three figures dressed almost identical to her in black assassin's attire stood before them. Tina gripped her daggers tightly.

It was the Assassins of the West, looking like the true assassins they were.

'Stand, Arthur, your fight has only just begun,' Mind's voice erupted into the wreck. 'We're here to even the odds.'

They split in three different directions, too fast for most people to see. Tina watched as Raita fired arrows at Knox, who quickly shifted her feet to avoid them. Riley had thrown a dagger at Mare, who parried it with his hook, whilst Mind grabbed Eve.

Just as quickly as they had arrived, they disappeared.

'Tsk.' Knox made a sound. 'These ruffians better not hurt Eve. Assassins of the West or not, I'll kill them.'

Eve had vanished, leaving Knox and Mare void of their earlier threat. The assassins never got involved in business that did not concern them, she knew that. But they had still helped them. Why? Did it have something to do with Arthur? Tina pushed all her questions aside.

She looked at Arthur, hoping he would catch her signal. The exchange of eyes was enough for him to understand. It was time to make a move. Tina rushed at Knox, daggers in both hands. Her nemesis parried Tina's lunge.

Behind her, she could hear Arthur's rusted pipe clattering with Mare's hook. As much as she worried about Arthur going up against one of the Shadows, she knew she had to deal with Knox first. He would be fine if he could tap into his memory; all his training would come down to this moment.

Knox's lance came crashing down onto her daggers. She used her legs to propel the force of the attack back. Knox leapt back towards a dark tunnel, and Tina followed relentlessly, not letting the purple-lipped woman catch her breath—she didn't deserve it. Tina continued to strike without giving any respect to her father's killer.

She would not forgive her. This was the moment she had lived for.

27. The Pacifist's Sword

Arthur

The clanking of metal reverberated around the archaic train garage as Mare's steel hook met Arthur's lead pipe. Arthur braced his legs for the impact of metal. The vibrations sent a tingling sensation through his body. He leapt back to create some distance between them.

You are my hope.

He needed to snap out of it. Now wasn't the time to think about Lucy's words, not when his life was on the line.

The smell of rust and decay added to his nausea as it wafted into the pebble-filled site from the tunnels beyond him. Sweat trickled down his brow, staining his white collar. The effects of being trapped in a dark cellar for a day still lingered in his muscles. He gripped his pipe tightly and remembered back to all the times he was bruised and beaten by Tina's so-called training. He couldn't see where Knox and Tina had gone to, but Arthur stood alone against Mare. Mary-Anne lay unconscious behind him.

Arthur would never have imagined himself to be fighting a man with a hook for a hand, let alone with a piece of metal debris as his only weapon. Mare didn't look like he was built for fighting; his body was almost the complete opposite of Arthur's. Where Arthur was tall and somewhat sturdy-looking, Lukas—Mare—looked malnourished and skinny. In fact, the only thing that really frightened Arthur was the silver hook that replaced his hand.

'Ever the thoughtful one, Arthur.' Mare's voice changed, turning softer—it was Arthur's voice. Mare chuckled at the surprise on his face. 'What? Did you think the Master of

211

Disguises would only have one voice? Must I always sound like Lukas? Does no one write about me?' He rolled his eyes. 'I guess that's the price I'll have to pay for having so many identities.'

Arthur felt like he was talking out loud to himself as he heard the member of the Shadows speak in a voice that was uncanny, and yet strangely his.

Mare reached into his pocket and produced a small item. Lipstick. He watched as Mare fiddled with his lips before stowing the item back in his pocket. A purple sneer.

He lunged at Arthur, catching his arm with his hook. Arthur gasped as pain seared through his body and his shirt tore at his arm, revealing a line of blood-red. Mare didn't give him time to gauge the pain as he spun on the spot and swung his left foot at Arthur's ribs. Arthur winced, clutching his sides. The impact felt stronger than any impact Tina had inflicted on him. This scrawny-looking man was not going to take it easy on him. He meant to hurt him, to kill him.

His voice reverted back to the Eastern-European accent he used as Lukas. 'Looks like this will be over before it even starts. I didn't know what to expect with you really. Like I said when I first met you, you could have been a Peacekeeper with your body. What a waste.' He leapt for Arthur again.

Arthur jerked to his side, narrowly avoiding a flurry of swings from the sharp point of the hook. He couldn't let Mare's taunts get to him. If he wanted to survive this, he would need to draw on every ounce of experience he had gained. He slid back into his memories and remembered every moment he had spent with Tina, watching her flawless movements.

'Too late, Arthur. Seems like you're daydreaming.' Mare made for a kick towards his chest, just like the kick Tina had tried to inflict on him back at the school.

Just like then, he remembered how to catch it and smother the impact in his hands. It worked; Arthur had grabbed hold of Mare's foot. A look of shock struck Mare's face, before turning to frustration. Arthur expected him to use his other foot to free himself from the grip, just as Tina had done. But this didn't happen. He didn't have the flexibility that assassins had. Sensing his advantage, Arthur held on tight and leaned back. Slowly moving his feet in a circular motion, he began to spin Mare's body in a circle.

'What. Are. You. Doing?' Mare's teeth gritted against each other in frustration as he flailed.

Arthur let go of his foot, letting the force of his circular swing take Mare into the air. His body flew several metres before crashing into a train with a loud glass-splintering crash. Crows above them dispersed in panic. A nervous bead of sweat dropped from Arthur's chin. He didn't mean to kill him.

A deep, husky voice started to cackle. 'Looks like you've changed a little since we last met.' Mare stood up and walked towards him, a gash on his face accompanied his malicious grin. He wiped the blood away from his eyes with his hook-free hand. 'I'll have to work a little harder to dig you a grave.' Arthur's eyes widened; now it was Draga's voice coming out of Mare's mouth.

Mare pelted towards him, swivelling away from Arthur's swing. Before he knew it, the so-called Jack the Ripper was standing behind him, locking his arms around his torso in a tightening grip. It all happened in such a quick motion. Arthur felt him squeeze like a python, making it unbearable for him to breathe. How was it possible that someone with his body could hold him like this? A scary thought struck him, was Mare able to—

'Have you figured it out yet? That's right, I'm pretty good at copying people. I sparred with that thug Draga a few times to learn how to hold someone like this.' He brought his hook closer to Arthur's neck. 'Say, shall I show you how I killed those pathetic women? After all, you were the source of my inspiration, you just kept rambling on and on about this Ripper.'

Mare's grip was unbelievably strong. Arthur's breath became shorter and more ragged as he continued to struggle.

'*You* helped me create one of my favourite identities,' Mare said.

'Why-why did you kill them?' Arthur choked.

'It's a bit pointless telling you now Arthur, you're about to die.' He paused, as if he was contemplating something. 'But as I'm a little offended that you don't know anything about *Mare*, I'll tell you. Besides, by the time I finish telling you, your lungs will probably have been crushed. Call it my mercy for entertaining me on the dumps.'

Why did he do it? Why would he even bother working at the dumps? Was this all part of a greater façade or the imposter's own ego playing the part?

Arthur expected him to relax his grip as he spoke, but he didn't budge. He winced; he felt as if his ribs were being crushed from the inside out, as if his organs were imploding. It was a struggle to even remain conscious. Mare's grip was like that of the bandit's a few days ago, except this time Arthur wouldn't be saved by Tina.

'My mother was an activist, her whole life she fought for women's rights. She was imprisoned several times during the First Revolution. My grandmother before her was a professional fighter, an Olympian before the Olympics were disbanded. She was an inspiration to thousands of women. They were both champions in their own ways. They fought their own battles and they did it for the liberty of women. Both of them were murdered during the White Arrow purges.'

Arthur was now slipping in and out of consciousness, but he could still hear Mare talking, still understand the anger in his voice.

'I just can't stand women who can't fight for themselves. I detest women who give up and believe they don't deserve justice. In order for this world to fight back against inequality, it needs strong women. Not these feeble and weak-spirited women. That's why I even have some respect for the little assassin. Unlike you, she's strong and has her wits about her. Perhaps I'll get Knox to spare her and she could make for a young bride.'

Arthur's eyes snapped open.

'But I don't think she'll agree to that. I guess I'll settle for making her my fourth victim.' Mare sneered, his purple lips dangerously close to Arthur's neck. 'Don't worry, I'm sure I'll be able to convince Bathory to not drink her blood.'

All shades of red crashed through Arthur's mind. Why was he being so selfish? Tina had spent her time teaching him to defend himself. All his life he'd believed he could get by without hurting others—he had done it up until today. But things were different now. Some violence was necessary to achieve peace. He needed to protect the people he cared for. That was all that mattered.

He let the pipe slide through his fingers a little, before turning it and finding a firm grip. He then summoned his strength and dug it at Mare's stomach. The Ripper let out a sharp gasp before reeling back in pain, clutching his gut.

Arthur felt his body collapse to the floor; his head was ringing from being starved of oxygen and he was sure something was broken inside him. He wondered how different the situation would have been if he hadn't been able to endure Tina's training.

He staggered to his feet, finding himself crawling towards a train. Mare stumbled after him. His brows told a furious story as he glared at Arthur.

'Just how long will you keep struggling against me?' He sounded more annoyed at himself than at Arthur.

He got to his feet, he needed to buy some time, to think of a way to defeat him. He launched himself towards the closest train. The inside was narrow. Arthur had never been in one before and possibly after today, never wanted to be in one again. The patterned seats were stained and covered in dust, and long green poles stationed themselves after every row.

Mare swung his hook and missed again. The metal scraped the paper advertisements off the train walls instead. His melee continued. They rushed in through one metallic arched-door and out through another. Arthur was breathing heavily, and he found the gap between them closing fast. Mare easily had more combat experience. Arthur needed to think of another way to defeat him.

He gasped as the hook struck him on the arm. Tears stung his eyes and the fear of Mare's hook touching a vital organ sent tremors across his body. A small hole now bore into his shoulder, leaving a chunk of flesh hanging and a line of blood dripping from his arm. It reminded him of all the times he had seen the necks of the murdered victims.

Mare smiled and licked his red hook. The pain was excruciating, making Arthur recoil back into a pole, clutching his arm. His body begged to give in to the pain, but his mind urged him to stand. He had to continue—falling now would be the end.

Quick.

He forced himself to stand.

Mare came at him once more. This time Arthur met him head on, metal on metal. He was gasping for breath, praying for the strength in his body to not leave him yet. The sound of steel resumed.

They weaved in and out of the train, jumping in from one carriage and leaving from another. Arthur was beginning to identify a pattern in Mare's movements. His regular fighting style relied heavily on the left side of his body. He would leap to his right to avoid being hit, and attack with his hook from his left.

'Don't get cocky, kid.' He threw a surprise punch with his hook-free hand, connecting with his temple. Arthur groaned and spat the red residue that had built in his mouth.

He could feel the weight of his body slowly giving in. He had to do something now; he didn't have enough strength to endure the fight much longer. There was one thing he hadn't tried yet, the last thing Tina had taught him and urged him not to do if he could avoid it. Before he let himself sink into a storm of thought he decided he would do it. It would take all his strength to pull it off, and if he failed it would mean the end.

He would have to attempt to Shadow-Step.

He had finally memorised Mare's pattern of movement as

they weaved through the carriages. This time, instead of leaving the carriage, Arthur grabbed onto a pole and swung himself 'round, connecting his foot with Mare's chest. The hook-handed man flew out of the train and into the clearing they'd started from. His body rolled to a halt.

Arthur bit his bottom lip. He relaxed and let his mind take him to the time Tina had taught him how to Shadow-Step. He let his mind will for his body to move, drew on his energy, and found himself walking towards Mare. He knew he lacked training; he knew he wasn't an assassin; he wasn't Tina. But in spite of all her scorn and sceptical comments, he *knew* she believed in him.

'Poor Arthur, you're actually trying to use aura against me? You, who has never wielded a sword and is too afraid to kill in this dog-eat-dog world?' A hint of pity enveloped Mare's voice.

Arthur was drawing closer to him. The energy that coursed through his body concentrated itself into his legs. His other senses began to weaken. He couldn't hear what Mare was saying clearly anymore; his sight became blurred and his fingers felt numb. Tina had explained it to him, how aura would take a toll on his other senses. Throughout their last training session, he had barely been able to harness the energy in his legs, let alone do a full Shadow-Step. Even if he did pull it off, Mare was already expecting something.

He leaned back and threw his pipe high in the air, letting it drift towards Mare in a slow and endless arching descent. The art of misdirection, he would need to rely on a trick. Memories of Raita's performance of misdirection filled his mind, followed by the way Tina moved.

'Oh my.' Mare's impression of Eve sounded in his voice. 'Is Arthur going to hurt me with a measly throw like that? Is that even something to throw?' Mare's eyes finally caught up with Arthur's movement. 'Wait, how did you get so clos—'

Arthur punched him in the throat. He had covered the distance between them in an instant. Mare fell to the floor, clutching his throat.

Arthur didn't give him a chance to get up; he began a flurry of punches. His fist connected with Mare's body—ribs, jaw, temple. Everything he touched made him feel sick. He hated the idea of hurting someone like this. Arthur stepped back and looked down at his masterpiece. Mare's body was covered in purple and red, and he groaned, showing signs of life. Arthur sighed. He wouldn't do any more than this; to kill was not in his capabilities.

Just stay down.

Everything around him started to darken. He felt his body grow stiff and sway. Aura consumed too much energy, especially on someone who wasn't trained to use it. His body commanded itself to meet the pebble-laid floor, and this time he complied as his limbs felt like they weren't his anymore. Only his mind remained, questioning.

Did he just see Mare get up? Something stirred near him, sending chills through his body.

Mare was walking toward him now.

'You should have killed me when you had the chance.' He stumbled towards Arthur with his hook pointing dangerously.

This was the end. Even after all his efforts, Arthur couldn't finish the job. His mouth moved as if it were ready to function for the last time. If these were going to be his last words he would rather they be voiced out loud, even though it ached him to move his jaw and made his throat throb against his tonsil. He felt a desert in his mouth. He didn't care if Mare was the only one listening; he wasn't speaking to him.

'Any last words?' Mare spat to the floor beside him.

Oh shut up, I was going to say them anyway.

He had failed Tina, failed Lucy, failed the Murrays. But who was he to really have hoped for anything better? He wasn't the Peacekeeper, nor the mayor, neither warrior nor pacifist.

'At least I fought with everything I had. I'm not a graduate of NIMAS, or an assassin. I just wish I could have been more helpful, Tina. Wish I could have said what I've been meaning to say for a while. Wish I could've been your camouflage, and your decoy, and your umbrella, and your pizza guy. But I'm just a street cleaner who doesn't like to see people getting hurt, and I couldn't even be that properly.'

Arthur closed his eyes, waiting for all the pain to end. Praying that Mare wouldn't cut open his throat the way he did to those poor women. A simple blow to the head would suffice.

'Really? Just a street cleaner? That's not what she wrote about in her letters.' Arthur didn't recognise this voice. It didn't come from Mare, but from behind Arthur.

A gush of wind brushed him as the figure of a man in a trench coat swept past. Arthur forced his head up. He heard Mare groan, before his body fell to the floor. A pool of blood erupted from the gaping hole in his body. A man stood over him, wiping his enormous sword with a cloth before throwing the red rag over Mare's corpse.

'You fought well. Who would've thought you could learn Tina's Shadow-Step so quickly.'

Everything about this man made Arthur feel on edge. From the metal shoulder pads on his black coat to his unruly black hair, to his large black blade. A claymore. But he stood there smiling, as if he knew who Arthur was. He walked over to Arthur and helped him to his feet.

'I'm sure Tina would have mentioned me. My name's Lars.'

***

It hurt to breathe, hurt to move every limb. Cuts and bruises decorated Arthur's body in a way that seemed unfamiliar, even by his standards. He cast a glance over at Mare's lifeless body. The vacant eyes bore furiously into the sky as if his last action was to curse the world. He bent down gingerly and shut Mare's eyes. Wrong as he was, he did share similar views to Arthur. Deep down, he wanted to restore equality between men and women. If violence didn't dominate this world perhaps he could have gotten along with him.

Arthur found himself leaning against the man that Tina had

once called her brother, someone she loved, her closest remaining family member, and one not by blood. At last, he could see it; Tina and Lars were like a parallel to Arthur and Lucy. As he studied him, Arthur couldn't see the physical similarities. He stood an inch taller than Lars. A small cut ran across Lars' cheek, from his eye to lip, scarred into the very tissue of his sturdy-looking skin. His eyes looked as if he were hiding a deep and dormant fury, yet his lips contracted into a smile that made Arthur feel comfortable. His body was muscular and broad, trained for a perfect Peacekeeper. It must have taken him years of training to get to this level. He looked battle-worn and experienced, nothing like Arthur.

'Did you happen to see which way Tina and Knox went?'

So he knew that Knox was here too.

Arthur shook his head. 'I lost sight of them when the fighting started. How did you get here?'

He grinned sheepishly and placed a hand on the back of his head. 'Well, I was told to come and back you guys up, but I think I got lost in one of these tunnels. I heard fighting, so I decided to check this area out.'

Arthur frowned. Who told him to come here? How would they have known that they were even here?

Lars continued, 'Me even being here to save you from Mare was…' He held up his thumb and smirked. 'Pure luck.' He burst into awkward laughter, which echoed along the walls and tunnels. He may have looked like a fully-fledged man, but he was still a teenager at heart.

The sound of wheels followed a flurry of movement from one of the tunnels ahead, interrupting Arthur's thoughts. The moon now presided as the officer of the sky, enforcing a white glow on the ground. Arthur squinted to see the familiar figures of Percy and his friends skating their way out of a tunnel. He waved the four of them over.

'What are you guys doing here?' Arthur coughed.

'Friends of yours?' Lars had his hands on his hips.

'Man, like Arthur, everyone in town was talking about you

hitting Greg. Some townsfolk overheard you guys talking about going undergrou—You look trashed, you good G?' Percy asked, peering at the patches of red that stained Arthur's clothes.

It must have only been hours since they were in town. Had news travelled so fast?

'I'm fine. I need you guys to do me a favour though.' Arthur pointed to where Mary-Anne lay. 'I need you to get her out of here.'

Jerome—or Wreckless—flipped his skateboard and held it by his side. 'No problem.' His eyes widened at the sight of Lars, who beamed back at them.

'Yo, the name's Lars. You from these ends, yeah?' Did he speak the same slang as these teenagers, or was he simply changing the way he spoke to match their lingo?

They nodded, too intimidated to say anything. Arthur turned back to the four of them.

'Wait, how did you guys deal with Gareth and his men?' Arthur could only imagine what these youngsters had been up to the whole day.

'We've known about these tunnels for ages. They act as a good place for us to practice music sometimes, so we gave him the slip but...' Percy's brows knitted together, 'he's kinda cornered us now. He's probably outside Whitechapel Station trying to open the entrances again as we speak. Let's just say that all of us might end up locked up soon.'

Arthur sighed. As much as Gareth was a pain, he would still prioritise the safety of Mary-Anne. If the boys were to leave with her, surely he wouldn't lock them up?

'Woah, there's a bunch of bodies here... I think I might be—' One of the boys vomited.

Lars walked over to the mass of corpses and lifted Mary-Anne's body. He walked straight past the odious scene with no emotion on his face, as if death didn't stir an ounce of fear in him.

'My brudda, how're you walking through these bodies like it's nothing?' Percy asked.

'Oh, this? This is minor. Try walking through a pile of crawlers. It's worse.'

Shivers ran down Arthur's spine. Just what had Lars experienced in his short time in this world?

Mary-Anne stirred in her sleep. Her skin was pale and her breath short. 'You need to get her out quickly, be careful.' Lars passed her over to the biggest looking boy, who held her body gingerly. A concerned look passed between them.

'We'll be careful. We owe everything to Miss Murray.' Percy led the way back towards the tunnel.

Movement from above them suddenly caught their attention. Loud cawing punished the sky, as two crows flew overhead. They were matching each other's speed and moving in a breath-taking fashion, changing directions and speed as if they were the masters of the sky.

'The way they're flying...it looks so cool,' Percy whispered as he walked away.

Lars looked over at Arthur. 'Can you see it?'

'See the crows flying?' Of course he could see them.

'No...they're not just flying around... they're fighting each other in the sky. A big one is fighting a smaller one. Look closely.' Lars looked towards them as if he was watching a completely different scene unfold in front of him.

28. The Silver Lining

Tina

Blood trickled down the side of Knox's face. She wiped it on her sleeve and sighed. Her dress was torn, revealing her long light-brown legs.

'I'm surprised, you actually put up a fight,' Knox said.

Tina struggled to her feet, placing a hand on her fractured rib, wincing. The pain was excruciating. They had been fighting non-stop for the past half hour. Weaving in and out of tunnels that smothered them with darkness. Marble pillars that held up the deteriorating station were the only obstacle between them as they stood on the old platform of Whitechapel Train Station. She could hear the frightened scurrying of rats by the train tracks. Archaic advertisements for shampoo and other hair products stained the walls. A purple sign decorated the station, representing the old train company—*Crossrail*.

Tina held a dagger in one hand; the other lay broken by her feet. She breathed out, tasting blood in her mouth. Her frazzled hair crossed her vision, so she swept it aside. Even though Tina had matched Knox's movements, Knox had kept the upper hand. There was no denying that she had a bank of fighting experience that Tina lacked. Knox moved as agile as if she were in her twenties. The idea that she had maintained her youth for such a long time by consuming blood was still hard to believe.

Tina shifted her feet as Knox Shadow-Stepped towards her, batting her lance away. She had lost count on how many times she had done this now. The skirmish of steel continued. Of all the skills she had learned at the Martial Arts school, one-on-one combat was not her speciality. It was better suited for someone like Lars. She ducked as Knox thrust her lance at her head, missing her eyes, only by inches. Tina swung and managed to graze Knox's arm. The fighting continued, neither side relenting in their attempts to end their opponent's life.

'You're still trying to avenge your family? You need to think bigger, little girl.' Knox continued her barrage of attacks, both verbal and physical. 'This world is constantly in a war of morals and ideologies, a tug-of-war if you'd like to call it that. Peace against freedom.'

What is she talking about? Tina wondered. They both leapt back to recuperate their breaths.

'This is why the Shadows do what we do—we want to end this war, this constant futile repetition. For hundreds of years, humans have fought one another over these two basic privileges. One side rises and fights against the other, sugar-coating their own ideologies like they were heaven-sent. Screaming and promoting ideas of peace; and when there is peace, the other side crawls out of the dirt and revolts with ideas of freedom. And when freedom becomes too free, ideas of peace resurrect themselves.'

'And Shadow-Hat has a solution for all of this?' Tina shot at her.

'Yes, he does. But first he needs to accumulate all the necessary power for himself; and knowledge is power, after all. He's gifted just like Arthur, except he's not afraid to use that knowledge in a way that benefits the world. Do you even know which side you stand on? Is it peace or is it freedom? Or is it whatever Arthur chooses?'

Tina bit her lip at the sound of Arthur's name being used by Knox. She wouldn't forgive what she'd done to him.

'What exactly did you hope for when you befriended him? Don't tell me you've actually got feelings for him?' Knox cooed in the dark.

Tina ignored her. Knox edged closer as she spoke.

'Wait, haven't you told him you'll be leaving soon? Assassins don't stay in one place for long, after all.'

This much was true; she wouldn't be staying in Whitechapel

for long. But her time with Arthur and the bond she had made with him was not in vain. She was sure they would cross paths again even after she left. Part of her wanted to ask him to come with her, but the life she lived wasn't for him. She wouldn't dare propose such a thing to him.

The silver lining in the clouds was that Mare hadn't joined them yet, which meant that Arthur had succeeded in holding his own against him. She hoped he was okay, hoped that they could go back to the school and eat pizza together, hoped that he was alive.

'Don't count on it,' Knox said, as if she could read her mind. 'Even if that boy defeats Mare, I'll make sure to slice his throat the moment he steps foot here.'

Tina gritted her teeth. She wouldn't allow that. She leapt back, narrowly avoiding a pillar. Knox pursued her, jabbing her spear-like weapon repeatedly.

'This ends here,' Tina breathed out. Focusing more of her aura into her legs as she shadow-stepped left, then right, trying to find the right opening to strike.

'It certainly does.' She stepped behind Tina, catching her off guard, before launching her lance at Tina's side. The sharp point grazed her side, creating a gash that flushed red with blood. Tina rolled to the floor before jumping back to her feet. She winced and clutched her side gingerly.

Knox threw something into the air. A sharp bang pierced the air, followed by fire. Tina could hear the woman laughing behind the glowing blaze. Heat and light brought the tunnels to life; the distant moonlight that had barely made them visible was now overpowered by the fire. Towering shadows danced along the arched walls, and the smell of smoke brought back unwanted memories. The fire created a barrier between them.

'How do you like the new flare-bombs they've developed in the city? We hijacked a White Arrow convoy a while back and confiscated a good number of these new-tech devices.'

Tina wasn't paying attention to her; her mind was too busy reminiscing about the similarities between the fire and the one that killed her family. The same colours, the same prickling heat, the same smell of smoke and ash.

'If you want to kill me so badly, get through this fire,' Knox sneered, licking some blood off her fingers.

Tina shook her head, fighting away her memories. She had lived for this very moment. She began to walk towards the burning wave; the heat began to prickle against her skin, before sending a sharper pain. She focused her aura lightly across her body, acting as a coat around her.

'I've let this fire eat away at me for four years already,' Tina said. 'I've felt these flames at the age of fourteen. You don't scare me anymore, Knox.'

She crossed the fire and leapt for Knox's neck. The woman's eyes widened. She missed by an inch, but quickly flipped her dagger around and aimed for Knox's back. She managed to wound her before the dagger clattered to the marble. Not letting Knox recoil, Tina hurtled towards her. She connected her fists to Knox's stomach with full force, knocking her off the platform. Her body clattered onto the train tracks. Tina picked her dagger from the floor and jumped from the platform.

Before she could strike a fatal blow, she caught the movement of another shadow. She leapt back just in time to avoid being hit. A slim figure revealed himself into the flickering light of the fire, he was dressed in all black, with a top-hat resting on his head and a purple painted smile dressing his face.

'M-master,' Knox croaked.

'Hush now, Elizabeth. There's no time to show weakness. Can you stand?' The man brought Knox to his feet. He held a walking stick in one hand.

The air felt heavy, as if the presence of the leader of the Shadows had brought about a heavy atmosphere with him. 'So, you're Shadow-Hat?' Tina asked.

Goosebumps rippled through her skin and she could feel the hair on the back of her neck stand. This was no ordinary man. She frowned, the old man's aura was strange, it was nothing like the malevolence of Knox, nor was it like anyone from the Ruh. She stifled a gasp. It was like Arthur's, except at least a hundred times more defined. There was something so majestic and pure about him. Who exactly was he?

'Indeed, young miss. I'm glad to make your acquaintance at last. I trust Lars has told you about me.' He tipped his hat towards her; his tone was strangely polite.

'Master, is it done?' Knox asked him.

He raised a finger to his temple. 'It's all here. I've burned the books already. We're done here.'

Things had just gone from bad to worse. Tina certainly didn't want to take her chances on a close combat fight with someone way above her skill level. She leapt back and drew her bow; in a quick motion, she fired two arrows at him. There was a gush of wind as she fired, then a clattering sound as Shadow-Hat parried both the arrows with his walking stick. Tina's eyes widened as she contemplated what the man had just done. She was clearly no match for him in this condition.

'If I were you, I would settle down now.' The old man motioned to either side of the tunnel.

The sound of dogs barking filled the area. The fire illuminated the tunnels enough for her to see shadowy figures approaching. Within a few seconds, hordes of mercenaries dressed in black had joined the fray. Each carrying weapons, some armed with large dogs that bared their teeth at her. The Minions of the Shadows. Things had turned from worse to disastrous. An ominous atmosphere now filled the moonlit platform. Tina found herself backed against the wall. The thugs crept closer, approaching her from either side.

Her heart was thudding fast. How many could she take on by herself? Maybe six? Before she would ultimately succumb to their slaughter. She searched the moving crowd frantically; her eyes lit up as she found a gap. Striking one of the men closest to her on the neck, she forced her way through the horde. She wasn't moving as fast as she could anymore, her breath was ragged, and her body felt as if it were pushed to the utmost limit.

She managed one last Shadow-Step away from a pursuer and thrust herself into the darkness of the tunnels.

And then she ran for her life. Pain clung to her body and pride. She'd had a chance to avenge her family, and she had let it slip. She forced her body towards the light at the end of the tunnel. Her legs felt like large sack of bricks dragging behind her. She staggered forward, seeing one of the trains from the old era. The moonlight hugged her as she entered the pebble-filled site where the tracks connected. The coloured stripes of pink and green welcomed her body as she collapsed against the metal snake-like carriage.

This was her limit; she couldn't move any farther.

Where was Arthur?

This was where she would meet her maker. She placed her dagger by her side and checked her quiver. One arrow left.

Please let him be alive, please.

One arrow to stop the horde of probably more than thirty mercenaries. Perhaps even Kisuke would have struggled in this situation. She could hear them getting closer. Glancing back, she spotted a dozen of them, swords, knives and axes all in hand. They circled around her. She drew back an arrow, but which one should she fire at?

Please.

Several shadows appeared in front of her as the stationary train jerked suddenly. The mercenaries all looked above Tina. What were they looking at? It hurt to even move her head. But the moment she heard the voice behind her, she swivelled on the spot and craned towards the light.

'Need a hand?'

A smile forced its way onto Tina's face. Her heart started to beat furiously. Sebastian grinned at her from atop the mechanical structure.

'Wait…what are you doing here? How did you even know where to come?'

'Well, you sent me your reports, didn't you? I just had to quickly sketch the map of Whitechapel and analyse all your findings. Easy-peasy.' His voice was smooth and full of logic, as to be expected of a genius.

Sebastian was dressed in his combat-wear: a dark green battle suit with his katana by his side. His bleached hair crowned his head in generous fashion, blending magnificently into the moonlight. Behind Sebastian stood the tall figure of Rayhan. His moustache had grown, curling at the end, a spear accompanied his hand. Next to him was Kisuke, the Japanese marksmen, holding his bow primed and ready for battle. The train rocked again, almost causing the three of them to lose balance.

'Toby, I told you the train isn't going to support your weight!' Kisuke snapped.

A large shadow engulfed Tina—the shadow of the giant, Toby. A hat cushioned his head, and a large black axe comforted his hand.

'For God's sake, Kisuke. Why do you guys get to always make the cool entrance?'

He tried to hoist himself onto the train again, but only managed to rock it further. The mercenaries were frozen to the spot, watching the giant rock the train with surprising ease.

Toby turned towards them. His eyes narrowed.

'The Ruh is here.' His voice would've sounded a lot more impressive had it been deeper. But the twenty-year-old giant still held a piercing stare that would send shivers into the souls of the mercenaries.

Two more figures now joined them from another tunnel. A warm feeling grew in Tina's stomach as she recognised Arthur staggering towards her. He was holding onto someone as he walked. A man with unruly hair, a black trench coat, and a large sword on his back. Lars waved at her.

Indeed, the Ruh were here.

'Sorry, we got lost.' He beamed.

Arthur scowled. '*You* got lost. I'm the one with the memory, we would've been out if you followed my directions.'

Lars met Tina's gaze and shrugged. 'I like him.'

29. The Ruh

Arthur

Even his imagination wouldn't have dared to create the scene that unfolded before him. Far to his left, next to the tunnels that headed west, was a swarm of bandits and thugs. Dressed in black and wielding weapons of various sizes, the horde looked menacing. Their monstrously large dogs growled. Yet to Arthur's right was Tina, accompanied by a group of warriors. Each one grinning at the other as if they were more entertained by their reunion than concerned with the threat in front of them.

His eyes struggled to scan the area; he noticed the stairs to his right. They were probably standing just inside the main platforms of the old station. Maybe if they all dashed towards the stairs they could make it out. But the exit was sealed—it had been for years. It would take people on both sides to open it.

Tina stood against one of the trains, leaning her back against the glass for support. If Arthur thought his body was in a poor state, then Tina's looked like she'd been hit by a working train. How was she still standing? He moved towards her. He wanted to hug her, to hold her, to tell her all about his fight with Mare and how much the thought of her had gotten him through it. God, he sounded so soppy, she would definitely hit him. He was able to stumble forward without Lars' support.

A man leapt down from the train and faced him. His hair was white like snow and spiked like a tropical palm tree that Arthur had seen on a poster in the third tunnel he had passed. An oddly shaped thin blade clung to the man's waist. He was shorter than Lars and looked younger, too. He had never seen someone like him before.

He held out his hand. 'My name is Sebastian Armstrong.'

Arthur shook it, his eyes widening. This was the person he had read about so many times. The young genius from a rebel family of hackers. 'My name is Arthur.' He paused, before deciding to use his full name just as Sebastian had done. 'Arthur Hudson.'

Sebastian's warm green eyes stole into him, as if he was searching deep into Arthur's mind. Unravelling the labyrinth that held his every waking thought and memory. He felt like he was reaching into him with his eyes, numbing his senses. Perhaps this wasn't aura but simply awe? Sebastian reached out and placed a hand on Arthur's shoulder. Leaning closer, he whispered into his ear.

'Are you sure that's your name?'

Am I sure about my name? Arthur frowned. What did he mean by that?

A shuffling movement from the crowd of mercenaries broke Sebastian's gaze on him. One of them stepped forward with their monstrously large dog. Saliva dripped from its jagged teeth, and it looked as if it took a lot of strength to hold the beast by the leash. A large steel chain swung in the man's other hand. 'Come on,' he barked at the other thugs. 'We easily outnumber them by at least five to one.'

'Actually, its seven to one, not counting Tina and the blond kid,' said the Asian archer, prodding his fingers as he counted each person in his view.

'I take it you're Kisuke, the marksman of the Ruh?' Arthur asked.

'Oh, am I famous?' he asked nonchalantly, loading an arrow into his bow.

'Oh, OH. YOU MUST KNOW ME TOO THEN, RIGHT?' The giant figure of Toby beamed down, his woollen hat making him look like a child; a very big child. He probably had no clue how loud he was in his excitement for acknowledgement, or perhaps that was his usual volume.

Arthur nodded at Toby, before noticing Tina swaying towards him. She was in no state to move anymore. He dashed to her and took her into his arms before her body wobbled any further. She felt cold. She leaned closer, drawing her weight on him.

'You're still alive, huh?' she muttered.

'Well, either that or you're holding onto a zombie. Hey, maybe I'm one of Eve's experiments. I wonder where she got to.'

Tina looked around at the mercenaries. They looked menacing, but perhaps everything to him was menacing in this shade of the world.

'They're all at least ten times stronger than any bandit.' Tina shook her head. 'It's all over now.'

'Hey, don't give up hope just yet. Didn't you tell me the Ruh were unbelievably strong?' Arthur was surprised. Was Tina this far mentally defeated?

She lifted her hand and reached towards his head. She flicked him, hard.

Arthur winced.

'You idiot. It's over for *them*. Sebastian and Lars are both here. Shadows of London or not, the result won't change.'

The mercenaries shifted, many of them looking behind them at the sight of two figures approaching them.

'WHAT ARE YOU LOT STANDING THERE FOR?' Knox bellowed. Her voice was hoarse and sounded as if she would keel over any second. The crowd parted as she limped towards them. A slim and elderly looking gentleman accompanied her. His top-hat made him look as if he were an ordinary, smartly dressed senior citizen of London. A silver walking stick led his steps. His eyes were dark and wrinkled; Arthur couldn't tell if they were even open or not. A dark shade of purple on his face identified him as another member of the Shadows.

'Where is Mare?' Knox asked.

The mercenaries looked at them, then back at the Ruh.

One of the bandits whispered something in her ear. Her eyes widened and looked towards the Ruh, searching and resting on

Lars.

Lars was oblivious to all this, as his gaze was focused on the old man.

'Old man Shadow-Hat is here too? Things are about to get interesting.' He reached for his claymore. Lifting it over his head, he pointed it towards the horde of black. The black blade shined against the moonlight like a weapon of ice, but his eyes stole the fury of a summer's sun. Larsson Denith, the warrior born from fire. If Arthur's body weren't aching so much he would've been giddy from finally meeting the Ruh in person.

'Focus on Knox first, Larsson.' Sebastian stood a little ahead of the rest of the Ruh. 'Toby. Kisuke. You guys are support. Rayhan, you protect Arthur and Tina.' He turned to Tina and smiled the same warm smile that made Arthur feel safe, as if his presence alone was enough to bring peace to the world. His instructions were simple, and not one member of the group responded differently. It was as if they had complete trust in this odd-looking man.

The mercenaries edged closer. Sebastian hadn't even drawn his sword yet. Arthur could feel his heart beat furiously. His mouthed opened, then closed.

'Relax,' Tina whispered. 'Just watch. You've seen how King's Paralysis worked, right? Now watch Sebastian. I don't know anyone with a stronger aura than his. They call it the King's Aura.'

Arthur squinted, watching Sebastian draw closer and closer to the crowd. He still hadn't armed himself. The closest thugs began their attack, surrounding him from almost every angle. Before they could touch him, they fell backwards, as if struck by some invisible force of nature. Their bodies fell to the ground, unconscious. Even the dogs stopped barking; they refused to move forward, refused to obey their masters. Their mouths closed, their eyes wise to the threat that stood before them.

Arthur's eyes widened as he searched for a rational reason for this spectacle. The rings of mercenaries were all rooted to the spot, seeing the collapse of their comrades. Were they trying to strategise and formulate a method to fight with Sebastian? The thought immediately left him as he looked at their faces; they looked awe-struck, intimidated, fearful. It wasn't that they were thinking at all—they were simply unable to move. Every step Sebastian took towards the centre of the horde followed with the dropping of bodies. This was King's Paralysis on a different level than Knox's.

At least a dozen bodies now decorated the hard pebble-filled surface. Yet, no blood was spilled. The few who managed to hold on to their senses were immediately struck down by the arrows of Kisuke or sent flying by the marauding figure of Toby, who simply flung his arms at them. Their bodies collided with either stone or metal; regardless, they were unable to move afterwards. Before long, the swarm of thugs began to decline. Sebastian drew closer to Knox and the man with the top-hat.

'Is that Shadow-Hat you spoke of earlier?' Arthur asked Tina.

She nodded. She was getting heavier by the minute, leaning more and more against him. She needed treatment fast. He looked over at Rayhan. The tall quiet figure stood by them in a relaxed manner, his arms folded, watching the other's fight, until he noticed Arthur looking and turned his attention to the pair of them.

'You both need medical attention. I can't help either of you guys here, though. Do you know the way out?' he asked Arthur.

Arthur pointed to the stairs he had seen earlier. 'But it's sealed up, it's been barricaded from both sides for several years now. They're trying to open it from the outside but—'

Rayhan nodded. 'I'll have to open it from this side.' Without waiting for a response, he dashed towards the stairs. Arthur didn't know much about Rayhan, since he wasn't spoken about as one of the fighters in the Ruh.

Arthur turned back to see a pile of black bodies sprawled across the wreckage. Tina was right; those mercenaries had no chance against the Ruh. Far at the back, Arthur could see the stumbling figure of Knox. She was slowly creeping towards another tunnel, one that would surely ensure her escape.

Tina groaned weakly. 'She's getting away.'

'No… she's not,' Arthur replied.

As he began to remember everything he had ever read about Sebastian and Larsson in journals, Arthur found himself frowning at the sight before him. He realised the differences between the two leaders of the Ruh. Sebastian came across as a gentle figure, a young man—a boy—brimming with a sense of control and reason, someone thoughtful and kind. Lars, on the other hand, was a large sword-wielding warrior that moved like an expert in several forms of fighting. He moved with a recklessness that frightened Arthur, like an individual carrying the burdens and troubles of hundreds on his shoulders, someone that wouldn't think twice about taking a life.

He watched Lars dash towards Knox, cutting his way past a few mercenaries, before Shadow-Stepping with such a large gap between each step that he made up the ground in a couple of seconds. It was like watching an adult race with a toddler as each mercenary tried their best to stop Lars from reaching Knox. He let loose a roar and swung his claymore in the air as if it didn't weigh a tonne. Blood whipped into the air like a fountain of water.

Sebastian had now drawn his sword, clashing furiously with Shadow-Hat. The old man didn't show any signs of age as he moved with breath-taking speed and flexibility. Toby and Kisuke picked off the remaining mercenaries. How they had defeated over thirty people with only four was beyond Arthur.

Cawing from the crows he saw earlier caught his attention. His eyes widened as he saw a whole new scene unfold in the sky. It was the same two crows, except this time the smaller one was joined by half a dozen more birds, all uniting against their oppressor, working in unison to bring the large crow down. They swept across the sky, swooping so low that they almost touched Toby.

As much as he opposed fighting, as much as his morals screamed at him with disgust for the sight in front of him, he stood in undeniable awe. The Ruh had defended them and showcased an unbelievable amount of strength. No journal or writing could have prepared him for this. They were like a murder of crows.

30. The Truth

Tina

A blinding pain coursed through her body. She could taste the scent of blood with every breath she took. Although her battle with Knox had ended, she continued to fight her mind and body for consciousness. She wasn't able to avenge her family, unable to kill the woman responsible for her burning nightmares, unable to fill the gaping hole that bore into her core. It was in Lars' hands now.

She wanted to see Lars defeat Knox once and for all. After all, he had suffered at her hands too. His home, the Soulhaven, was burned to rubble and ash by Knox. The students at NIMAS still spoke about it in their stories, stories that started as rumours to tease Lars, stories that now stood as inspiration for the new generation of Peacekeepers. Stories of a boy who died in the flames, to be reborn as a man, a warrior birthed from fire. The irony of it drew a small smile on Tina's face. It was Knox who had burned down their home four years ago. Knox who had driven Lars to the brink of physical and mental extremities, just as she had done to Tina. Knox who had made his mother homeless. Knox who had taunted them both, provoking them to grow stronger. And it was Knox's body Tina saw—behind her blurring tears—being cut in two by a swing of Gilgamesh.

Toby and Kisuke roared in delight. Arthur turned away at the sight but still gripped her shoulder firmly, he knew this meant a lot to her. Shadow-Hat and Sebastian were locked fiercely in combat. The old man glanced at Knox from the corner of his vision and Tina briefly saw a few tears release from the leader's eyes, before he fixed Sebastian with a determined look. A part of Tina almost dared to pity the old man.

It was the end. The finale. Satisfaction would warm her stomach. Assassins weren't meant to take pride in killing, nor feel anything towards death itself. But this one would burn at her core. If she died here and now, she would be satisfied with the fact that they had avenged her family. An everlasting satisfaction for the suffering of these past few years.

That's what she was supposed to feel. But she didn't.

The thoughts disappeared as fast as they arrived. Something else stirred inside her, something that stained her mind. Was revenge not enough? Or was she aching for something else altogether? Her eyes fell on the hands that were wrapped around her shoulders, holding her upright, supporting her. Arthur's hands. His eyes scanned the field as if he were a new-born experiencing the light of the world for the very first time. His lips trembled with delicacy, opening then closing, smiling. He was witnessing what Tina had seen too many times amongst this band of warriors.

Then it struck her, the clarity beneath the raging ocean of feelings inside her. Perhaps all this time, revenge wasn't the cure for her emptiness. Perhaps she longed for something that would replace the gaping hole that her father and brother had left inside her. A form of love that she had not been able to replicate or reciprocate since. But one that was slightly different. A frightening form of love, one that felt like thunder and the movement of the very earth itself, one that she hadn't truly thought was possible. She cursed the thought of thinking she could die happily at this moment. She knew the man who held her right this very moment, the pacifist who stared into her soul, was one that loved her fiercely.

An assassin was not meant to feel this. But she did. She had lost her battle.

She turned to face him, her body close to his. She could feel his heartbeat and his gentle heat. As she looked towards his eyes her heart skipped a beat, perhaps literally. In the corner of her vision, from the very depths of the shadows surrounding them, was the figure of Eve creeping towards them. A long knife protruded from her hand, pointing straight at Arthur. The irony came to eat at her. How had she not noticed her?

Tina's mind screamed but her mouth was too slow. Arthur gazed into Tina's eyes, before her body did the one thing that she wished it hadn't. It gave in to the pain. Her eyes closed at the wrong time. *Not now. God, not now.*

The last thing she felt was the rounded hard texture of the pebbles below her. Arthur had thrown her out of harm's way.

31. A Fact

Arthur

The only thing that struck his mind was a cold fact; not anything remotely close to a guess, a suggestion or an attempt. Not a *what if* or a *maybe*. A fact not written in any journal he had ever read but written down into the very fibres of his essence and purpose of existence. He would not let Tina die.

He could feel the gentle grip of Tina's fingertips as she gazed over his shoulder. A frosty look of terror crystallised into her eyes. Inside them was the bitter, twisted figure of Eve, a doomed spectre of malice. It was all it took to shake Arthur into a mind-tearing twist; he threw Tina away from him and swivelled on the spot. Managing to avoid a fatal blow from the sharp end of the knife—instead, it pierced his already-maimed shoulder. Blinding red pain rippled through him. He felt like his throat was bursting with a blood-curdling scream but beneath the ambience of the battle before him, no one seemed to hear him.

Eve pulled the knife out and attempted a second jab, but this time his hands reached for hers before she could enforce her wrath. He struggled against her as their bodies came close; he held her wrists to stop her from plunging the knife into his chest. An inch or two was the difference between this world and the greater Beyond. She snarled like a beast as the weight of her body pressed against his. His mind raced instinctively—if he hesitated now, it would be the end of him.

He didn't want to die now, not after coming this far. In the corner of his eyes, he could see that Tina had lost consciousness. He needed to live. For her.

'You spoiled everything,' Eve spat through gritted teeth.

Everything about her demeanour signalled danger. Her hair

was wild and frenzied across her face, like curtains shrouding a monster. Her clothes were ripped, and her skin covered in dirt.

'I had to find my way here through the godforsaken darkness those assassins had left me in. And the first thing I see when I arrive is that scoundrel killing my aunt.' Her eyes glared into his. 'It's all your fault. I swear I will kill you Arthur, if it's the last thing I do.'

She pushed forward, unrelenting from her mission. Arthur could feel his strength waning. Only around a month ago he was a simple street cleaner with no stomach for violence, no desire to inflict pain and no urge to struggle for his life. A pacifist is all he had hoped to remain when the world stole everything else. But could he remain like that when the world had started giving back? He finally had a purpose, and he didn't want to lose it all now. Dying was not an option. All he could do was let the force of her movement find its natural momentum. To let her plunge forward. He remembered when Tina had taught him how to act against those who were stronger than him. He felt no embarrassment towards the idea of Eve being stronger than him. Over the past few weeks, if there was anything he'd learned and accepted quickly, it was that women were strong and fierce when push came to shove.

'I wish it didn't have to come to this, Eve.' A tear bloomed at his eyes before he shifted his body, letting gravity pull Eve away from him. He twisted her arm to poise the knife towards her own body, and thrust his arms forward, letting the knife sink deep into her stomach.

His body collapsed to the floor with hers. He could hear the voice of Rayhan rushing back to him. The voices of Percy and Gareth accompanied him. He could hear Percy frantically calling his name, but the voices were dulled out by his own thoughts. The world turned to grey before it turned to black. Just as his morals did.

Did I just kill someone?

32. Remember Me

Tina

Tina woke in a place unfamiliar to her. The walls were painted white and a clock ticked to her right. *10:27 am*. That couldn't be right, could it?

The bed she was lying on was firm. A small pillow cradled her head and the sheets were white as the walls. Beside her stood a small table with a cup of water, and one silver dagger with a black hilt was positioned in a small drawer. The windows across the room held the keys to the wretched sunlight that shone directly at her. The bright light burned at her pupils, forcing her arms up for shade.

A man paced by her bedside. Rayhan. He was checking her for signs of whatever fake doctors checked for nowadays. He studied her eyes, her face, her pulse, and her wounds. Bandages were wrapped across several parts of her body, the parts that Knox had managed to cut into. She struggled to a seating position, noticing her ribs and stomach were wrapped in white too. She struggled for memory. Where was she? Why was she here?

'You'll have questions, but I need you to remain calm as I give you answers. Nod if you understand me, Tina Roberto.' Rayhan had always been so stiff and formal.

He was the patron of the Ruh; his duty was to always ensure they were in good condition. He was someone who always got on her nerves in New India, but at this point, she was glad to see him.

She nodded.

'You're in one of the old wards of the Royal London Hospital, we've had to reopen it and clean it all up. A whole day has passed since the fight.'

Emotions and memories burst from both her mind and chest. Her mouth opened as she struggled for words, but her eyes did the most talking.

'Relax, Arthur is resting right now. He should wake up soon enough. The local Peacekeeper and his men are dealing with all the bodies in the station. I expect them to ask us for a full statement soon enough,' he said this with a sigh. 'More headache for Sebastian to lump me with.'

The furious beating from Tina's heart began to subside. Rayhan offered her a sip of water before resuming.

'You've got several wounds and burns from your fight with Knox.' He held up a hand to pause her futile attempts to speak. 'Lars has ended her. In regards to Shadow-Hat…' She looked at the composed figure; it was as if he was reading from an old newspaper. 'Unfortunately, even with the joint efforts of both Sebastian and Larsson, they could not apprehend him. He escaped.'

Tina's eyes widened. She always knew Shadow-Hat, the leader of the Shadows, was a formidable opponent. But to clash with both Lars and Sebastian and still escape was simply unimaginable.

'You'll rest for another few hours before you can join the rest of us downstairs for lunch.' He stood up and moved towards the door. 'Oh, and your friend Mary-Anne has made a full recovery, she came by earlier and left some food for you over on that table.' He pointed at a table at the far end of the room. This was just like Rayhan—he wouldn't bring the food to her of course, that would be too easy. 'When you're able to walk, you can help yourself.'

Rayhan opened the door.

'Rayhan,' she called out. 'What about Eve?' The last person she had seen before her body shut down. A dozen questions raced through her mind that only Arthur would be able to answer. Like how he had even survived after Eve's sneak attack. But the answer she received didn't fill her with any relief or assurance towards Arthur's health at all.

'Eve is dead, by the hands of Arthur.' He closed the door, leaving Tina to ponder in silence. Arthur may have survived physically, but how he fared mentally was another question altogether.

***

After a few hours, Tina limped out of her room. The neglected corridors of the old hospitals were stained with cobwebs and damp, a complete contrast to her spotless room. It seemed they had cleaned the wards but hadn't reached all the corridors. She listened to the sound of voices and manoeuvred her way through the hallways. A rush of nerves fluttered through her stomach, making every step slow and difficult. It had been a year since she had been amongst the Ruh.

She climbed down the stairs and pushed past a large door, entering a room that looked like an old reception area for the hospital. This room smelled better, cleaner. Rows of chairs circled the room, and a group of people sat there in deep discussion. As Tina made her way towards them, Lars noticed her first. He shot up and ran towards her, engulfing her in a hug.

'Lars. You're. Squeezing. Too. Hard.'

He leapt back, tears forming in his eyes. 'I'm sorry! I'm just so glad you're okay. Come, let me help you over.'

She felt as if she was still in Master John's room, sitting by the fireplace with her friends, listening to his stories. Each person came over to her and hugged her. Toby lifted her into the air before Rayhan scolded him. They were all happy to see her.

'I'm glad to see you on your feet again, Tina.' Sebastian offered her a sandwich and a glass of juice.

'You had us worried, Tina, but we got the gist of it from your letter.' Kisuke waved the piece of paper Tina had asked the wood merchant to deliver to them. She had told them what was happening in Whitechapel, whom she had met and what she had learned from the Assassins of the West.

'I'm still surprised you came.'

Sebastian shook his head. 'If good old Raita, Mind, and Riley said the Shadows were coming to Whitechapel, then we weren't going to ignore it.' He spoke of the Assassins of the West as if he knew them well. 'Plus, if the town of Whitechapel didn't care for the deaths that were taking place here, then it was up to us.'

'Who's in charge here anyway? They're doing a lousy job,' Lars said.

Rayhan squeezed his eyes. 'I told you already. That big oaf of a man, Gareth. He's cleaning up the station as we speak.'

'He's in charge? What happened to old man Murray?'

Tina swallowed her mouthful. 'Mr Murray has been ill for over a year now. Dr Dovedi was filling-in in his stead until his untimely death.'

'Right, we'll have to change a few things then,' Sebastian concluded. He spoke like a true leader, something that Gareth never was.

Tina studied him. His knuckles were purple, cuts and bruises decorated his face. Souvenirs from Shadow-Hat.

'You were all amazing,' Tina said. The Ruh smiled back at her.

'So were you,' Sebastian replied. 'But we all need to keep getting stronger. Shadow-Hat is simply stronger than us, even with both myself and Lars fighting against him. He's only going to scout for new warriors to join the Shadows now.' He looked at each person's face as he spoke. 'But...we did well. Especially Tina and Arthur, to take on two of the Shadows by themselves is commendable.'

Tina felt herself blush slightly. Praise from Sebastian was always something worthy of remembering.

Lars, who still had tears in his eyes, prodded Tina. She knew what he wanted to say, and knew how he felt deep down. She smiled at him.

'It's over now. Papa and brother can rest soundly,' she said.

Lars nodded.

'Guys, Tina said in her letter that the pizza was nice here. Can we get some?' Toby asked. His fingers clasped around each other in a humble manner, as if the giant were asking permission like a toddler.

'Toby, we've just had lunch.' Kisuke scowled at him.

'I'm still hungry,' he moaned.

'Speaking of the letter. Did anyone notice the merchant's name?' Sebastian smiled widely as he spoke, as if he found something amusing. They all shook their heads. 'His name was Magnah...and he had a cart. Magna Carta get it?'

They all stared back at him blankly. Tina frowned. Sometimes Sebastian said things that made a lot of sense, and other times he spoke a different language.

He shook his head. 'Never mind, maybe Arthur will get it. Anyway, I'm off to pay a visit to Mr Murray. Unfortunately, Dr Bathory's work never had my mind applied to it. Perhaps Mr Murray could still benefit from it after I'm done.'

Tina wasn't sure what Sebastian could do to help Mr Murray at this point, but whenever it came to Sebastian, nothing could be ruled out. She turned her attention to Rayhan.

'Rayhan. Can you take me to Arthur?' she asked. He and Sebastian passed fleeting looks at each other before Rayhan nodded.

Why did they do that?

***

Rayhan led her into a room that was fitted with curtains, enshrouding the small hospital ward in a darker feel. Along the way, he apologised profusely for leaving her and Arthur to find a way out. Tina shook her head.

'We were lucky you guys even came. Besides, we both lived. That's all that matters.'

Rayhan wasn't the type to simply accept that, though, so she knew he was probably more disappointed with himself than he was showing.

When they got closer, they found Arthur sitting up in bed.

'He wouldn't be able to handle the shock light treatment I gave you earlier,' Rayhan muttered.

A look of confusion painted Arthur's face. Tina had to hold in a gasp as she saw the number of bandages he had wrapped around him. He must have fought to his very limit. As a warrior, she was proud of him. But he wasn't a warrior. Something was wrong; she could feel it in the way he looked at them. His grey eyes looked at her blankly, as if there were no colour or warmth towards her. Even the most hurtful blows that Knox had inflicted on her didn't come close to the pain she was feeling in her gut right now.

This is why Assassins shouldn't feel, shouldn't get close.

Arthur opened his mouth and said three words. Words that stabbed at her, and twisted like a knife deep in her chest. Words that made her feel as if she had been thrown off the rooftop towards a concrete death. All without meaning to do so.

Words that breached her soul and made her eyes glaze over.

'Who are you?'

33. The Pacifist's Soul

Tina

Her heart pumped with the wind, racing with every step she took across the roofs of Whitechapel. She had ignored the calls from Rayhan to rest and departed from the old hospital building to find her way to Arthur's room. She didn't bother using the door; instead, she unlocked the window from the outside with relative ease and slipped her small body in.

She spent little time there, rummaging through his closets and desk before lifting up suspicious-looking floorboards. He would definitely have hidden his personal journals somewhere difficult. After her fifth attempt at a floorboard—by which time she began to feel guilty for ruining his room—she found it. A singular black leather journal wrapped in a cloth that had begun to build up with dust.

Rayhan and Tina had asked him a few questions to test his memory. Arthur could remember most of the general aspects of his life, most things before Tina had arrived in Whitechapel. He knew he was a street cleaner, he knew of Mary-Anne and Mr Murray, he even knew Gareth and Eve. But he didn't remember himself killing her. He had forgotten most things that had occurred in the past few months. He had completely forgotten about Jack the Ripper, Mare, Knox and even Tina. She wondered if it were even wise to help him remember the brutal murders, the fighting, the Shadows. Or even her. She could leave him now and he wouldn't even feel anything towards it.

She bit her bottom lip. She couldn't let him forget—he wouldn't want that either. *He wouldn't*, she convinced herself.

The sun was beating down on the town as she dashed back to the hospital, not caring for her heavy steps and ragged breaths and the noise she was making, not caring for the eyes of the townsfolk who were watching her as she jumped from rooftop to rooftop. She could hear people gasp as she cast a shadow across them. Something that she wouldn't usually do, an amateur mistake of an assassin. But she didn't care. Children in the street cheered, probably thinking she was a gymnast from the circus they had witnessed over a week ago. She didn't care.

By the time Tina reached the hospital she was dripping in sweat, or was it tears? Or both, perhaps? She didn't care. She forced her legs towards Arthur's ward and only slowed down when she approached his door. She didn't want to freak him out.

His eyes lit up as he saw the journal in her hand.

A hooded figure dressed in a dark cloak stood beside his bed. The figure raised their hand and smiled.

'Salaam,' Mind said, taking her hood off, revealing her short brunette hair. This was the first time she wasn't wearing a clown's wig or an assassin's attire.

Tina's finger lingered over her concealed dagger. 'What are you doing here?'

'I came to help Arthur.'

Arthur looked from Mind to Tina. 'Is anything wrong?' he asked Tina.

Tina stowed the journal away from sight and shook her head as she took her position on the other side of Arthur's bed.

'I heard that Arthur was having trouble remembering things. Even if we feed him information about his memories, his mind will simply associate all the information as separate pieces of information. I can help him thread them all together,' Mind said. 'If you'd allow me to help?'

'How?' Tina asked.

'As you should know by now, I'm a skilled hypnotist. I know a thing or two about the mind.' She beckoned with her hand.

'Do it,' Arthur replied without even so much as a glance towards Tina.

Tina bit her lip.

'Stop worrying so much, Tina Roberto,' Mind whispered.

Tina frowned. It annoyed her that the Assassins of the West knew so much about her and the Ruh, but she knew very little about them. Just who was this woman and why did she want to help Arthur?

'Favours are valuable currency in this age.' She spoke as she passed a hand over Arthur's eyes.

'So, you want us to be indebted to you this time around?'

Mind nodded, moving her hands in a circular motion. Arthur's eyes moved obediently. His breath was deep and slow.

A few minutes passed as Tina watched Mind put Arthur into a hypnosis.

'It may take a day for his memories to fully recover.' She got up and walked towards the open door. Arthur's brows pulled together as if he were in deep thought.

'I don't believe a favour is all you're after.' Tina said, following her to the door.

'And what do you believe?' Mind replied.

'I don't have the foggiest. Tell me, why are you helping Arthur so much? You came to our aid with Knox. You come to our aid now. Why?'

'You owe us a favour. The next time we meet, we may call on your assistance.' Mind passed Arthur a fleeting look before turning to Tina. 'He interests me. If you knew who he really was, you would love him in a whole different way.'

'What?' What was she talking about? What did she mean *love him*? Could she really read minds?

'Don't be silly, it's not like I can really read minds,' Mind said, her eyes analysing all the expressions Tina's face was making. 'He loved you too—I saw it on his face back at the circus. It's up to you now. Make him remember. We will meet again, Tina of the Ruh.'

Tina's stomach churned as she gazed at the man decorated with injuries. He was staring at his hands as if he were wondering who they belonged to. He looked up.

Did it really matter who he really was?

Tina turned back to Mind—gone. Disappearing into the air as assassins do—or just stepping really quickly out of the door when nobody was looking. She sighed. Mind had left Tina to face her toughest challenge yet.

'Have you got something for me?' Arthur asked.

Tina nodded, revealing his journal. 'How do you feel?'

'Like I'm about to piece together a puzzle. I'm ready. Is this my journal you were telling me about?'

She nodded. 'Can…can I sit with you as you read?'

'Is that something we used to do?' he asked.

She nodded, passing the journal to his outstretched hands. He made space for her on his bed as he sat up to face the light. His fingers brushed the side of the journal, as if he hoped each touch would trigger a memory. He turned to the first page. She could see his eyes glow as they moved from left to right. The first page was infuriatingly slow. As he sifted through each page, his speed increased, as if he was learning how he usually read.

Ten minutes passed in infuriating silence. He passed the journal back to her and closed his eyes. Tina propped up his pillow to ease his back against the bed-frame.

She waited patiently. The others had probably realised how difficult this was for her. None of them knew Arthur the way she did. Only *she* would be able to help him now. She said she would. She promised.

A few minutes passed before his eyes sprang open. He rubbed his head. 'Oh, that hurt.'

'Arthur?' Hope clawed at her throat dangerously. 'Tell me what you remember.' She didn't know what he had even written in that journal, not daring to take a peek on the way.

'I remember meeting you in an alleyway as we saw Eve cutting up poor Amy's bruised body.' A familiar smile and warm gaze breached his face. He spoke fast, as if he were reciting. 'I remember the colours of the pizza we had when I met you at the school. I remember the sight of you sitting on top of Mary-Anne's roof in the rain. I remember meeting the clowns, the Assassins of the West. I remember being stuck in a godforsaken cell. I remember walking through a dark tunnel by myself before finding Knox and Eve. I remember fighting Mare, I remember Lars killing him. I remember the Ruh fighting against the mercenaries.' He smiled. 'God, they're brilliant. I remember how badly both of us looked before we both fell unconscious. And…'

'Yes?'

'I remember pushing a knife into…' He couldn't bring himself to say more.

Tina nodded. 'Arthur, you were defending yourself. You had no choice—you saved us both.'

He stared into his open palms, at the bandage wrapped around his right hand.

'I don't feel bad about killing her…'

Tina watched as he seemed to struggle to piece together what he really wanted to say. He had, after all, been betrayed and attacked by someone he regarded a friend for many years.

Arthur continued, 'She was responsible for the deaths in Whitechapel, too. As much as Mare was the Ripper, she was too. There had to have been more than one Ripper, maybe that's how it was in the 1800s too.'

'Do you remember anything else?'

She wanted to ask him if he remembered her, and everything they'd been through and everything he felt towards her. Or was she wrong? Maybe he didn't feel any special way towards her. Maybe Mind was lying. Maybe it was always her own imagination poisoning her.

'You mean anything about you?' he asked. 'Well, I remember you teaching me how to fight in that old basketball court. I remember us walking all over Whitechapel in search of clues to find the Jack copycat.' He paused, turning towards her. 'Was… was I supposed to remember anything else?'

She could feel tears welling up again. For God's sake, why did she ever get this close to someone? She felt her blood pump despairingly, a deep and tightening knot forming in her gut, writhing and twisting its way through her body like a worm eating away at the earth.

Steady yourself, Tina, you're an assassin. You're not meant to— Why didn't he write about his feelings in his stupid journal if he really loved me?

She had told him that she would never let him forget her, and yet here she was, struggling to stir his memories and emotions towards her. But maybe he didn't write anything because he didn't really feel anything towards her.

His glistening eyes were still staring at hers for understanding. If this was the end of her journey in Whitechapel, she didn't want to leave it like this. Understanding was what she'd give him. No, not understanding—the truth. She would deliver him what she felt was the truest feelings she had felt in a very long time.

Without another thought, she leaned forward and kissed him. An unfamiliar sensation burned inside her. Her heart leapt to her throat and continued to batter against her body. Is this what a kiss felt like?

How wretched. How painful. How beautiful and bitter.

Seconds passed in this close embrace, and each second felt equally painful and liberating. Arthur's hands drew to her face, wiping a tear away from her eyes. A smile formed on his face.

'What?' she whispered. Tina's heart pumped with sorrow and thoughts of what could have been, if only he—.

'I wouldn't forget you so easily, Tina. Of course I remember you. *Everything* about how I feel about you.'

Silence breached into their intimacy.

Tina scowled. 'Wait, so when you said...' She paused to gather her thoughts. Realisation dawned on her. 'Wait, you remember *everything*?' Her feelings turned to molten rage.

Arthur's smile vanished, he knew what was coming next.

'Wait...it was a joke. Honest, I only remembered things a few minutes ago—Please...no wait, I'm already injured as it is. Hey...' He began to shout for help.

But nothing would save Arthur Hudson from her now.

He was hers.

34. Revelations

Arthur

Hail descended with a furious scorn, an unrelenting barrage of water and stone cascaded against the dark road. The sky never discriminated, nor did it care for those below. Yet as the wind continued its brutality, there was a special care in the way Arthur was being carried. He looked back at the man that held him close to his stiff chest. A blond beard shined white in the moonlight, yet the light itself never revealed his face. *How did his eyes look? Were they cold like the night or warm like the sun? Who was this man? Where was he? Why didn't it feel cold? Why was he being carried?* A plethora of questions erupted in Arthur's mind, but none exited his mouth.

'Please, they're after me. I must leave him in your care.' The man's voice was almost hushed by the wind.

'What's his name?' Mr Hudson's voice replied.

Arthur stretched his hands as they passed him over. His heart drummed wildly, and his eyes refused to accept what he saw. His hands were small, a small child's hands.

'His name is Arthur,' the voice spoke, before pure white started to burn at his eyes. *What was happening?*

Arthur awoke with a shudder, light poured into the room and drew his focus back to the hospital ward. Tina sat by his bedside, her brows knitted in a frown.

'You were moaning in your sleep, Arthur,' she said before placing her hand on his. 'It was probably just a bad dream.'

'Yeah.' He wiped the sweat from his forehead and covered his eyes from the brutal light. 'Probably.'

***

Memories flooded back to him throughout the quick journey to the centre of the town. He could remember everything that had happened in the past few weeks, everything that Tina had quizzed him on. From Mr Hudson to the evil figure of Elizabeth Bathory—Knox. He hoped, at least, he had remembered everything that was a blank to him only a few hours earlier.

A few minutes' walk from the Wayward Inn, passed Bart's barber shop, at the town centre, people from all over the area had gathered. News had circulated that Mr Murray had called for everyone's presence. It was deep in the afternoon now. All the shops closed early, and the weather kept to its good faith, casting a warm glow on Whitechapel.

The Ruh found themselves standing on a stage that had been built up only a few hours ago. The lonesome figure of a tree stood behind them, casting a slight shadow over them as the sun conducted business. The branches were decorated with golden-brown leaves and the lowest branch touched Toby's hat.

He did his best to not look at the crowd, but he could tell the townsfolk were all looking at them, their eyes passing from Sebastian, to Larsson, to Kisuke, to Toby, to Rayhan, and then to him. Unsurprisingly, not many seemed to notice Tina standing beside him. Kisuke scolded Toby quietly for attempting to move around too much.

'You're already attracting too much attention,' he snapped at him.

Gareth and his men stood to the other side of the stage. They looked towards the Ruh with distaste. Arthur could understand why, as Gareth was forced to clear up their mess, and what a mess it was. Several dozen bodies had been left unconscious or dead for him to deal with, including the ones Knox and Mare had created.

Bart was furiously staring at Gareth, his eyes swollen and his demeanour sullen. He had been hit with the death of Mrs Gower the most. Many people in the crowd had lost loved ones. It was Gareth that bore the brunt of their anger. Everything had occurred under his watch. Why didn't he notice people going missing? Why didn't he listen when Arthur had warned him? Why didn't he take action sooner? These were just some of the questions that Gareth had to face now.

Tina squeezed his arm when Gareth's eyes flitted towards her.

'What's the matter, Tina?' Arthur looked from Gareth to Tina.

'Nothing,' she muttered before casting her eyes away from Gareth. It looked like she was trying her best to stifle her rage about something.

Arthur wasn't the only one to notice Tina's behaviour.

'You said you guys were imprisoned by him. Did he hurt you, Tina?' Lars' voice was nothing like that when Arthur had met him. A cold tone caressed his voice in a way that sent shivers down Arthur's spine. Lars wasn't even looking at Tina.

Arthur could feel a dangerous tension brewing around them. The crowd had now begun to notice the movement on stage too. This was bad.

'Did you hurt Tina?' Lars addressed Gareth this time.

Arthur noticed Sebastian turn away from them, as if he knew something was about to happen, and he wouldn't intervene.

Gareth stepped forward. 'I merely questioned the girl. I admit my methods may be harsh, but I needed to understand the situation better. It's my duty as a Peacekeeper.'

The crowd looked from Gareth to Lars to Tina.

'I apologise…I—' he began.

Lars walked over to him, his hands reached for his sword.

The large figure of Toby quickly intervened, restraining Lars' attempt to unsheathe his weapon.

'Lars, this isn't good. Let me handle this 'kay?' The biggest figure of the Ruh spoke in a calm and assuring manner, which surprised Arthur. All he had ever heard from Toby were his child-like comments.

They looked at each other for a moment. Arthur imagined

Lars to protest, but he didn't. He simply stepped back and continued to glower at Gareth.

Toby towered over Peacekeeper, smiling.

'I'm not sure Tina will forgive you.' He brought his colossus body lower to whisper into Gareth's ear, although the idea of whispering was lost to his naturally booming voice, as everyone on stage could still hear him. 'Nobody hurts one of the Ruh and gets away with it. Especially not little Tina. Lars would have cut your limbs off.' A bead of sweat dripped from Gareth's forehead as he stared up at the giant. 'But don't worry, I'll offer you some mercy.' Toby straightened up.

People in the crowd were craning their necks for a better view. Gareth looked relieved, as if a huge weight had lifted off his shoulders. He wiped his sweaty forehead and hid a smile. Toby grinned back at him.

'I'll only crush one of your limbs instead.'

The giant swung a fist at Gareth's shoulder.

One, two, three.

For three seconds Gareth's body defied the laws of gravity. His face contorted in pain as he twisted in the air. His men stood aghast, not knowing whether to move or to wait for his body to fall to the floor. The crowd watched the spectacle in terrifying awe. Toby's strength was immense; to lift a large body like Gareth's into the air was unimaginable—until now.

He fell to the ground away from the stage with a rough thud. Stu, Greg, and some other men rushed over to Gareth's body.

Arthur felt Tina leave his side. She walked up to Toby and kicked him. He didn't react, though—he couldn't feel it—so she had to shout to get his attention.

'You didn't need to do that!' she scowled.

Toby embraced her with a large hand. 'We made a promise, didn't we? All those years ago in NIMAS.'

The Ruh all exchanged looks with each other and nodded. They now attracted the full attention of the crowd that stared at them in awe. They didn't seem to care for Gareth.

Tina walked back to Arthur, looking at him with a brow

raised.

'Are you okay?'

'Yeah, why wouldn't I be?' He frowned at her.

'Uhm…I don't know. Maybe because you hate violence? Mr Pacifist,' she said with scorn.

'Pacifist?'

What is she talking about?

Tina gave him a funny look, like she thought he was joking around. She was about to say something but stopped as Mr Murray took to the stage.

The old man called for calm, choosing to ignore the groans of Gareth. Mr Murray wasn't fully recovered—he still looked frail—but he looked around the street and the crowd as if he wasn't suffering from signs of aging. An afternoon with Sebastian and some New India chai tea had done the trick, Rayhan had told Arthur. But he wondered what exactly Sebastian had done. Either way, he was glad to see the old man on his feet again. Mary-Anne stood beside him.

An hour earlier, she had thanked Arthur and Tina profusely—with tears glittering from her eyes—for all their efforts. She had also apologised for causing them so much trouble. Tina, to Arthur's astonishment, hugged her. Was the little assassin coming out of her shell a little?

The people beckoned towards Mr Murray, many nodding at him respectfully. Others reached up and shook his hand. As usual, the townsfolk still held the old man with admiration and respect. He was their Mayor, even if he had been away for a year. He raised his hand, calling for silence.

'To my friends and family of Whitechapel. I humbly request your attention for a few minutes. Many of you may have noticed that I have not been at the best of my health as of recent times. No, I've been bed-bound for too long. I ask you to forgive me. I left you for too long, and I feel I left Whitechapel without a proper leader to love you the way I did.' He cast a cold glance towards Gareth, who was now holding his shoulder gingerly. 'But not anymore. I will take Whitechapel back into my hands from today forward. Many of you have suffered, and therefore I too have suffered. I say to you from today, NO MORE.'

For a man well into his latter half of life, he spoke with volume that turned the heads of those who were still distracted, and even those far back in the crowd. There must have been just under a hundred people who had come to hear him speak, practically everyone in town. His voice was calm and slowed when it needed to and sped up when he willed. The man was an experienced orator.

'NO MORE shall the atmosphere of Whitechapel be littered with petty thieves, thugs, mercenaries, brothels, and unpleasant sights. All this time, the Peacekeeper Gareth has averted your attention from all the blemishes of society, it was his way of keeping the peace. But this is the worst way. For centuries we have had people ruling over us who did the same; they averted our attention from all the issues that threatened our world. The world of poverty today is the result of such actions. We don't need to lie to one another anymore, we must be true to ourselves and we must face our problems with integrity, together. NO MORE shall we forget the old ways, the good ways of our forefathers who maintained the peace and prosperity of this town. NO MORE SHALL WE STAND WITH THE TYRANNY OF THE WHITE ARROW—'

Arthur and every member of the Ruh shot a look at Sebastian, who simply smiled back at the crowd. This was his plan all along, to bring Whitechapel under his banner of influence, to lead the town into diplomacy with the other areas that the Ruh had influence over. This would be a new start for Whitechapel.

Mr Murray's voice continued to ripple through the crowd.

'NO MORE shall we ignore the mistreatment of women. NOT ON MY WATCH.' His voice caused both pigeon and crow to take flight. 'We must embody the qualities and traits of the best of humanity. We may be in an era of stagnation, we may be living in poverty, and we may be struggling for supplies and material, BUT WE WILL NEVER LOSE OUR MORALS.

Remember the people who have died in the past month, and do not let their deaths be in vain. Remember what I've said today. Write it down if you must.' His wrinkled eyes passed over Arthur. 'We must stand together, we must ALWAYS remember.'

The crowd erupted into a roar. Tears swam in the eyes of many and even Arthur had to compose himself. Tina's hands wrapped around his. She had warmed up to him again after he had pretended to not remember her earlier. He would never make a mistake like that again. He found himself smiling. After all those dark times, he believed he deserved a little more of these kinds of moments. Moments of victory.

Mr Murray brought the Ruh on to the stage, one by one He showered them with glowing praise and expressed his gratitude for arriving at Whitechapel in the nick of time to save the town and his daughter. He saved Arthur for the end.

'It is with great delight that I present you all with our own local boy—no, a fine young man. A man who held fast to his beliefs when nobody believed. A man who cleans up after you and cleans our streets with nothing but sweat, dirt, and pride on his face. A man who believed in us at times when we didn't believe in him. A man who has earned my respect, and I hope yours too.'

Arthur was now on the brink of tears. The crowd burst into a loud cheer. He could see Percy and his boys screaming and waving at him. He had never felt this before, and he'd never needed to before. He was a man who did what needed to be done for the sake of the community. Everyone must play their part, right?

Mr Murray and Sebastian now stood at the centre stage.

'After much careful consideration, I officially relinquish the title of Peacekeeper from Gareth Demont.' The crowd's eyes swept to Gareth, who looked disgruntled but not totally surprised by this news. 'We need to strengthen ourselves, and we will. Starting tomorrow, we will be starting a new school here in Whitechapel. We will form a new group of Peacekeepers to protect us.'

Loud cheers accompanied the applause.

'YES!' Screamed Percy, attracting some odd looks from the crowd. Arthur and Tina couldn't help but laugh.

Sebastian stepped forward. His demeanour and physical presence demanded the crowd's attention, silencing them.

'As the leader of the Ruh, and as a graduate of the New India Martial Arts School, I have but a few words for you all.' The hairs on the back of Arthur's neck stood, as if Sebastian's voice carried a prickling aura that commanded the atmosphere. The tension became electric and yet soothing, all at once. 'We live in an age where power has been stripped from us, simply by restricting us from expressing ourselves. I am here to remind you that there existed an age not so long ago that allowed for the freedom of speech, that allowed for the flourishing of culture and the tolerance of all creeds. Mark my words, this age will return. For you, for your children, and for their children. I, Sebastian Armstrong, declare Whitechapel, as of today, UNDER THE PROTECTION OF THE RUH.'

35. Arthur Hudson

Lars

The sun waned and crept behind the grey skies. The air felt brisk and invited sharp gusts across the tents that had hosted the circus a few weeks ago, causing the plastic sheets outside to sway violently. Only one large tent still stood, housing the Assassins of the West.

'Are you ready Lars?' Sebastian asked.

'What's there to be ready about? You're the one doing all the talking. I'm just here in case a fight breaks out,' he replied with a lazy smile.

Gilgamesh rested on his back, ready for any action. The claymore was his trusted ally and quite literally had his back.

'It won't come to that—if God wills.' Sebastian pushed past the drapes and entered the large staging area.

God indeed.

The inside of the tent was barely visible, the only source of light came from the few candles placed around the edge of the stage. Rows of empty seats directed them towards the light, where five wooden chairs were placed in the middle, centring around a circular dark-brown table.

'Come,' said a voice in the dark.

'How eerie…show yourselves Assassins of the West,' Lars called out.

Sebastian shook his head and placed a hand over his eyes. 'Lars.'

'What?'

But Lars finally noticed them; sitting on three of the chairs were the assassins. He had met them in person only once before—a strange yet interesting meeting years ago, whilst they were still learning at NIMAS. The hooded figures were only distinguished by a few features; Raita's unusually long legs and stark voice, Riley's slightly larger body which Lars had had the pleasure of testing his strength against years ago, and Mind; whose face still looked too young for her. The famed assassins from a western guild. He should have known better, he should have used his aura earlier to notice them. He couldn't let his guard down again.

They took their seats, each warrior eyeing the next.

'Shall we begin?' Sebastian took out a withered journal from his cloak and placed it on the table. 'This is Wilfred Armstrong's journal. I'm sure you'll gain so much from it.'

Immediately, the three assassins gawked at the item on the desk as if Sebastian had dropped a bag of gold—or several bags of gold.

'If this is indeed your father's journal,' Raita began cautiously, 'then you're about to ask us for something of a great magnitude.'

'Simply three questions,' Sebastian replied.

'Very well. But before that, we need to give you something too.' Raita placed a creased envelope on the table, before slowly pushing it towards Lars.

'What's—' Lars went to ask. Sebastian shot Lars a fierce look to stop him from speaking. Questions were a privilege to ask these people, he knew better.

'We were told to deliver this to a Larsson Dennith. Feel free to read it in your own time.' The gruff voice of Riley spoke into the darkness.

'Let's begin,' Raita said.

Lars pocketed the letter before silently observing the tension that stung the air. Each warrior knew something for certain at this point; whatever information was shared now would ultimately define the next move for both guilds.

The candlelight weakened and wavered, giving strength to the darkness that now surrounded the five of them.

Sebastian shifted in his seat. 'First, allow me to adjust the ambience of the room.'

The assassins all nodded simultaneously, almost as if they were waiting for some display of power.

Lars watched as Sebastian closed his eyes. He could tell that he was gathering his aura, letting it accumulate in one place before dispersing it into the tent. He felt a tingling sensation waft through him and turned to see the room get brighter; the candles now stuck out as if they had new heads, unusually large and bright flames perched themselves atop the wax items. Lars blinked and for a split-second, he could see Sebastian's silver-white hair reflect the colour of fire.

Lars had seen Sebastian's powerful aura a countless number of times, but even after these four years around him, it still resonated as sharp and untainted as the first time. The limit to his aura was still a mystery.

'Wow!' Mind clapped her hands excitedly. 'You should *so* join our circus!'

Sebastian smiled at her, but his eyes bore no amusement. 'You hypnotised Arthur earlier, what did you learn?'

The first question.

Mind's demeanour changed immediately, her hand brushed aside a trailing strand of hair and her excitement faded into caution.

'The reason why Arthur has episodes and loses his memory at times, is because some of his memories had been suppressed and hidden away by *that man's* power. His mind is fighting to unlock these memories and—in the process—he faces collateral damage to the rest of his memories. It was hypnotism on a level greater than mine, unfortunately.'

What did she mean by *that man?* Had someone intentionally stopped Arthur from remembering something?

Mind continued. 'Before I tell you everything I know about Arthur. Allow me to hear your two remaining questions.'

Sebastian leaned forward, his elbows rested on the table-top and his fingers weaved together under his chin.

'What did you learn from interrogating the nurse? And

where can I find the Anonymous?'

Arthur

Later that evening, the Ruh gathered for dinner. Mary-Anne and Mr Murray had cooked them up quite a feast. The long table was filled with long rows of colourful and mouth-watering dishes. Toby helped himself to several.

Rayhan was in deep conversation with Mr Murray, discussing the contract of agreement between the Ruh and Whitechapel. Arthur could overhear them negotiating, settling on a monthly payment of eighteen pounds. This was how guilds worked, and it made perfect sense. It worked for both parties; the townsfolk would be happy as they would have a strong group of people protecting them, and the guild would also be happy with the money they would receive and the influence they would hold.

Tina and Mary-Anne were whispering to each other, casting Arthur strange looks and giggling. Arthur raised a brow at them. No doubt the girls were talking about him and Tina.

'For God's sake Toby, leave some for others.' Kisuke did his usual duty of trying to keep Toby under control.

'So…what next?' Lars asked Arthur.

Arthur hadn't really thought about it. All he wanted to do at this stage was spend more time reading—and of course, spend time with Tina. But he felt strangely comfortable with the Ruh as well, even though he had only just gotten to know them.

He shrugged. 'What will you guys be doing?' he asked Sebastian.

Sebastian swallowed his helping of potato. 'Well, there's so much happening out there, Arthur. Things that you aren't aware of. So many people to help, so many slums to fix.'

Arthur's eyes glowed with interest. He nodded, beckoning Sebastian to continue.

'Tina tells me you've been looking for your sister?'

Bread, chicken, and surprise tangled in Arthur's throat. He gulped down some water before nodding back. 'Yes, and I've not had much luck. I don't think she's in Whitechapel anyway, so…' He turned to Lars. 'I guess that's my next step. I'm going to leave Whitechapel and search for her.'

Lars raised an eyebrow. 'You're going to do this by yourself?'

Arthur hadn't thought about that. He wouldn't want to burden others with the search for his sister. But could he really venture into the dangerous slums of London by himself?

'Arthur.' Sebastian's voice became stern and demanded his full focus. 'I've spoken to the Assassins of the West…'

Arthur recollected his time in the circus.

Isn't it worth anything to know that she still lives?

He remembered what Mind had said to him, and hoped she was right.

Sebastian continued. 'They managed to get little out of Eve, but what she did let slip was that Lucy figured out the King was alive and was being held in the city. I'm not sure what happened to her after she found out, but if these claims are true, then she'll be in the City too.' He paused as everyone looked at him with wide eyes and dropped jaws. 'If these claims are true… then this is news that could shake the foundations of both the city and the slums.'

'In the City? You mean my sister is actually *behind* the walls? And how could there still be a King in this era?'

Questions flooded his temple and his mind raced back to all the journals he had read about the walls of London, but he knew immediately he had never read anything about a King that still lived in this era.

'Well, then there's hope for the slums yet.' Lars helped himself to more chicken. 'Both the King and Lucy are in the City, and the only person from the slums that is known to have breached the walls is—'

Tina interrupted him with a sigh. 'Lennart Chance.'

'So, we just need to get into the City to find them?' Arthur asked.

Lars shifted, his eyes looking towards Sebastian, then back at him. 'You can't just get into the City. It's a fortress and there's White Knights everywhere.'

'In order to get into the City we need to find Lennart,' Rayhan muttered, he had been quietly listening to everyone until now.

Silence finally introduced itself to the dinner table. Mr Murray and Mary-Anne silently watched the rest of the Ruh in awe, perhaps they were surprised by the level of verbal treason from a group of people that were barely a few years into adulthood.

'We'll find a way.' Sebastian fixed his eyes on Arthur. 'We're looking for Lennart, and as you're looking for Lucy, it would only make sense if you—'

'Yes.' Everyone's eyes bore down on him, some looked surprised and some cautious.

Sebastian raised a brow. 'Our path is dangerous. Death will only be one of the many vile things you'll experience, and you'll never forget.' He pointed to his own temple. 'Will you be able to handle it?'

He didn't need to think anymore, he just needed to make decisions. To take a leap of faith and not have to live with any regrets afterwards.

'Yes. My best chances of finding my sister is with you guys. Please take me with you.'

Sebastian rose to his feet. 'I think it's time the rest of us introduce ourselves properly then.' He nodded at Kisuke, who similarly rose to his feet.

'My name is Kisuke Neel, marksmen of the Ruh.' He bowed slightly before sitting down.

The table rattled as Toby stood. 'My name is Toby Welder, the strong arm of the Ruh.' He grinned.

'My name is Rayhan Zulfiqar, I'm the patron of the Ruh... I basically look after them.' Arthur wondered if he had ever seen Rayhan look anything but serious.

Lars gave the patron a friendly nudge. 'He's our nanny.'

Toby chuckled, rattling the table in the process.

'I'm Larsson Dennith—but call me Lars—I'm second-in-command of the Ruh. I'm the man that will change the slums one day. I'll create a place where everyone can live together in harmony.'

It was just as Tina had mentioned weeks back, Lars was serious about changing the slums.

'So, what would my role be in the Ruh? I'm not that good with any weapons…'

Sebastian put a hand on his shoulder. 'You're going to be our investigator. Your weapon is the most powerful of all; knowledge, and you have the ability to recall far more than me.' Arthur found himself speechless, he couldn't imagine being better than Sebastian at anything. 'Well then. All in favour of Arthur joining the Ruh?'

Tina raised her hand, and Lars followed. One by one, each member of the Ruh raised their hand. Acknowledging Arthur, the street cleaner, as a new member of their family.

Toby shook the table as his hands stretched upwards, touching the low ceiling with his tips.

'I want seconds, too,' the friendly giant boomed.

'You're on your sixth helping already!' Kisuke snapped again.

Laughter cascaded across the dinner table. Arthur couldn't help but lose his appetite in the excitement. He was going to be useful, far more useful with these people, helping more people. Surely this would be the best way to find Lucy too.

The evening was spent with Mary-Anne playing the piano, and Lars and Kisuke dancing and drinking. Toby slept through most of it, digesting his eight helpings of food. Tina leaned against Arthur, staring out the window. Mr Murray curled up on the sofa and was singing along to his daughter's song.

Sebastian came and sat beside Arthur. He knew Sebastian came from a rebel family, a family persecuted and deemed as a massive threat by the White Arrow. He knew Sebastian studied the past like him. But he was still curious.

'Sebastian, Lucy was the person who made me interested in learning about the past. She gathered so much information from years of reading, and I've been reading for years now too. But...' He turned towards him. 'Just how much of the past have you uncovered?'

The young man looked at him with eyes that appeared double his age. He leaned forward and whispered.

'Ever heard of Gandhi?'

Arthur shook his head.

'Mandela? Douglass? Malcolm X? Castro?'

Arthur shook his head at each name.

Sebastian had a glint in his eye, a look that made things clear for Arthur. He knew too much. So much that Arthur could understand why the White Arrow Party would deem him a threat. Arthur wanted to follow a man like him. A cool shiver ran through his arms. Tina raised her head and looked at him upside down.

'Well then.' Sebastian's eyes glanced from Tina to Arthur. It was as if he was wondering how long it would take them to realise something he had known for a very long time. 'There's a lot to learn. Arthur Alexander George, or should I call you, Prince?'

The End

Epilogue

Dear Larsson,

I hope this letter finds you well, and I hope I haven't worried you too much.

Let me start by apologising for my disappearance. I truly am sorry. After the Battle of the Bridge, struck with grief and my own issues—that you are aware about—I voluntarily gave myself up to the USA. I'm currently being held in their stronghold in the Grey Ward; I hear the Annual Slum Tournament is almost here, that would be the perfect opportunity. It's time for me to leave this place. Be on your guard.

I'll be awaiting your arrival.
Art.

P.S. I can only hold Lenny off for so long, beware.

About The Author

M. S. Uddin was born and raised in London, England, hailing from a Bangladeshi migrant family. He grew up in Stratford and spent much of his childhood life experiencing the world-changing effects of the Internet. He soon found a thrilling love for writing; allowing him to express his thoughts and emotions through the medium of poetry. At the age of twenty-one, he published his first book: a poetry compilation called *UNSHACKLED*.

After graduating from SOAS University in History and the Study of Religions, Uddin entered the challenging and rewarding world of teaching. On the eve of 2018, he decided to pursue his dream of becoming a novelist. He wanted to write a story that would be relatable to many, a story that would allow the reader to question their world and their surroundings, to wonder about the very fabric of ideologies that govern and dictate our perspectives. But most importantly, to fall in love with the characters and their very extreme values of equality, tolerance, pacifism and heroism.

Uddin, who turns twenty-four this year, lives with his family, including his loving and supportive migrant parents, his two younger sisters and his little brother. In the upcoming years, he hopes to continue his passion of working with the youth and travelling the world.

***

THE PACIFIST'S SWORD is the first of the *Ruh Series*, the sequel is to be released in 2019. The main thought process behind Uddin's creation of the *Ruh Series* was to give the reader a glimpse of the many thrilling societies and cultures that exist in both the past and the potential future. The idea for this world came from many different influences; from George Orwell's 1984 to the film, V for Vendetta. His real-life experiences of travelling and growing up in London also played a major role, from the London Riots of 2011 to the Grenfell Fire of 2017. Uddin didn't just write a novel, he challenged the readers to put the pieces of history together to understand the *current* world better, whilst reading about another. His aim is to take you through a journey that will be both thrilling and fulfilling.

To keep up with all the news regarding the Ruh and their upcoming journeys—or to get in touch with M.S.Uddin, make sure to visit his website **www.SaifTheWriter.co.uk**.

Printed in Great Britain
by Amazon